Kevin Spencer is a first time author. The eldest of four children was born on the Isle of man on May 22 1969. Now residing in North Wales, the father of two, unsure of what to with his time during the difficult times of 2020, spent his days on furlough writing about an idea he had fifteen years previous. Six months later, his dream of publishing his work became a reality.

I would like to thank my family and friends who have been extremely patient with me while writing this book. My many days of solitude and one word answers, whilst barely lifting my head from my laptop have taken its toll on them. I would also like to thank, Austin Macauley Publishers for working with me and making my dream become a reality.

Kevin Spencer

Molly Miggins and the Hidden World

Austin Macauley Publishers™

LONDON • CAMBRIDGE • NEW YORK • SHARJAH

A CIP catalogue record for this title is available from the British Library.

ISBN 9781398428935 (Paperback)
ISBN 9781398428942 (ePub e-book)

www.austinmacauley.com

First Published 2022
Austin Macauley Publishers Ltd®
1 Canada Square
Canary Wharf
London
E14 5AA

Chapter One

The search for Norman Miggins was one of the biggest and most intense nationwide missing persons' investigations in decades. A well-known and talented solicitor suddenly disappeared whilst away with a friend, visiting family on the Isle of Man.

The disappearance was as baffling as it was strange. Local police and coastguard, along with the combined efforts from mainland Britain, had searched for more than a month without finding any clues as to what had happened to him. A well-respected and high-profile professional, loved by family, friends and colleagues alike, had vanished without a trace.

The only witness to the disappearance was James Wittleworth. Norman and James were good friends and fishing buddies, who'd gone on a short break/work trip to the Isle of Man. They both lived in the same village and became close friends after discovering they had a mutual love for fishing. Although there was around twenty years' age difference between them, they clicked almost immediately. On many occasions, they would chat about the pair of them going fishing on the Island where Norman grew up and tell cider fuelled stories of catching the biggest mackerel he would ever see.

Police and detectives questioned James for weeks. He was their only real lead and was treated as a suspect for a while (although there was no motive) as he was the last one to see Norman before he disappeared. Eventually, with no evidence against him, James was released without charge.

His story, although very strange, couldn't be disproved. With no body and no signs of a struggle, along with the fact that James was in his mid-fifties and physically was considerably smaller than Norman, the authorities were left with no other option than to let him go. It had a devastating effect on James and had left him feeling isolated for years after. Although the police had no evidence against him, public opinion was of the impression that, as he was the only person with Norman at the time of his disappearance, he must have known something.

Even Norman's family had their suspicions. James knew something. How could two men go fishing together and one disappear with no trace? It was impossible.

After a month of searching and no leads, the case was scaled down to the minimum resources available.

Until any fresh evidence was found, there was little more they could do.

Norman's disappearance was a mystery and remained so.

Born on the Isle of Man in the mid-eighties, Norman Miggins came from a modest family and was well educated, attending the only public school on the island, King William's college.

His calm and, alluring manner made him extremely popular with all that made his acquaintance. His jet-black hair and, big brown eyes, along with his chiselled jawbone and olive complexion made him somewhat of a hit with the ladies through his college and university years much to the annoyance and jealousy of his friends. Norman's chosen career path wasn't so popular though. One person made it noticeably clear where his future lay.

His father (Robert Miggins) had made his money in property development, which back in the sixties, was an uncertain and risky business venture to take on. Infer structure, along with a fluctuating market in those days, was a bit hit and miss. Robert was a hard-working man, with a dogged determination and, never say die attitude that eventually, after the inevitable ups and downs he had expected, made him a relatively successful businessman. And come the mid-eighties, around the time his son was born, the business was secured, as property prices took an unexpected and, dramatic turn for the better.

The relationship between father and son, although never visibly strained, was both cold and distant. Warmth and affection were emotions that were difficult for Robert to show. Work had always come first, which was hard for Norman to understand. His friends would always go out with their families at the weekends or taking holidays together, whilst Norman was made to sit in his father's office and take care understanding the family business. Trips to the beach or park, were few and far between. Even a run out in the car, no matter how short, was a welcome treat to get excited about.

Robert had high hopes for his son. But Norman was as headstrong as his father (Although Norman vowed that, if he were, one day to ever have children of his own, would give them the love and attention they deserved) and, had little intention of following in his footsteps. So, when Norman made the unpopular decision to study law at university, Robert was furious. He felt betrayed by his son. Their relationship, if not entirely broken was, hanging by a thread. A thread that was completely severed when, Norman, after refusing to come home after finishing university to spend a year or two, helping his father run the business, took the opportunity to work as a clerk at a well-known partner's firm in Chester.

As far as Robert was concerned, it was the final insult. He felt his son had disrespected not only him but had taken for granted all the advantages that very few were privileged to, without any gratification whatsoever.

The truth was Norman wanted to make his own way in life. He had no interest in capitalising on his father's money or business. The fact that he had the opportunity to attend a public school, and then university, was something he believed all parents wanted for their children, if they had the means to do so. Norman would have given anything for a normal childhood. All he ever wanted was to be close to his father. Do things a normal dad would do with their son's. Kick a ball around, go to the beach, play fight and all the other cool stuff his friends did with their dads.

Normality for him was, keep your room tidy, take off your shoes at the door, do your chores, do not answer back, never go into the office if he was not there. These were all commands. Discipline was akin to a military barracks. All these things, you might say, are lessons that any child should have to ensure a decent upbringing. But discipline was all there was. Love and affection were seen as weakness by Robert.

The only love, Norman received was from his mother, Violet. A farmer's daughter. Small and petite, but deceptively strong. She was pleasant to look at, without being beautiful, with long golden hair that flowed down the full length of her back. Her eyes were pale blue that had a calmness to them that made you feel warm inside.

Work on the farm growing up was hard which had toughened her physically over the years. She had a gentle nature and infectious personality that those around her found difficult not to love.

Norman and his mum were close, as close as they could be considering they needed to walk on eggshells whenever Robert was home.

On the rare occasions Robert worked away from home, Norman would love to spend time with his mum in the garden. It was of a decent size and was more like a mini farmyard than a garden. One of the few pleasures, Violet and Norman shared together. Large parts of the garden were filled with livestock. Chickens, a couple of pigs, a sheep and a goat. Robert would only allow animals on the property that were of practical use. 'There was no room for pets,' he would say. If it didn't lay something or process anything of use, it had no business on their property. It made little difference to, Violet and Norman what Robert said, they loved spending time with their animals. It was release for them. A time to let go from the strict, disciplined regimental life they were used to. And they made the most of the fun they had.

Life was so much harder for Violet after Norman moved to the mainland. Robert was sore and bitter, which made life at home unbearable at times for his long-suffering wife. If he couldn't get to his son, then his poor wife would bear the brunt of his frustration. But Violet was made of stern stuff and although it was extremely difficult at times, she cared deeply for Robert. She understood a lot of the bitterness he had inside was due to the animosity he felt towards Norman, a relationship she tried, but failed to mend.

A little over a year into his clerkship, life for Norman was to take a dramatic turn when he received a frantic call from his mother. Robert had succumbed to a massive stroke and, after some consultation, was given little hope of any recovery.

It was a huge blow to both, Norman and Violet, when Robert passed away a couple of days later. Irrespective of his faults, Robert was a big part of their lives and did what he thought was right for his family.

The budding young lawyer had no choice but to put his career on hold and return home to help his mum with the business. He had no interest in giving it any more time than was necessary. Long enough to sell the business and, help his mother through the worst.

It mattered little to Violet what Norman did with the business. She was simply happy to have him home for however long it was. She knew, that like Robert, Norman was his own man and would sooner or later resume his own path. But, as long as he remained, she would enjoy every minute.

Chapter Two

'Molly, it's time to get up now sweetheart, you'll be late for school.' hollered Molly's mother from the kitchen.

'Monday morning again. Why do they always come around so quickly? Oh well, only a week to go, then seven fun filled weeks off. I can't wait,' said Molly, stumbling out of bed.

Molly Miggins was the only child of Gina and Norman. Mature for her age, but a little naïve at times.

She was of slender build, with long wavy golden hair that resembled the colour of a winter sun.

Her features were delicate and innocent, with big bright blue eyes that when provoked could give a look that would make the toughest of those offending her feel small.

They lived in a small village on the coast of north Wales called Deganwy. A small but well sort after place where most of the community's residents had their own businesses.

Molly and her parents had moved to north Wales from the Isle of Man, shortly after she was born, when her father had the opportunity to branch out their modest solicitor business to mainland Britain.

Unfortunately, following the disappearance of her father, Molly's mum had to scale down their business substantially and leave most of the work to the other solicitors left in the firm. She got involved as much as possible, but raising Molly was Gina's number one priority.

'Come along, Molly, and stop being lazy, you're going to be late,' said her mum anxiously. 'Now what would you like for breakfast?'

'Could I have pancakes with syrup please?' said Molly, the only thing she deemed worthy of getting up for on a Monday morning or on any school morning, come to think of it.

After a quick refreshing shower, Molly got dressed into her school uniform and made her way down the stairs to the dining room.

'Thanks mum. They look and smell delicious.' She said tucking into her warm breakfast.

'Hurry and finish now, that will be Peter,' said Molly's mum, on hearing the door knocker pounding for longer than it should, in the only manner that would tell you who the caller was.

'Hello Peter, come on in. She's almost ready,' said Molly's mum, smiling to herself knowing she was right. 'Tell her to move herself will you or you'll both be late for school.'

Peter Hughes was Molly's oldest friend. A pleasant enough lad who had a habit of being a bit of a tell-tale. He was never malicious with it but was always trying to please others by insisting on telling them things that was best kept to himself, despite being sworn to secrecy.

Peter was quite well built for a lad his age, due to the intense amount of training he did. Football and boxing seemed to be the two sports he excelled in the most.

He had jet black hair, with a fringe that fell just below his eyebrows, that he was constantly having to move away from his face. Molly, took enormous amounts of pleasure, teasing him about getting his hair cut properly. Calling him names like, heir flick or Mr Curtains which, Peter mostly took in good humour, as he'd usually return the compliment by commenting that the, three bears would find her one day for eating their porridge and sleeping in their beds.

Peter Hughes was from a middle-class family. Both his parents were also, successful solicitors. (Which is how the two families first met.) In fact, it was Peter's father that recommended they look at a property that was available on the very same street. The house turned out to be just what they were looking for. Molly's parents were delighted with the property. A three-bedroom detached house that had already an extension built that was perfect for an office, so her parents could work from home whilst their business took time to grow. An offer was quickly placed, so they would be sure not lose out on the opportunity. After a little negotiation, the deal was sealed and their new life began.

The families became close friends over the years which meant, Molly and Peter were pretty much inseparable. They were only a couple of months apart in age, Molly being the oldest. A fact she took a great deal of pleasure reminding, Peter of, whenever he stepped out of line. They attended the same schools, went to birthday parties together, as well as hanging out at one another's homes whenever they had the chance.

They were a team. Their lives entwined by circumstances beyond their control. And it would take a force of nature to separate them.

I bet he's telling tales on me again, for going into Mr Wittleworth's garden. Thought Molly, as Peter was taking longer than usual to come through to the dining room.

'Molly!' Shouted her mother from the hallway.

'Oh no here we go,' muttered Molly. 'What have I told you about going into Mr Wittleworth's Garden?' asked her mum, hands on hips and a look of disappointment on her face.

'But mum, I was only getting Dasher's Frisbee, it's no big deal.'

'I know Molly, but how many times have I told you? He's a very private man and doesn't like people going into his garden.'

'I know mum. And I'm sorry. But how else was I meant to get it back? I couldn't just leave it there. And I certainly wouldn't knock on his door to ask for it back. He gives me the creeps,' said Molly, feeling a little annoyed herself. But more so with Peter as she watched him skulking cowardly behind her mother.

'Well maybe you should think about playing with, Dasher a little further away from his property.

That way, you won't get yourself into any trouble.'

Molly shrugged her shoulders in a manner that might suggest her mum may have a point. Although she would never acknowledge it openly.

Her mum gave a wry smile, indicating they both understood she'd won this particular argument.

'I've got to go to the shops now, so off you go to school before you miss the bus. And don't forget your lunch again or you'll be snacking as soon as you walk through the door after school and spoil your dinner.'

Molly grabbed her lunch bag from the dining room table, crammed the last piece of pancake into her mouth whilst sucking the sticky maple syrup from her fingers.

'Ok, bye mum. See you later,' said Molly as she took Peter by the arm and marched him through the Front door.

As they walked down the street to the bus stop, Peter felt Molly's eyes burrowing through the back of his head, in the way only she could.

'What's wrong Molly? Is something bothering you?' He said, hesitantly. 'I think you know only too well what's wrong!' Said Molly, confirming the anger he suspected. Peter lowered his head, embarrassed at the curt tone of her voice.

'Why do you do that? Every opportunity you get you can't wait to drop me in it. Is it deliberate?' asked Molly, her reaction evident to, Peter that he'd snitched on her one time too many. Peter slowly raised his head to see her expression was as he feared, a mixture of hurt and anger.

'I'm really sorry Molly, I just can't help myself; I open my mouth and the words just come out. I don't mean any harm by it, really I don't.'

'That may be true,' snapped Molly. 'But I'm beginning to wonder if you do it on purpose, just to score points with my mum. You really must understand that you can't keep telling tales on people whenever you have the urge. One of these days it will get you into a lot of trouble. We've been best friends since we were at pre-school together. We're now into our fourth year of high school and you still insist on making my life more difficult by saying things that should only be between you and me. If you're going to come away on holiday with us, then I don't want us falling out with each other just because you can't keep your mouth shut.'

'I really am sorry,' said Peter, feeling extremely guilty and realising that this might indeed be his last chance before their friendship is gone. 'I promise it'll be the last time.'

Molly looked at him, wondering if this really would be the last time. But knowing Peter as she did, it was doubtful. Molly knew she could never cut him off completely. They'd been inseparable for more than a decade now. And for all his faults, he'd had her back and bailed her out of more sticky situations than she'd like to admit.

Certainly, on one occasion a little more than a year ago. They both knew a boy called Callum James. A bit of a scrawny lad. Pleasant to look at, with thick spikey black hair. Not very bright, and some would say, a bit of a jack the lad. He and Molly would give each other the odd glance across the classroom where they had history lessons together. Molly wasn't sure if she liked him or not. He was forever finding himself in bother at school. On one occasion at lunch break, Molly was busy eating her sandwiches in the cafeteria when, Callum walked straight up to her and asked if he could sit with her. Molly, taken a back at his presumptuousness, almost choked on her ham and tomato sandwich.

After a little small talk, mostly from Callum whilst, Molly was busy trying to persuade her lunch to pass down her throat, by continually swallowing her food without trying to look like an epileptic swan, he asked her if she would like to go for a walk with him after school. Feeling somewhat embarrassed and a little flustered not knowing what to say, she reluctantly agreed.

After a few more minutes of awkward small talk, Callum went over to join his friends. No sooner had the cocky individual left, Molly spotted Peter heading towards her with a puzzled look on his face. Not really knowing what had happened herself, Molly tried to explain to him that, Callum had asked her out on a date after school. Molly could tell Peter was somewhat confused by it all. Let's face it, she was a little confused herself if she were being entirely honest. In her haste in accepting Callum's proposal, she realised that her mum would be non-too pleased if she found out that her daughter gone on a date with someone she barely knew. (Or more importantly, someone her mum didn't know). And that she would have some, awkward explaining to do.

After a little persuasion, Peter reluctantly agreed to cover for her by explaining to her mum (if she called to check) that they were at, Peter's house studying. (which they did from time to time) Fortunately for Molly, Peter didn't trust Callum one bit and being very protective of her, decided to keep an eye out and follow them after school.

As the bell sounded at the end of the day, Molly made her way to the main school gates where she saw, Callum was waiting.

He was leaning against the fence with one leg crossed over the other trying to look cool. Molly felt a little self-conscious as he watched her walk towards him, whilst wondering all the time, if this was such a good idea.

In the meantime, Peter hurried as quickly as he could from class, just in time to see them walking away from the school gates.

Making sure that he was at a safe distance, but close enough to be sure not to lose sight of them, Peter began to follow Molly and Callum.

It wasn't too long before they'd reached one of the local parks. This particular park was mainly occupied with trees and bushes, along with all sorts of winding pathways.

Losing them wouldn't be difficult, so, Peter had to be careful they didn't take a turn he was unable to see. Unfortunately, by the time Peter had reached the park entrance, Molly and Callum were out of sight. In fact, Peter had no idea which direction they had taken.

Desperate to catch up with them, Peter made a calculated decision to take the pathway in the direction that was closest to home.

Peter frantically searched the park, whilst trying extremely hard to be as quiet as possible without looking suspicious. But with every turn he took, there was still no sign of them.

Suddenly, he heard a voice coming from one of the bushes nearby. As he got closer to where the sounds were coming from, it became clear it was Molly's voice. It sounded as though she was in some kind of trouble.

As Peter stepped through the gap of two menacing looking bushes, he saw that Callum had Molly pinned up against a tree, attempting to kiss her. She was clearly trying to avoid his advances, by twisting her neck from side to side and attempting (without much success) to push him away.

Without hesitation, Peter ran full steam towards them. Through all of the commotion between the two of them, Callum failed hear Peter coming up behind him.

Grabbing Callum's school bag (that was dangling over his shoulders) Peter dragged the unsuspecting assailant off of Molly and threw him to the ground.

Both Callum and Molly were in total shock to see him there. More so, Callum as he was left staring up in disbelief at his rival, wondering how on earth he'd found them. Molly, looking a little dishevelled, seemed embarrassed, but relieved to see her friend.

Although Callum had a reputation of being a bit of a trouble maker, he was physically no match for Peter who proceeded to pick the culprit up by the scruff of his neck and warn him that, if he ever came near Molly again or speak a word of what happened to anyone, he would make it his mission in life to make the rest of his school days a complete misery.

Callum could see from the look in Peter's eyes that he was deadly serious. So, with Peter's threat ringing in his ears and his tail tucked firmly between his legs, Callum nodded his head unable to speak and scuttled his way from the bushes as quickly as he could.

Still feeling very embarrassed to say the least, but more than grateful that he'd been there to save her, Molly begged Peter to keep the incident to himself. I suppose Peter realised that he could hardly insist that Callum keep it a secret if he couldn't do the same. Which he did. With no more said about it to this day.

'Alright Peter, I'll forgive you…. again! But please believe me when I say this. If you ever betray my confidence to anyone, especially my mum ever again then I'm sorry, but I will have to think long and hard regarding our friendship.'

Peter looked into Molly's eyes. Those big, bright blue eyes that seemed to captivate him every time he looked into them. He'd do anything for her. All she had to do was look at him with those eyes and submission was inevitable. He could never tell her how he really felt. The fear of losing her compelled him to keep his true feelings well-guarded. Friendship was enough for now and to put that in jeopardy by revealing something that was not reciprocated terrified him.

'Ok goldilocks,' said Peter, trying to pull himself together. 'Message received and understood. And you're right, I shouldn't say things to your mum that could get you into trouble. I'm an idiot. But you already know this, don't you?'

Molly laughed. He always had a way of changing her mood. She could never stay mad at him for too long. 'Yes, you are heir flick. As well as a massive pain in the neck,' said Molly, flicking Peter's fringe from his face. 'Come on, let's try and get through this final week as quickly and painlessly as possible. I'm so looking forward to this holiday. It's been almost two years since we've been back to the island. We used to go at least twice a year before dad's disappearance. I miss him so much, Peter. It's been difficult for mum too. I know she misses the family, but the thought of going back home after what happened to dad was unthinkable for her. But I think she needs this now. As do we all.'

Peter placed his hand gently on Molly's shoulder. It had been a tough two years for everyone. But for Molly, it had been torture. She knew little of the details. Only what she could find out from newspapers and social media.

As difficult as it was, her mum tried to protect her by keeping as much information as possible away from Molly. But she was curious by nature and the older she got, the more she wanted to know.

'I know Molly,' said Peter sympathetically. 'And I'm sure they are missing her and you, too. Your dad was a great guy, Moll's. It'll take time for everyone to come to terms with it.'

'I don't think I'll ever come to terms with it Peter!' said Molly, starting to feel the anger flow through her once more. 'He's out there somewhere. And until he's found, I'll never accept it.'

Peter was relieved to notice the bus appearing in the distance. 'I know Molly and I get it. There's nothing I'd love more than for you to see your dad again. But it's been a long time now and there's been nothing, not a trace. Someday, and I hate to say it, sooner or later you will have to face the fact that he's gone and not coming back.'

Molly turned to Peter and gave him a look that made his legs buckle slightly. 'I know you mean well Peter, but there's no way I'll face that fact! Not while there's a chance he's alive. If they'd found his body or some sort of clue that may have established foul play, then I would move on. But something's not right. People don't just vanish without a clue to their whereabouts.'

A pained expression came over Peter's face. He knew it was useless to try and convince her he was never coming back. All he could do is give his support, like he always did. Hope was all she had. And in a way she was right. Until he was found, there was always hope.

'I know Molly. And I don't expect you too. Come on, let's get school done and dusted, so we can have some well-earned fun.'

Molly smiled. Peter always had a knack of changing the subject at the right time. 'Cool. Are you ok to walk Dasher with me after school?' She said, showing the driver her bus pass. 'Yip, no worries. I'll see you at lunch anyway,' said Peter as they settled in their seats, ready to endure their final week of torture.

The school bus ground to a halt, as an out of breath Peter climbed the steps. 'That Mr Mcsheffrey really got on my nerves today,' he said out of breath as he sat down next to his friend.

'Why, what have you done this time?' asked Molly, with that accusing tone she used when she knew Peter has been up to no good. 'Nothing!' Shrieked Peter, still a little out of breath. 'He had me wait after class while he went through long, bloody, division with me again! I just don't get it Molly. It's doing my head in. No matter how many times he tries to explain it to me, I don't understand it. Or maybe it's him I don't understand. That broad Scottish accent. I can't make out much of what he says half of the time.'

Molly began to giggle, followed shortly with a burst of uncontrollable laughter which sent Peter's head in a spin. 'What's so funny?' He said, folding his arms tightly over his chest like a petulant child.

'It's you, ya noggin! We did long division over a year ago now, Peter. How on earth are you still struggling with it?' Peter turned to her and looked her right in the face, noticing she was struggling not to laugh at him. 'Look Miss high and mighty! We're not all teachers pet ya know. Just because, brain of Britain, Miggins knows her long division, doesn't mean the rest of us are all dummies!' Said Peter, shifting uncomfortably in his chair.

Molly grinned at Peter from ear to ear, whilst trying really hard not to giggle. 'What do you mean, the rest of us? I think you must be one of the few that doesn't understand it by now. That's probably the reason why he's keeping you in late after school. I'd be happy that he's not suggested one on one lessons if I were you.' Peter went cold with the thought of one on one lessons with Mr, Mcsheffrey. An intimidating larger than life, brash loud Scotsman, looming over him. It was hard enough trying to concentrate in a class full, let alone having to get through a whole lesson on his own with him.

'Wow! That's a nightmare I could do without thank you very much. Can we change the subject please? What are we up to later?' Molly had a sly chuckle to herself. She got a kick out of winding him up. A little pay back for getting her into trouble. 'I've got to take Dasher out for a walk. If you want to come along, meet me at mine after you've changed.'

Peter stood up after ringing the bell for the next stop. 'Okay great. But after we get back, could you please give me a hand with understanding these, head wrecking maths problems?'

Molly sighed in frustration. A part of her loved the idea of watching him squirm. The thought of him attending extra maths lessons with big Mr Mac, gave her great satisfaction. 'I don't know, Peter. Mr Mcsheffrey is a far better teacher than I am.' She said, trying hard not to laugh.

'You're enjoying this, aren't you?' said Peter, with a sense of dread, not knowing if she were winding him up or being serious.

Molly coughed, trying to stifle the imminent laughter that was fighting to get out. 'If we have time later, then I'll see. But you have to promise to concentrate. No messing about or changing the subject to try and avoid the problem. Do we have a deal?'

Peter let out a huge sigh of relief. 'Deal. You had me going there for a while, Goldilocks. See you in about half an hour.'

Molly nodded as her friend disembarked, waving cheekily, pleased with her wind up.

Chapter Three

'What's in the rucksack,' said Molly curiously, greeting Peter at the front door.

'My maths books,' said Peter, a little confused after their last conversation. 'Remember? You said you'd help me with my long division.'

'If I have time I said. Besides, knowing you like I do, it's going to take a lot longer than an hour to grasp the concept of it before your next lesson. Which is when, tomorrow?'

Peter's shoulder's slumped in disappointment. The last thing he wanted to do was be a pain, but knew it was more preferable than facing a one on one with the big fella. 'I'm desperate, Molly! I promise I'll concentrate. I won't take any more of your time than absolutely necessary.'

Molly sensed the desperation in his voice. And although there were a hundred and one thing's she'd rather do than teach Peter long division, she could see that he needed her help. 'Okay. Leave your bag in the study. We'll give it a go when we get back.' Before she could change her mind, Peter threw his bag into the study and closed the door.

'Good grief, Peter! I hope you're as quick at learning as you are at moving when it suits you,' laughed Molly, grabbing Dasher's lead and Frisbee.

The daily dog walking routine consisted of a quick jaunt up to the local park, which took about ten minutes, with a twenty-minute game of catch the Frisbee. Dasher was a cross breed rescue dog that Molly fell instantly in love with. He was a mishmash of Jack Russell, Border Terrier, with a hint of Collie mixed in. Molly needed something to focus on after her dad went missing. And Dasher was the perfect distraction.

After a good thirty minutes' exercise, satisfied the dog was spent, the trio made their way back home. Peter stared as he noticed there were an unusual large amount of black birds, swirling low in the sky a short distance away. Being the impulsive person, he was, he snatched the Frisbee from Molly's hand before she could react and launched it towards the black mass. Molly stood rooted to the spot as she watched Dasher's Frisbee sail straight through the parting flock and float right into Mr Wittleworth's garden. 'Oh my god, you complete idiot! What have you done?' complained Molly, cupping her hands over her mouth. 'Are you completely insane?' Even Dasher stood still, staring straight at Molly, as if he knew how serious the situation was.

Peter leant forward with hands on knees, mouth wide open. 'Oops!' He said, standing up straight to meet Molly's angry looking face. 'Well, that wasn't meant to happen.'

Molly's eyes widened as her cheeks flushed scarlet red. 'No, it wasn't, you absolute moron! You can damn well get your backside in there and get it back!' Peter stiffened with panic as Molly's command rang in his ears.

'Not on your Nelly! I'm going nowhere near that garden!' He replied, trying to determine what was worse; Molly's wrath or getting caught then murdered by Mr Wittleworth.

'Oh yes, you are,' said Molly, trying extremely hard to restrain herself from ripping his ridiculous curtains from his head. 'Because if you don't, there'll be no help from me with your maths, I can promise you that!'

But Peter's mind was made up. One on one lessons with big Mac were far more appealing than death. 'Sorry Moll's, but I like living a lot more.'

'Right! I'll get it myself! You're so dramatic!' screamed Molly as she made her way towards the back gate.

James Wittleworth mainly kept to himself since the disappearance, which only fuelled speculation of his involvement. Rumours and Chinese whispers over the last couple of years of people entering his house but never coming out, grew, amongst the children in the neighbourhood. Kids would tell stories to each other of people locked in his basement, never to be seen again.

'Please don't let him be in,' muttered Molly, as she approached the gate. 'Make sure you keep a look out, Peter. It's the least you can do since you're too much of a coward to go yourself.'

Peter felt a little embarrassed and hurt from her taunt. 'I'm not a coward! I just don't fancy being dragged down that bloody cellar to have, god knows what done to me.'

Molly shook her head at him in disbelief. 'Don't talk twaddle! You don't seriously believe all of that nonsense, do you?'

'Weather it's true or not, I'm not taking any chances! Why don't you just leave it? It's only a stupid Frisbee. You can always get another one. Why put yourself through this for a chewed-up piece of plastic?'

Molly looked at Dasher as he tilted his head to one side. 'Because he's had it since he was a pup. It might be all chewed and dirty but he loves it; and so do I. Besides, mum will only ask where it is. If I tell her I've lost it and then Mr Wittleworth finds it, I'll be in all sorts of hot water. So, I've got no choice.'

Molly tentatively raised the latch on the gate. Desperately trying not to make any noise, she slowly opened the door. 'Make sure Dasher stays where he is,' whispered Molly as she peered through the gap to see where the Frisbee had landed.

'Oh my god! It's at the other end of the garden. Just under the window!' She said, damming her bad luck.

'Molly, it's not safe,' said Peter, grabbing onto her coat, hoping she'd change her mind.

'You're going to get caught for sure.' Molly brushed Peter's hand from her coat and slowly crept inside closing the gate behind her, putting one finger to her lips as she did so.

'Be careful,' whispered Peter as the latch clicked into its resting place.

Molly crouched down as low as she could, so as to not be seen. 'Well, this isn't the best idea I've had.' She whispered to herself as she began to shuffle her way towards the dark grey eerie looking house at the end of the garden. The place looked tired. A shadow of the house she remembered when visiting regularly with her dad, years ago. The grass, where there was once a lush lawn, with bordering flowerbeds and beautiful red rose bushes situated in each corner to emphasise its splendour was tall and unkempt. The house itself, looked drab and dirty where it was once a bright whitewashed stone dwelling, with black borders around the windows that made it stand out from all others. A place, that was once inviting and colourful, was now cold and intimidating.

Molly noticed her breathing was getting faster and shallower and the beat of her heart accelerating with it. 'No turning back now.' She said to herself, whilst all the time her eyes, searching for any signs of life coming from within the house. Molly was smart enough to know that the rumours about, Mr Wittleworth that were circulating around the village were just that. But it was difficult not to feel extremely vulnerable. Crouching down low, like she was looked suspicious at best. It would be difficult to believe, if caught, that she was only trying to retrieve a Frisbee.

'Molly! Hurry up will you,' said Peter, as loudly as he could without giving her away. 'Dasher is starting to whimper. I'm afraid he'll start barking if you're not out soon.' Molly's heart skipped a beat on hearing Dasher whining outside the garden.

'Keep him quiet, Peter for god's sake. I'm going as fast as I can.' Eventually, after what seemed like an eternity, she reached the house. But the hardest part was yet to come. Unfortunately, the Frisbee was situated directly under the living room window. It was only about twenty feet from her but, might as well have been a million miles away. How was she going to reach Dasher's toy without being seen? The only thing that made her feel a little easier was, she had noticed the curtains were drawn. 'Come on Molly. Don't think. Just go.' She whispered to herself. Knowing one last push, and it would all be over.

Staying as low down as she could, Molly shuffled along tight against the house. She was no more than halfway when, the hackles went up on the back of her neck. Maybe it was a sixth sense or a part of her peripheral vision. But there was definitely some sort of movement coming from directly above her. Molly's heart accelerated to a gallop, that she was sure, if it beat any faster, would jump straight out of her chest. She pushed herself hard against the house. Any harder and she would certainly become part of its structure. The window was barely three feet above her head. Molly slowly tilted her head up towards the window. Horror and panic set in as she could just make out, what looked like a hand pressed firmly against the glass. 'Oh my god!' came a stifled squeak from the depths of her soul. 'I'm dead.'

What Molly failed to hear, because the beat of her heart was so loud, was that Dasher was now whimpering constantly and trying to get to her through the small gap at the bottom of the gate. 'I'm done for.' She said, realising there was no point trying to hide anymore. 'I've no choice but to make a run for it.'

Taking a deep breath and grabbing hold of the Frisbee, Molly took to her heels and sprinted towards the gate. Everything seemed like it was in slow motion. Was she in a dream? Would she get out of there alive? Were all questions invading her mind.

'Not far now. I'm almost there.' She said to herself as panic and fear rose to a crescendo. Molly was no more than ten feet from the gate, when all of a sudden, a loud and deep voice coming from behind her, stopped her in her tracks. 'Stay exactly where you are young lady!' Molly stood frozen to the spot. Unable to move or cry for help. 'What do you think you are doing in my garden?' Was the question that seemed to be a lot closer to her than it was a few seconds ago. Molly's hackles stood up on the back of her neck as she slowly began to turn her head around towards the towering figure of a man, that was now, no further than three feet away from her. Molly stood there, looking up at a man that she thought she knew. He had changed so much since she last saw him.

Mr Wittleworth looked old. He must only have been in his late fifties but looked at least ten years older. An old grey tatty beard, stained around the mouth, covered his wrinkled face where it once was clean shaven. Deep, trench like lines etched into his forehead with huge crow's feet around his eye, showed the pain of the last few years. His clothes appeared worn and threadbare. His posture looked laboured and frail, as though he'd spent all of his life picking up heavy materials.

Molly looked curiously at the old man. 'Mr Wittleworth?' She asked. Not quite sure this was the same man she knew only a few years ago.

The old man winced in pain as he tried to straighten his back too quickly, shocked a little by the question. 'Of course, it is Molly,' he said with a half-smile whilst rubbing his back to ease the discomfort. 'Who did you think it was? I have to say, you've grown so much since I last saw you. What are you doing here?' Molly, still a little bewildered by the appearance of the man, that looked a shadow of the person she used to know, slowly started to relax. 'I'm really sorry, Mr Wittleworth. We accidently threw our Frisbee into your garden.'

'Oh,' said the old man, scratching his head a little bemused by her response. 'Why didn't you just knock on my door and ask for it back? I am fully aware what most say about me around here, but I thought you of all people, knew me better than that.'

'Err, we didn't want to disturb you, Mr Wittleworth,' said Molly, feeling somewhat embarrassed, not really knowing what else to say.

'We?' he asked, his eyes searching the overgrown garden.

'Yes. Peter is just outside the gate waiting for me with my dog. It was he, who threw the Frisbee into your garden.'

'Oh, I see. Well, why don't you let them in. I can see that your dog is getting a little restless. He's almost burrowed his way under my gate,' laughed the old man, noticing the Jack Russell's snout was eagerly sniffing out its master.

Molly lifted the latch on the gate and opened the door, where Dasher preceded to jump up into her arms, growling a warning towards the stranger. 'What's going on Molly?' asked Peter, standing sheepishly just out of eyeshot, ready to make a run for it.

'It's ok Peter. Come on in,' said Molly, amused by his cowardice. 'Are you mad?' Replied Peter, taking two steps back. 'You've got the Frisbee. Now let's get out of here.'

Molly laughed as she reached out for him. 'It's fine. Come on, he's not going to bite you. I think he's lonely and just wants someone to talk to,' whispered the girl, so as not to embarrass the old man.

'Are you sure?' replied her friend, trying to peer around the gate to catch a glimpse of him. 'I don't fancy joining the others in his basement.'

Molly laughed at the absurd notion. 'Don't be ridiculous. He's in no condition to over-power a baby, let alone us,' said Molly, dragging him reluctantly through the gate.

'Hello, Peter. How are you?' asked Mr Wittleworth, causing the young man to freeze. 'You've grown into a big lad.'

Peter stood there dumbstruck for a few moments, trying to get his head around how different he looked. 'I'm okay thank you Mr Wittleworth,' replied Peter awkwardly.

Like Molly, Peter also couldn't quite believe how much he'd changed. How could this old frail man, who everyone thought was hiding people in his basement, go through such a transformation in only a couple of years. 'I've been going to boxing for a while now,' said Peter, letting him know he was more than capable of handling himself if there was any funny business. Mr Wittleworth smiled at him, knowing exactly what he was trying to insinuate. 'It's okay Peter. There's nothing to fear here. I'm quite harmless. Would you all like to come inside and have some lemonade and biscuits?' Molly and Peter looked at each other without saying a word but knowing exactly what the other was thinking. 'There's something important I need to tell you Molly. I promise, you're completely safe.'

The way Peter looked at his friend, told her exactly what he thought about that idea. But Molly needed answers. Answers she knew only James Wittleworth could provide. 'Thank you, Mr Wittleworth, that's kind of you. What about my dog. Is it okay if he comes in too? If I leave him in your garden on his own, I'm afraid he'll alert the whole neighbourhood.'

'Of course, he can,' replied the old man, smiling down at Dasher. 'I'm sure we can find a few treats for him too.'

Chapter Four

The house seemed different to how Molly remembered it. How could this once bright, welcoming place, that hosted a variety of freshly picked flowers, mixed with the sweet smell of herbs and spices that used to drift in from the kitchen, now seem like it resembled Mrs Havisham's home from Great Expectations? The flowers that once filled the air with the scent of summer all year round, were now a sorry sight of withered stems, that barely protruded their vases, half filled with a dark cloudy liquid once resembling the water that gave them life.

The carpet that used to feel like you were walking on a soft, newly cut lawn, now felt sticky and hard under foot. Dust and mildew filled the air, so thick that it was difficult to focus on anything. Even breathing it felt like your lungs were being contaminated. The house had pretty much the same layout as the others on the same road. This one seemed different though. There was no familiarity to it, even though it looked similar, it felt dark and claustrophobic.

'Please, sit down and make yourselves comfortable while I get us some refreshments,' said Mr Wittleworth as he left the living-room.

Molly and Peter looked at each other, a little bemused as to how they found themselves here. How on earth had they managed to go from walking the dog, to being in the one place in the world they'd rather not be, in less than half an hour? It all seemed a bit surreal.

'Molly; this is madness! What the hell are we doing here? Your mum would go absolutely mental if she knew where we were! And my parents would ground me for the rest of my life.'

Molly scanned the room, trying to take everything in. 'I know Peter, but I've a feeling we're here for a reason. I don't know but, my senses are telling me that I need to be here.'

'Yeah? Well, mine are telling me to get the hell out! Look, even Dasher is acting strange.'

Molly turned to see Dasher standing upright on his hind legs, staring up at a photograph that was hanging on the wall. 'What's the matter boy?' asked Molly as she walked towards the hypnotised dog.

'How can he be staring at a picture?' asked Peter, following closely behind. 'I'm sure I read somewhere that animals can't see two dimensional.'

'What? Where did you get that information?' asked Molly, doubting Peter had read anything that didn't have something to do with sport. 'I don't know. Maybe I saw it on tv or something. Never mind, what is it anyway?'

As she got closer to the picture, Molly began to feel a little lightheaded as she recognised the person that was right next to Mr Wittleworth. 'That's my dad!' said Molly in disbelief. 'But I've not seen this picture before.'

Peter leant forward to get a closer look, convinced she were seeing things. 'Oh my god you're right! What is a picture of your dad doing here?'

'That's the last photograph there is of your dad,' came the response from behind them.

Startled, they both spun around to see Mr Wittleworth, standing in the centre of the living room holding a tray with a jug of cloudy lemonade, alongside a plate of cookies. 'There's so much I need to tell you, Molly. Please sit down, won't you? You both must be thirsty.'

Molly and Peter, a little lost for words, sat down while the old man placed the tray of refreshments on the coffee table. 'Let me start by saying, you have nothing to worry about. I've no intension of harming you. Like I said earlier, I'm aware of the rumours that are circulating, but look at me. Do I look like I'm capable of hurting anyone? All I want to do, is tell you my side of the story. I think it's what your dad would have wanted.'

Molly looked at the old man realising there was no malice behind those eyes. There was a sadness to him that she sensed had lived deep inside over the last few years. 'Please Mr Wittleworth. Where was that picture taken?'

'Help yourselves to the refreshments,' said the old man as he took the picture off the wall, staring at it as he walked back to the couch. 'This picture was taken the day before your dad went missing Molly. It was taken by your aunt, at her farm.'

'Aunt Olivia took this photo?' asked Molly, as she reached out to take the picture from him. 'She did indeed. I had it developed about six months ago. It's the only thing I have left to remind me of him.' Molly watched his hand tremble, as he tried to pour the ice laden lemonade into the glasses. 'Please, let me help you with that.' She said, gently taking the jug from his unsteady hand.

'Thank you, young lady. Unfortunately, I've a touch of arthritis, which makes lifting, a little painful at times.'

Molly finished pouring the cold beverages and placed the jug on the table. 'Dasher! That's naughty!' Shouted Molly as one of the cookies swiftly vanished from the plate.

The old man laughed as the dog skulked away in shame; crumbs spilling from his chops onto the floor. 'It's quite alright. He's more than welcome. I guess the smell was too much for him to bear. Here boy, have another one,' he said, tossing a cookie over to where the eager dog sat drooling.

'You said earlier that you wanted to tell Molly what had happened,' said Peter, getting a little impatient, not to mention feeling more than uneasy.

Molly glared at Peter, letting him know under no uncertain terms that he was being extremely rude. 'That I did, Peter. Please accept my apologies. I appreciate you'd like to leave as soon as possible. I was only trying to make you feel as comfortable as I could before I begin.'

The old man picked up the picture, staring longingly at it, before turning his gaze towards the young lady, that sat patiently waiting, to get the answers she'd been longing for. 'You have your father's eyes, Molly,' he said with a warm smile that sent her heart into a hop, skip and a jump. 'I apologise for staring. You look like your mum, but your eyes are your fathers. Of that there is no doubt.'

Molly's eyes began to glaze over. The memories of her dad tucking her into bed at night. The sweet smell of his after shave as he leant forward to kiss her goodnight as clear as day in her mind. She took a deep breath, stealing herself whilst wiping the moisture from her eyes before it began to flow out of control. Peter placed a hand gently on her shoulder for comfort. A gentle shrug suggested that sympathy was not what was wanted. The only thing Molly needed right now, was to hear the whole story.

'Let me start by reiterating that your dad was (is) my best friend. All the accusations that I had anything to do with his disappearance, had a huge effect on me over the last two years. I've had a lot of time to think. To try and make sense of it. There's no logical explanation I'm afraid. All I can tell you is, what I know. The events leading up to and after he disappeared.'

'Please, tell me everything. Leave nothing out. I want to know every detail,' insisted Molly, now perched on the edge of the couch in anticipation.

'I'll do my best Molly. To be honest with you, unusual things started to happen the day before. As you are probably aware, your dad and I were staying at your aunt's farm. The whole idea of the trip was to fish. You know what a keen fisherman he was. What you may not be aware of is, he loved to explore. He'd tell me stories, of when he was a kid, exploring the caves that surrounded the beach of port Soderick. He was strangely drawn to them, he'd tell me. Spending many hours searching aimlessly through the small caves and cracks that lined the cliff face. Searching for what? I couldn't say. Neither could he really.

'Anyway, on this particular day, your dad insisted on showing me these caves. I wasn't so keen I'm afraid. I was no spring chicken even then and the thought of climbing over rocks at my age, was about as appealing as a trek across the Antarctic! Besides, all I was interested in was catching some of the big fish your dad would boast about for years. Maybe he wanted someone else to confirm that he wasn't the only one that felt these urges. Maybe he needed to know if the lure of this place was as strong as it was when he was a child. I don't know. Whatever it was, there was no deterring him from it.

'Eventually I agreed, with the promise that we'd enjoy a full day's fishing the next day. So off we went. We set off from the farm late morning. It was roughly a couple of miles from Loch Nedd to Port Soderick. It was a beautiful summer's day, with a light north westerly breeze to cool us on our way. The scenery was lovely, as I'm sure you know. I spent most of my life in the city, so taking in the splendours of the countryside were a novelty for me.

'I was amazed at the sight of the fields, covered in bright yellow rape seed flowers, that stretched as far as the eye could see. Blackberry bushes lined the way as we made small talk about the Island's history and sights it had to offer. Your dad took great pleasure telling me about the Island's past. A mixture of what was fact, and what was folk law.

'Folk law has it, that thousands of years ago, at the time of battles of the giants in Ireland, Finn Mac Cooil was fighting with a great, red-haired Scottish giant who had come over to challenge him. After beating him, Finn Mac Cooil chased him eastwards towards the sea. But the Scottish giant was a faster runner and began to pull ahead of him. So, Finn who was afraid he would jump into the sea and escape, stooped down and clutched a great handful of soil of Ireland to throw at him.

'He cast it at him but missed his enemy and the great lump of earth fell into the midst of the Irish sea.

'That lump of earth became the Isle of Man and the hole which Finn made, where he tore it up, is Lough Neagh.

'Apparently, the Isle of Man has the oldest parliament in the world, Tynwald. Started over a thousand years ago by the Vikings in 979 AD. After colonising the Island, the Vikings established their own laws separate from the mainland, that still exist to this day. Every year on the 5th of July, the Islands elected representatives gather at a ceremony called Tynwald, held at the parish of St. Johns, to finalise the many changes to the Islands laws, where incidentally stands the church where your dad was christened.

'The Isle of Man also has the oldest tram system in the world drawn by horses that has been in existence since 1876 and still runs to this day along with electric railway that can take you to the peak of the island's only mountain, Snaefell. It's said that on a clear day you can see the seven kingdoms from the summit. Mann, England, Ireland, Scotland, Wales and rather more fancifully kingdoms of Neptune and Heaven.

'The island has the largest working water wheel in the world. The Laxey wheel, also known as the lady Isabella, created to mine the Island's copper and is, also home to the world-renowned Manx cat. Famous because it had no tail. Legend has it that when, Noah was calling the animals into the ark, there was one cat that was out moussing and took no notice when he was calling her. She was a great hunter, but on this occasion, she was having trouble finding a mouse and wouldn't enter the ark without a catch.

'So, when all of the animals were safely inside and the rain began to fall and there was no sign of her, he said. 'Who's out is out and who's in is in!' And with that, he began to close the door when the cat came running up, half drowned. Which is why cats hate the water. She just managed to squeeze her body inside, but Noah slammed the door shut on her tail, cutting it clean off. The cat said, 'Bee bo bend it, my tails ended. I'll go to Mann, get copper nails and mend it.'

'The Manx Folk are a very superstitious people. From the 1950's it was reportedly custom to advise a visitor to greet the Fairies on the journey south from, Douglas or north from the airport whilst travelling over the Fairy bridge, situated over the Santon Burn. Failure to pay your respects, by either saluting or a verbal greeting according to locals would result in angering the Fairies, (or little people, as they preferred to be addressed) which would lead to extreme bad luck. This was more worrying for visitors that were travelling to the airport, as it was more preferable not to take any chances whether you believed the superstition or not, for obvious reasons.

'I was fascinated. The fact he knew all this stuff was very impressive. I could listen to your dad tell stories for hours. He had an enthusiasm about him that would hold your attention and hang on his every word.

'By the time we got to the beach, I felt like a native.

'It was a beautiful place that seemed a million miles from civilisation surrounded by cliffs that were strangely clean in appearance, considering the vast number of sea birds decorating its facade. It was almost like they went elsewhere to do their business out of respect for its beauty. The only thing that looked out of place, was this old and derelict amusement arcade that was built into the cliff around mid to late twentieth century. When allowed, your dad would spend time there playing skittles, a miniature version of what you now call ten pin bowling.

'He paused for a while before telling me about the masses of tourists that used to pack the beauty spot throughout the summer, enjoying the beach and the winding pathways that lead around the headland. Unfortunately, the arcade shut down due to it being deemed unsafe because of erosion from the constant incoming tides. Over the years that followed, tourist numbers declined heavily until only dog walkers were the only ones that frequented the once bustling resort.

'As we made our way towards the rocks, he pointed out a crack in the cliff face. It must have been ten feet wide at the bottom and got narrower the further it climbed. Getting there was a nightmare, especially for me. Like I've already said, I was no spring chicken, even then. Climbing over huge rocks and boulders was dangerous and I didn't fancy it one bit. But my curiosity got the better of me and I knew if I refused to go and check it out, we'd be back the next day, exploring instead of fishing. To be honest with you, I couldn't understand what the fuss was all about; at the end of the day, it was just a cave. It looked no different than any other.

'Your dad though was mesmerised; he couldn't take his eyes from it. He literally left me to fend for myself as he moved as quickly as he could over the jagged and slippery rocks, until he eventually reached the mouth of that cave. I on the other hand, took my time. There was no way I was rushing to get there. If he wanted me with him, before going inside, then he'd have to wait. It must have taken me at least ten minutes to get to him. Once I got there, all I could think about was, whether we'd have enough time to get back before the tide came in. There must have only been a couple of hours left before we would be cut off by the sea.

'The cave was dark, dank and wet. The fresh smell of the sea inside told me, that when the tide was at its highest, this cave would be flooded. There was no way on earth I was venturing far inside. Your dad assured me we didn't need to go too far inside. He only wanted to know if I could hear anything.

'We must have only been about twenty feet inside when he asked me if I could hear a noise? I told him, the only thing I could hear was the sound of the sea, amplified by the cave. He was wandering around like a man possessed, looking in all the nooks and cranny's trying to identify where this noise, only he could hear, was coming from. It was a little unnerving I can tell you. When I asked what the noise sounded like, he said it sounded similar to a foghorn, only deeper and constant. I thought he was going mad and begged him to leave, when suddenly he stopped. He took a step back and looked down, as if he felt something under his foot that was different to the shingles that covered the floor of the cave.

'Crouching down and brushing away the debris, he saw what looked like a small box made of some sort of metal. Maybe iron or copper. Using his fingertips, he dug around the edges so he could get a better look at it. It was definitely old. Looking at the markings that were carved on the surface, it was like nothing I had ever seen. He grabbed a sharp stone close by and began to dig out the box, taking care not to damage it.

'Who knows, this thing may have been hundreds of years old. It certainly seemed to have been in there for as long. We must have been there at least an hour or so. Although it was a warm summer's day, I was beginning to feel really cold. My bones felt chilled to the marrow and my feet were uncomfortable, as well as damp. Just as I was about to give up and insist that we leave, your dad dropped the stone he was using as a tool and pulled the box from the ground.

'Apparently, as soon as he took that thing out from the earth, the sound he was hearing had stopped. All I wanted to do at that point was get the hell out of there. Who knows how long we'd spend in that dungeon? For all we knew, the tide was close to cutting us off.

'On the way home, after taking me twice as long getting back over those rocks, I noticed your dad seemed different. He was chilled and relaxed. As you know, your dad was quite a hyperactive individual. Always rushing around, usually at a hundred miles an hour. But now, it seemed like someone had turned down the dial on him, to slow. We hardly spoke a word the whole way back. Focused solely on that box, running his fingers over the carvings etched into its surface, all the while trying to find a way inside. There was no keyhole either. No way to open it. The carvings were just as strange. Weird mythical creatures like, the Hydra, circling moons and planets were beautifully adorned around the surface. What was inside? What treasures would we find? All questions that would never be answered unless we could find a way to open it.

'As soon as we got back, all I wanted to do was lie in a hot bath and relax, but your dad was in no mood for any kind of relaxation. In fact, he seemed to be back to his old hyperactive self, insisting that we went straight to the barn to try and find a way to open the box. Although I was just as curious to find out what was inside, the thought of destroying the antique to discover its contents seemed wrong. I mean, the box itself must have been worth a fortune. But there was no reasoning with your dad. And nothing I would say could deter him from his goal.

'We must have tried for more than an hour with every tool we could find. We used drills, chisels, hacksaws, hammers. We even tried opening it with a jackhammer! We didn't make a scratch. Not a single blemish. It was impregnable. Finally, we gave up. It was clear to us that this thing was made of something far stronger than anything we'd ever come across, so decided we would take it to someone who might shed some light on what it might be as soon as we got back home.

'It had been an exceptionally long day. I was beat and after your dad had accepted defeat, all we wanted to do was sleep.'

Molly and Peter just sat there. Mesmerised by what they were listening too. Time was getting short and Molly's mum would be home soon, but there was no way they were leaving until, Mr Wittleworth had told her everything. She insisted on knowing every single detail and nothing less than the whole story would make her move from that couch.

'Molly. It's getting late,' said Peter, looking anxiously at his watch. 'And I'm as fascinated as you are to hear the rest of the story, but my parents will be wondering where I am very soon. Do you think we could come back tomorrow? I'm sure, Mr Wittleworth wouldn't mind if we came back then.'

Molly sat upright and gave Peter another one of those looks that said exactly what he feared. 'Not a chance! I'm not moving an inch until I know everything. You're more than welcome to leave if you want to. But I'm sorry, I have to stay.

Why don't you send your mum a message? Tell her you're at mine. Say, I'm helping you with your maths homework. You know, the thing we should be doing right now, before you launched Dasher's Frisbee into the garden!' Peter sighed in frustration, realising she was letting him know that it was his fault they were there in the first place.

'Okay. I'll text her now, but you know what my mum's like and if she calls me back to confirm where I am, then I'm putting her on to you.' Molly gave him a satisfied smile. She knew Peter would never leave her there on her own. Although convinced she was quite safe, the thought of someone finding out that she was alone at, Mr Wittleworth's house of all people, would have everyone in serious trouble. At least if Peter were there, there'd be no misunderstanding.

'Maybe Peter's right, Molly,' said the old man, just as aware of the implications that would surely be levelled at him, should any of their parents know where they were. 'I really don't want you to get into any bother. Like Peter said, we can finish this tomorrow.'

'Please Mr Wittleworth. I need to know now. If I go to bed tonight without finding out the truth, I won't sleep. I've got another half an hour before mum gets home and even then, she'll think I'm out walking the dog, so there's plenty of time,' said Molly, eager for him to agree to continue.

Mr Wittleworth paused for a moment, contemplating if it were a good idea to put himself in a position, (even though it was all quite innocent), that would open him up to even more speculation. 'Okay Molly, but we'll put a time limit on it. It's nearly 5.30. If by 6pm I haven't finished, then we'll have to call it a day, okay?'

'Deal,' replied Molly, letting out a deep breath as she settled back, anxious to get on with it.

'Well, although I was extremely tired that night, I had a lot of trouble sleeping. Tossing and turning most of the night, thinking about that box. What was it made of? Why couldn't we open it? What secrets did it hold inside? I think I managed to get about three hours sleep in total. I gave up hoping for any sleep at about 5 am, so I got out of bed and went to the bathroom to get cleaned up. I was halfway through brushing my teeth when I heard a tapping on the bathroom door.

'I slowly opened the door to find your dad standing there in his dressing gown, looking as excited as a schoolboy and breathing so fast that you'd be forgiven for thinking he'd just been on a five-mile run. Urging me to finish brushing my teeth, he asked me to follow him to his room. On entering the bedroom, he pointed, his hand trembling, to the box that was sat on his dressing table.

'To my astonishment, the box was open! I looked at your dad, who was still breathing heavily and noticed he was drenched in sweat. We slowly walked towards the box, not knowing exactly what to expect. As we peered inside its bright interior, sitting side by side, on top of a couple of raised plinths, were the two most beautiful gold bracelets I had ever seen in my life. They were captivating. Your dad and I looked at each other, knowing we were thinking exactly the same thing. Who was going to reach inside first? Your dad took a deep breath and slowly reached inside, picking up one of the bracelets.

'They were exquisite! Beautifully engraved with the same markings that were carved on the box. We were entranced for a few minutes. Marvelling at how perfect they looked. Being the impulsive person, your dad was, he proceeded to place the trinket over his hand. I tried to persuade him that it might not be such a good idea until we knew more about them. But it was like he was in a trance and couldn't hear a word I was saying.

'No sooner was the bracelet on his wrist, it began to tighten, moulding itself tight around the flesh without putting too much pressure that made it feel uncomfortable to wear. At first, we began to panic. Wrestling with it. Trying everything to get it off. Suddenly, your dad pulled away like he was happy to have it there, encouraging me to do the same with the other one.

'There was no way I was putting a self-retracting bracelet on my wrist without knowing what it was! I quickly placed it back in the box, left your father to get ready and went down for breakfast. Your aunt Olivia was in the kitchen making breakfast by this time and invited me to sit at the table and help myself to tea and coffee. I'd never seen so much food at a breakfast table. There were pancakes, bacon, sausages, fruit, bread and cereal adorned with all sorts of condiments. The smells were amazing, and as soon as your dad joined us, we put all thoughts of the previous events to the back our minds. All I wanted to do today was fish.

'After breakfast, we set about gathering everything we needed for the day and set off for the beach once more. I was excited. I'd never tried beach fishing before. All of our usual fishing trips were spent at the lake on, Conwy mountain in, North Wales where it was slightly easier to catch the little blighters. Beach fishing was a tad more difficult. More patience was needed, as the tides that you wouldn't necessarily have whilst lake fishing, took a little more skill.

'The walk to the beach was a pleasant one. There was no talk of the bracelet. I wasn't going to mention it and neither it seemed was your dad, which suited me fine. I'd had enough of adventure for one lifetime. Mostly, we chatted about passed fishing trips and teased each other about who would be going home with the most fish. Obviously, I knew it wouldn't be me, but I was happy the conversation was light-hearted. And getting back to reality was more than a welcome change.

'The beach was as deserted as it was the previous day. Not a soul in sight. There was a small jetty that I noticed the day before, in the centre of the beach that was used for small rowing boats, back when the resort was busy with visitors, that stretched out into the sea. The tide was at its lowest by this time, so we set up our rods close to the beach, so we had plenty of time to fish before the tide came back in. We baited our hooks with small pieces of, herring that we prepared earlier and cast our lines into the sea. It couldn't get much better than this, I thought. Chatting away with your dad, about life and generally solving the world's problems.

'The stress and anxiety of the last twenty-four hours seemed like a distant memory until, suddenly, without any warning, your dad jumped out of his skin, dropping his rod. At first, I thought he had a bite that was too strong to control. But my heart sank when he asked me once more if I could hear that noise. The noise that had plagued him every time he came near this place. At this point, I was begging to fear for his sanity. I could hear nothing.

'Maybe he had some kind of medical problem or a mental issue no one was aware of. Whatever it was, clearly had something to do with that cave. Determined to find the answers and rejecting all my suggestions to leave, he insisted on going back to the cave to find out once and for all what was happening. To this day, I deeply regret not going with him, but at the time, the thought of navigating those rocks again, filled me dread.

'After making him promise, to be extremely careful and come back as quickly as possible, he made his way back to the cave. As I watched him negotiate his way across the rocks, I told myself if he hadn't returned by the time it took me to pack up our stuff, then I would have choice but to go in after him. A thought that didn't inspire me one bit.

'It must only have taken me no more than fifteen minutes to dismantle the rods and pack everything away. Just as I was about to make the one decision I was dreading, came a call that chilled me to the core. Your dad, clearly in distress was shouting my name from inside the cave. In a sheer state of panic, I forgot all about my fears of potential injury and jumped like a man possessed from rock to rock, whilst screaming, I was on my way. As I got closer, the cries for help seemed to get further away, fading into the distance until, as I eventually arrived at the mouth of the cave, I heard his voice no more.

'I shouted out his name, over and over again, desperately seeking a response. Nothing! The silence was as deafening as it was eerie. I frantically searched the cave looking for any clues, constantly calling his name. There were no signs of him whatsoever. It was like he had vanished into thin air. I kept searching, looking for any gaps or tunnels he may have fallen into. But there were none. The cave was solid. The only way out, was the way in.

'I kept going over it in my mind. Could he have gotten out without me noticing? Questioning my own sanity. But it was impossible. Other than glancing at where my feet were going from time to time, my eyes were fixed solely on the entrance of the cave. Besides, I could hear him calling me right up until I arrived. I felt sick to my stomach. My first thought was to call the police but decided that it was best to let your aunt know what had happened. Maybe this was some sort of sick game they played as kids and I was the brunt of the joke. But this was no joke. Your aunt went into a blind state of panic. I could hardly find the words to explain what happened.

'To be honest, I didn't understand myself. Eventually, after we both calmed down a little, convincing each other there was a perfectly reasonable explanation for it all, Olivia told me to stay where I was while she contacted the authorities.

'It seemed like forever, waiting for the police to arrive. I kept on looking, inside and outside the cave. Constantly calling out to him. All sorts of emotions, one after the other running through my whole being. Panic, fear, confusion, anger and dread combined into one, so when the authorities eventually arrived, they found me exhausted, slumped at the mouth of the cave, with head in my hands, an emotional wreck.

'It must have been a few minutes before the sergeant in charge managed to get any sense from me. To be honest, there wasn't much I could tell him. I explained what had happened, from when we left your aunt's, right up until they arrived. He kept on insisting that there must be more to the story. That he couldn't just vanish into thin air. I totally agreed with his second point, but there was nothing else to say.

'That's exactly what happened. I could tell he was getting a little frustrated with me. His tone changed dramatically the more I told him, that was all I knew. I began to fear there was, more than a sense of accusation from the questions he was asking. He wanted to learn if there were any disagreements between us. Or if we had argued or fought about anything that morning. I explained that your dad and, I had never had a crossed word ever since we'd known one another.

'Your aunt Olivia, who had accompanied the police in order to direct them to the correct location, could hear the line of questioning the officer was levelling towards me and instantly came to my defence, extremely annoyed that there was any suspicion I might no more than I was letting on. The officer, aware of the sensitive nature of the questions, reassured us that it was only a formality.

'After I was questioned, we were told there was nothing more we could do and that we should go home and wait. If they managed to find him, then we'd be the first to know, but that I should remain on the, Island in case I was needed to help further with their enquiries.

'That's it, Molly. The rest you know. I was questioned multiple times over the weeks that followed and then the accusations began. Even your mum began to believe them. The newspapers, social media and local press hounded me. That's when I locked myself away. I couldn't take it anymore. I was receiving death threats in the post. People would heckle me as I went to the shops.

'Eventually, it got so bad that I barely opened my front door. Please don't take this the wrong way. But there were times I'd see you walk past my window and was desperate to call to you. Explain to you that the rumours were untrue. But I knew what that would look like to anyone that saw me approach you. I'd had enough of accusations. A bigger spotlight on me, I fear, would have been the end of me.'

Molly and Peter sat there dumbstruck for a moment, staring at the old man in disbelief at what they'd just heard.

'Until you told me, I wasn't aware of half of what you've said. I mean, I know that you were questioned by the police and there was a certain amount of suspicion at first. But to learn what you've been through is shocking. All my mum ever told me was, that you were to be left alone and that I should not, under any circumstances, bother you. I'm certainly unaware my mum blames you either.'

Peter lowered his head, staring at the floor, knowing he did have those suspicions. 'Peter?' said Molly, surprised by the way he was acting. 'Have you got something to say?'

'Err…. No, nothing,' said Peter, feeling a little embarrassed as he tried to look at the old man without giving away his true feelings. 'There is one question I have though, sir, if you don't mind,' continued Peter. 'I noticed you didn't say anything to the police about the bracelet.'

Molly looked at her friend, surprised that she hadn't remembered the bracelet herself. With everything she'd had to think about, she'd totally forgotten about it.

'I'm glad you asked me that, Peter,' said Mr Wittleworth as he got up off the chair. 'I asked myself the same question for a long time. I can't really give you a sensible answer if I'm being honest, other than, trying to explain to the authorities that we'd found a box that contained two, of what seemed like, out of this world golden bracelets that, when you put them on, magically shrank to fit the wearer; what else could I say? Besides, something told me, to keep it to myself.'

The old man slowly made his way towards the cabinet, standing at the far end of the room opening. Molly and Peter watched in amazement as, Mr Wittleworth opened one of the draws and took out the second golden bracelet.

It was as beautiful as he had said it was. Perfectly formed with the markings he described, beautifully engraved around it. He walked slowly over to molly and placed the golden trinket into her hands.

'I don't know why, but something tells me that this was meant for you. There's a connection between those bracelets, that cave and your father's disappearance. You may think I'm crazy Molly, but they are out of this world. Of that I have no doubt.'

Peter looked the old man, then at Molly as he indiscreetly tugged on her shirt, indicating it was time to get the hell out of there. 'Erm… Thanks, Mr Wittleworth. It's time we were on our way now. Our parents will be wondering where we are.'

'Don't be rude Peter,' snapped Molly. 'Thank you, sir. Thank you for everything. I'm grateful to you for telling me what I needed to hear. I think you should know, we're off to my aunt Olivia's at the weekend for the first time since dad's disappearance.'

Mr Wittleworth looked at Molly and smiled, knowing that fate was the reason why they were here at this moment. 'This was meant to be Molly. Go and find your dad. Bring him home. One word of advice though if I may.'

'What's that, sir?'

'Don't put the bracelet on your wrist until the time is right.'

'When will I know if the time is right?'

'You'll know. When the time is right, you'll know.'

Molly placed the trinket in her pocket as they said their goodbye's, promising she'd do all she could to find the answers that would clear his name.

'You didn't believe all that rubbish, did you?' mocked Peter as they walked home.

'Why, didn't you?' said Molly abruptly, hoping she wasn't being naïve.

'Don't be daft! What a load of rubbish! No wonder the police didn't believe him.'

'How do you explain this then,' scoffed Molly as she pulled the bracelet from her pocket.

'Easy,' said Peter as he crossed the road to his house. 'It's probably his mothers. A family air-loom or something, I don't know. I certainly don't believe it's a magic bracelet that had something to do with your dad's disappearance.'

With that, Peter waved his hand in the air as he opened the gate to his garden.

'Have you forgotten something?' hollered Molly as she put the bracelet back in her pocket. 'You forgot about the long division lessons!'

Peter's shoulders slumped in exasperation, knowing there was no time for them to study before, Mr Mac's class tomorrow. 'Great! I'll pick up my bag in the morning!' he shouted, closing the door behind him.

Chapter Five

The trip from Liverpool to Douglas was a rough one on Mannanan. Due to its twin hulls, the high-speed catamaran, with speeds capable of up to 42 knots, was generally only affective in calm waters. The unpredictability of the Irish sea meant the vessel was only in service during the spring and summer seasons.

Built in 1998 in Tasmania by Italian ship builders, it was originally used for commercial services in Australia and New Zealand. She was then charted to the US military in, 2001 as a joint venture (HSV-X1). A flight deck was added to accommodate various US military helicopters. It could ferry up to 325 combat personnel and 400 tons of cargo that could travel up to 3,000 nautical miles one way at a time, before eventually being sold to the Isle of Man steam packet in 2008 and refurbished to accommodate up to 850 passengers and 200 vehicles for commercial service once more from the ports of Douglas (Capital of the Isle of Man) and Liverpool.

Molly had sailed on Mannanan on many occasions and had experienced a few rough crossings from time to time. But this was Peter's first time on a ferry. He'd sailed on small boats before, like rowing boats in the lake when on holiday with his, family. But this was a whole new experience.

The weather forecast report for the day suggested it would be an uncomfortable crossing with wind speeds exceeding 35 knots (force 7). Pretty much the ferry's limit, before it was deemed too dangerous to sail.

Peter was extremely nervous to say the least, looking for reassurance from Molly the whole journey from north Wales to Liverpool.

Prior to setting sail, the captain made his regular announcement over the public address system, warning passengers that although the vessel was secure and ready to depart, they should take extra care whilst moving around the vessel due to the motion of the ferry whilst navigating the rough seas.

'I thought you said it would be safe Molly,' said Peter anxiously as he gripped tight hold of each of the armrests either side of his chair. Molly laughed, finding a hint of pleasure in Peter's unrest.

'It'll be fine Peter. Don't worry too much. There's plenty of life jackets to go around. In fact, if you look under your seat, you'll find yours.' Peter stiffened when the ferry suddenly lurched forward as the captain cranked up the speed on exiting the river Mersey.

'What! A life jacket! Why do I need a life jacket? Are we going to sink?' Molly laughed even harder, now making the most of the opportunity to wind him up.

'Who knows. You can never be certain. Maybe the captain had a few too many drinks last night.'

'Stop teasing Peter, Molly,' said the mischievous girl's mother sat one row in front, listening to every word. 'It's going to be fine Peter. The captain knows what he's doing. I've been on enough rough crossings over the years. If it were unsafe to sail, the captain would have postponed the crossing until it was. Don't listen to madam there, she's trying to wind you up.'

'Shut up, Molly. You know how nervous I am. You wouldn't like it if you were on the receiving end. Besides, I still owe you one for setting me up the other day. Asking Mr Mcsheffrey if he wouldn't mind giving me one on one tuition to help me with my long division. How could you? I know we like to play practical jokes on each other. But that one was a low blow, even for you.'

'She did what?' said Gina clearing her through, trying to disguise the giggle she was failing miserably to stifle. 'Molly, that's a terrible joke to play on your friend. What happened, Peter?'

Peter wasn't sure if he wanted to answer, suspicious if he were setting himself up to be ridiculed by both of them. Molly was certainly a chip off the old block. Her mother also well renowned for playing the odd joke on her dad back in the day.

On one occasion, Molly had told him that her mum, once pretended to have cut her hand badly with a knife while peeling potatoes. Bursting into fits of laughter after her dad rushed around looking for the first aid box, only to find out she'd squirted tomato ketchup on her hand as a joke.

'Erm… He approached me on the last day of term saying he'd be more than happy to give me one on one lessons and help with the maths questions I was struggling with. But was disappointed that I'd sent Molly to ask before coming to him myself.'

It was too much to bear. Both Molly and her mum burst into hysterics. 'Ha, ha, ha,' laughed Peter sarcastically. 'Big laugh, isn't it? Don't you worry, miss smarty pants; I'll get you back.'

Molly wiped her eyes, clearing the tears of laughter, before gathering her composure. 'Oh, wise up, misery chops. It was only a joke. Anyhow,' she whispered quietly under her breath. 'You deserve that, after all the times you've grassed me up.'

'I'm sorry, Peter,' said her mum trying to straighten her face. 'We're just trying to take your mind off the journey.'

Peter's Adam's apple began to bob up and down. A sure sign there was something trying to emerge from his mouth he would rather remain inside. 'I think I'm going to be sick,' he burbled as he leaped from his seat, clasping one hand over his mouth. 'I need the toilet!' He continued, now panicking and stamping his feet in some sort of mad ritual dance routine.

'Come with me. I'll take you,' said Molly as she grabbed his arm, trying hard to avoid of anything projecting from his mouth. Difficult as it was because the ferry was pitching in all directions.

'Quick, get in there!' insisted Molly as she shoved him through the toilet door. No sooner had door closed, there was a noise coming from inside the facilities that sounded as if someone were being strangled.

'Good grief Peter! I've not heard anyone make as much noise as you. What have you been eating?' The sound of retching mixed with interrupted moaning was too much to bear. 'I'm going back to my seat, Peter. You'll be okay. Take your time,' said Molly, scrunching up her face, feigning sympathy as she left her friend to fend for himself.

'Molly, it's been nearly half an hour now. Shouldn't you go and check on him? I'm getting a little worried. He's my responsibility at the end of the day. I don't want to have to explain to his parents how we left him stuck in a lavatory on the ferry over.'

'You go and check on him then if you're so worried,' huffed Molly, knowing what a drama queen Peter could be. 'Did you hear him in there? I'm surprised the whole boat didn't hear him. It's embarrassing.'

He's your friend. Besides, I'm not his mum. It'll look weird me standing outside, shouting through a toilet door.'

'And it won't look weird if I go?' laughed Molly, as she picked up her magazine, pretending to sift through the pages.

'Oh, look, there he is,' said Gina, looking a little concerned noticing Peter's pale complexion was less than healthy. 'Are you ok? You don't look particularly good; would you like some water?'

Peter looked at Gina with half open eyes that suggested the thought of anything passing his lips was the last thing he wanted. 'Err... No thanks, Mrs Miggins. I don't think I'd be able keep anything down right now.'

The ashen faced young man turned his attention towards his unsympathetic friend who was still busy pretending to check out the latest fashion items in her mag. 'Thanks very much for waiting. I've been all over the boat looking for you.' Molly forced herself to tilt her head to the side, whilst wetting her index finger ready to turn the page. 'What are on about? We were only twenty feet away from the toilet. How the hell could you get lost?'

'I was disorientated, wasn't I? Forgive me, but my mind was on other things at the time, like throwing my guts up. I was looking everywhere for you. One fella thought I was trying to nick his bag because I was looking intensely at who was sitting in the seats that looked similar to ours.

Molly burst out laughing again, dropping her magazine on the floor as she slapped her hands over her face. 'You idiot. Only you could cause so much drama in such a short space of time, now get your head down, there's only an hour to go before we dock. You can't get lost if you're asleep. Well, maybe in your head.'

There's no way Peter would be sleeping on this rollercoaster. He just prayed there was no unwanted trips to the toilet in the time that was left.

Chapter Six

Aunt Olivia was waiting to greet them as they disembarked. Gina's older sister of two years was a hard-working lady who had one son, Bailey. Between them, they took on the majority of the work load needed to keep the farm functioning at a sustainable level, after Olivia's ex-husband, (being a beer swilling, lazy, gambling degenerate) decided the grass was greener on the other side and hot-tailed it, a couple of miles down the road, into the arms of another less fortunate woman he was coveting for some time.

Gina had warned her sister for years that he was no good for her. Taking advantage of her mild manor and forgiving nature for most of their married life. Olivia was one for a quiet life. Confrontation and drama were situations she would avoid at all costs, so life for her and, 'The sponge' as Gina called him, drifted aimlessly for years without much dialog between them.

Olivia was a slightly larger version of her sister and a little shorter in height. Same colour eyes and hair although, Gina's hair colour changed, like the wind, depending on what fanciful shade was in fashion at the time. At least until a few year ago when everything changed.

The only common ground, Olivia and her ex-husband found between them, was their son. Bailey was a year younger than Molly, but extremely smart. An A-level student, who made a point of reminding, Molly of that fact whenever he had the opportunity. Molly was pretty smart herself, so the competition between them, made their relationship frosty to say the least. Bailey was a contradiction of what you might think an, A-level nerd might look like. He was fairly well built and roguish looking. Short cropped blond hair, with a cheeky way about him. Growing up on a farm all of his life had toughened him up some-what having to do, along with his mother, most of the work.

There was a mutual, (begrudged at times) respect between, Molly and Bailey. More begrudged by Molly as she usually came out second best to him whenever competing, against each other. He'd also make a habit of correcting, Molly whenever he thought she was wrong. Even if he knew she were right, Bailey would word it in a way that would sound as though she had made a mistake, which got right up, Molly's nose.

'How was your trip guys?' asked Olivia as they pulled out of the sea terminal. 'Flipping awful,' replied Peter, scrunched up in the backseat between, Molly and the door.

'Olivia, this is Peter,' said Gina, acknowledging his response with a wry smile. 'He's had a bit of a bad experience bless him. It's his first time on a ferry, so, not the best way to start his holiday.'

'You poor thing,' said Olivia sympathetically, catching a glimpse of him through the rear-view mirror. 'That's not an ideal start for your first time. I hope you were looking after him Molly.' She continued, averting her glance to the sniggering young lady sat next to him.

'No, she bloody well didn't,' complained Peter, fixing an accusing look at his tormenter. 'She shoved me into the toilet and left me there as I was about to throw my guts up. Then, I got lost trying to find our seats because she couldn't be bothered to wait for me.'

'Oh Molly! You and your practical jokes. Don't worry Peter. You've seen nothing yet. Wait until these two get started on each other. You can sit back and have a good laugh at her expense,' laughed Olivia, referring to the two adversaries sat next to him.

Molly shot upright and gave her aunt a look that should have cracked the rear-view mirror, before shooting, Bailey a warning glance that suggested, I dare you.

The ride home in the beat-up, Volvo V70 was mainly a quiet one. Mostly due to the fact it had been a long and arduous journey up to now. The only conversation, was a carefully disguised whisper between the two sisters. Molly guessed it was probably to do with, how everyone had been coping over the last couple of years.

' What's, that?' asked Peter, pointing at an old looking, arched stone landmark.

'That's Snotty bridge,' replied Gina as they passed under a bridge displaying thousands of what looked like gooey droplets hanging from under its arch.

'Snotty bridge?' chuckled Peter.

'Yeah, the locals named it, oh…. I don't know how many years ago, because the droplets looked like Droplets of Snot hanging from your nose.'

Peter blew his cheeks out and gulped. 'Please, if you want me to keep what's left of my stomach contents where they belong, can we dispense of any talk of human waste?' Everyone in the car burst out laughing. Even Peter, after composing himself saw the funny side.

The farmhouse was everything you'd expect a farmhouse to look like. The drive leading up to the large, whitewashed stone building was lined with tall oak trees that stood firm against the strong wind that seemed to swirl amongst the lofty canopies. The five-bedroom house itself stood majestically at the centre of a courtyard that offered ample parking space for a number of vehicles.

Estimated to have been built in the late eighteenth century, the family was said to have acquired the property over a hundred years ago through a number of gambling debts owed to their ancestors, that was handed down to sons and daughters over the years.

Significant restoration over the last fifty years gave the owners a reputation of high-standing in the borough. With two high chimney stacks on either side of the property and a central gablet that was added in the 1970's completing its splendour.

'Wow!' Remarked Peter as they pulled up to the front of the house. 'It doesn't look like any farmhouse I've ever seen.'

Molly laughed as she pulled her suitcase from the Volvo's huge boot. 'How many farmhouses have you seen in your many years on the earth?'

'Not many. But I don't remember seeing any as big as this one.'

'There's been a lot of restoration done over the years Peter,' said Olivia as she rummaged through the bunch of keys, finding the one that would gain entry. 'Parts of it were added much later and significant upgrades were needed due to its old age. Well I don't know about you lot, but I could do with a brew.' She said, changing the subject.

The inside of the, grand farmhouse was just as impressive. The living room extended at least half the length of the house. Two, three-seater chesterfield sofas sat opposite each other, with plenty of room spare to accommodate a large, handmade oak coffee table between them. An impressive old grandfather clock stood proud. Its large brass pendulum swinging hypnotically from side to side in the far corner of the room. The pier de resistance though, was a huge, stone fireplace that commanded most of the gable end of the house. A great oak plinth that rested almost six feet above a roaring fire, emphasised its grandeur. The heat generated, along with thick stone walls was enough to keep the entire house warm through the coldest of winters.

'Would you all like to go and get settled into your rooms and get cleaned up, while I make some dinner?' asked Olivia, wiping her feet as she closed the porch door. Molly will show you where you'll be sleeping, Peter.'

Molly lead the way up the solid oak stairs, aided by thick wooden banisters on either side. Large black and white framed photographs of what, Peter guessed, were of family ancestors, decorated the landing on the first floor.

'This one is you,' said Molly as she opened the bedroom-door.

Peter stood with his mouth wide open, like a Venus flytrap waiting for its unsuspecting pray. 'I'd have put you in the attic if it were up to me,' joked Molly, standing hands on hips.

'This is impressive,' said Peter as he took in the lavishly furnished bedroom.

At the far end stood a solid, hard wooden chest of draws that accommodated a large, porcelain wash basin and jug, as well as a double wardrobe of matching design. Long, blood red velvet curtains hung either-side of a sliding sash Georgian bar window that took in the majestic views of the landscape. The crowning glory though, was a sumptuous carved six-foot, oak super king size four poster bed in a mock, Tudor antique style, with canopy.

'Oh my god! This is amazing!' Gasped Peter as he leapt onto the soft, cotton filled mattress. 'Is this the master bedroom you've given me by mistake?'

'You wish. This is one of the smaller rooms. Wait till' you see mine,' scoffed Molly, checking the jug on the chest of draws was empty. 'Besides, you might want to sleep with one eye open tonight. Apparently, one of our ancestors hung himself from one of the beams in this room. It's said, you can sometimes hear the cracking of the beam, followed by the sound of his neck breaking.'

Peter bolted upright on the bed. The hackles on the back of his neck standing to attention. 'Are you kidding me? Are you saying this room is haunted? That's it. I'm not staying here tonight. I'd rather stay in that attic; You were eager for me to have!'

'That's even worse.' She replied getting immense pleasure from his increasing anxiety. 'Legend has it that…'

'Oh, pack it in will you!' Interrupted Peter, eventually realising it was another wind up. Molly burst out laughing, clapping her hands in appreciation of her own brilliance. 'You're so easy Peter. You fall for it every time.'

Peter climbed off the bed, secretly cursing himself and a little embarrassed that he'd fallen for one of her many wind ups again. 'How many is that now Peter?' She teased, lifting up her fingers one at a time. 'I've lost count waiting for you to catch up.'

'Yeah, yeah, yeah. Laugh it up. Trust me, your time will come soon enough smarty pants.

'Yeah? Well, be sure to give me a clue as soon as those cogs start turning, okay?' Baited Molly, ducking to avoid a gestured swing of his arm. 'Let me chuck my case into my room and we'll head down for something to eat. I bet you're starving. You haven't eaten since breakfast and 99% of that was left on the ferry.'

'I could definitely eat something,' said Peter, subconsciously wondering if his digestive system could handle a full meal.

Peter followed his friend as they ditched the girls bags in her room and made their way down to dinner.

'I hope chicken salad will suffice guys,' said aunt Olivia, placing a freshly cut loaf of bread on the kitchen table.

'Perfect for me. Thank you,' replied Peter, with a sense of relief. 'I'm not sure how my stomach would react to anything heavier.'

The kitchen was in keeping with the rest of the house. As traditional as expected with what a farm kitchen should look like. Standing proudly against the rear wall was a, pine Welsh dresser, decorated with floral painted plates, cups and sources on each of the three shelves. Built into the gable stone wall, sat an old, but fully functional solid fuel arguer, kept constantly lit that, as well as the main fireplace, maintained the house was warm throughout the day and night.

The rustic wooden surfaces at the front end of the kitchen, stretched the full width of the room which, at the centre, housed an old Belfast sink just below the window, offering ample views of the courtyard. The rectangular dining table, again, was made of solid oak. A common theme of most of the furniture in the farmhouse. Peter guessed most, if not all of it, came from the many oak trees that occupied their land. The smooth flag stone slabs that made up the kitchen floor, surprisingly felt warm under foot. Probably due to the constant heat generated by the impressive arguer.

'So, what have you lot got planned for tomorrow?' asked Gina as she offered the salad bowel around the table.

'Peter and I were thinking of just going for a walk around the countryside. Ya know, spend the day showing him around the headlands and places of interest.'

'Oh right,' replied her mum, a little surprised at her choice. 'I thought you might have wanted to go into town. There's certainly more going on in Douglas. Not that I'm complaining. The clean fresh air of the countryside is far better for you. Just stay away from, Port Soderick will you. I don't want any of you going anywhere near that place!'

Everyone stopped eating for a moment as the room fell silent. Everybody knew why, but no one would say.

'Why don't you go with them Bailey,' said Olivia, Eager to break the awkward silence.

Molly nearly chocked on a pickled onion trying to get her words out before Bailey came to her rescue. 'No thank you!' He shouted before anyone could scupper his plans. 'I'm off to town with my mates, tomorrow. There's a fair down on the promenade. Maybe another time ay.'

'Oh…. Okay,' said his mum, trying to remember if he'd mentioned it. 'Why don't you take, Molly and Peter along with you, to meet your friends. It'll be great for them to meet new people while they're hear.'

This time it was Molly's tern to intervene. 'Thanks aunt Olivia. But there'll be plenty of time for that. We'd much rather have a quiet day tomorrow if that's okay?'

Olivia looked at her sister, shrugging her shoulders in submission. 'If that's what you want. I just don't want you to miss out is all.'

'We're fine, honestly,' insisted Molly, all three of the teens breathing a huge sigh of relief.

'I'd like to go and unpack now if that's ok? Said Molly, pushing her plate to one side. It's been a long day. I need to get sorted so I can chill out.'

'Yeah, me too,' agreed Peter, anxious to re-acquaint himself with his amazing four-poster bed.

'Yes, of course. Your mum and I will clear up. This time!' Replied aunt Olivia, hinting they wouldn't get away without helping every day.

'Thanks, Molly's aunty,' said Peter as he handed her his empty plate.

'Just call me Olivia, Peter.' She laughed, placing the dirty dishes into the sink.

Unpacking wasn't the only reason, Molly wanted to get to her room. She'd been fascinated, no, obsessed with the bracelet, Mr Wittleworth had given her. Every night when she'd gone to bed, Molly had spent hours, hardly sleeping, entranced by the trinket. Studying every inch of its surface. The markings that surrounded it were like nothing she'd ever seen. Even googling its description gave no clues as to its origin and all the while, Mr Wittleworth's warning ringing in her ears.

What would happen if she put it on? She thought to herself. Would it react in the same way with her as it did with her father? The temptation was irresistible. Sitting on the end of the bed, with the bracelet laying in the palms of her hands, she felt an energy surging through her, almost electric like. A sense of invincibility running through her whole being. Was this how her father felt when he held its twin? If it were, then how could she hope to resist its pull, its need, its craving to be at one with its suiter? Mesmerised by its aura, Molly slowly moved the trinket with one hand and gently, began to slip it over her fingers. A strange pulling sensation, urging her to continue to place the trinket onto her wrist, like a magnetic force, becoming harder to resist.

'What the hell do you think you're doing!'

Molly jumped out of her skin, as she yanked the bracelet off her hand, quickly hiding it under her leg.

Peter was standing in the doorway in utter disbelief at what he had seen.

'I.... I.... I couldn't help it,' gasped Molly, breathing a little heavier than usual 'Could you not hear it calling?'

'Hear what calling? Don't you remember what the old man told you? You promised you wouldn't put that thing on unless. A, I was there with you. And B, we were at the exact place where your dad went missing. Put it away. It seems, every time you make physical contact with it, it takes over your inhibitions.'

'But couldn't you hear it Peter? It was like a whisper. I couldn't understand the language, but I knew what it meant.'

Peter shook his head, angrily. 'No, and you should know better under the circumstances.'

Peter suddenly made a move to grab the bracelet from her. 'What are you doing!' Snapped Molly, hiding the trinket behind her back.

'You need to put that away before it possesses you,' replied her friend, taking a step closer, carefully reaching out, gesturing her to hand it over.

'Leave it! I'll put it away now. Just step back will you.' She demanded as she opened the dressing table draw.

Peter did as she asked, taking a few steps back to make her feel a little more comfortable. 'Please don't touch it again until you're ready to use it. There's not long to wait now. Tomorrow, okay?'

Molly carefully wrapped the bracelet, as if it might break if she put any pressure on it. Placing it in a white handkerchief and shut it away in the draw.

Peter gave a gentle nod of approval and closed the door behind him.

Chapter Seven

A hand on her shoulder convinced her to run faster. Battling against the strong wind, the thick mud beneath her feet meant escape was futile. The door seemed close and yet so far away at the same time. The creature was almost upon her. Its long thin spindly arms reaching out. Gnarled bony fingers, with jagged hooked black claws swiping at her. Its head, so grotesque, with eyes wide and as black as coal, nose, long and pointed. Its mouth, with teeth like scythes, open, eager to receive its pray. A roar coming from either side of her. Galleries, filled with creatures, beings, blood thirsty monsters cried out in anticipation. 'Get her…. kill her…. eat her soul!'

Her arms, thrashed around, desperate to ward off the, what looked like, winged creatures from a movie, ducking and diving, tormenting her for their own amusement. The door only metres away now.

A little old man, wearing a robe, stood beckoning her with one of his tiny arms to move faster. Everything seemed in slow-motion. The devil like creature, ready to pounce and devour her at any moment.

'Speak the words…! Speak the words!' Was the message coming from the old man as he pointed to a sign above the huge iron door that spelt out the phrase. 'NIMINE MEO APERIRE IANUAM.'

Although the words seemed alien to her, she knew what they meant. 'Hurry! Speak the words before it's too late,' insisted the strange old man.

She could feel and smell the creature's breath on the back of her neck. Its scent was putrid! Like it had come from the bowels of hell itself.

The crowed was now at a frenzy, knowing that the end was imminent. Sensing their patience would soon be rewarded.

Again, the dwarf like figure bellowed his instructions. This was it. She had to do it now. Had she read the inscription, right? She had no choice but to trust her instincts. Exhausted, beaten and with all she had left she screamed the words. 'IN THE NAME OF MY FATHER OPEN THIS GATE!'

The great iron door's hinges began to creak. A gap started to appear. Beams of bright lights escaping from captivity, as if imprisoned for thousands of years, filling the dark arena with all colours of the spectrum, blinding those who were used to the darkness, sending them running for cover, afraid they'd be turned to ash. The door sprung wide open, revealing the spectre completely. Dazzling those who dared to look upon it. Not her though, to her It was magnificent. A warm and exhilarating sensation rushed through her, invigorating every part of her once depleted body. It was like drinking in the nectar of the gods. Without any more hesitation, she moved quickly towards the light. Salvation was certain. She'd won.

Suddenly, a sharp pain shot through her shoulder, like she'd been lanced by thousands of needles. She felt its presence, towering above her. The recent replenished energy quickly being sapped from her body as quickly as it came. She slowly lifted her head in time to see beasts, sinister teeth drooling with spittle, jaws wide open, ready to devour her, consume her.

Molly's whole body jumped, as she opened her eyes, expelling a terrified cry. The room was black. Dark shadows filled the corners of the room. She blinked continuously, trying to catch any light. Searching for a hint of comfort the moon had to offer from the gap in the curtains. Her eyes, still capturing the hideous creature from her dream every time she closed them.

The frightened girl, sat hard against the large wooden headboard, her arms hugging tight around her legs, pulled up to her chest, heaving from the horror she'd woken from.

'Molly, are you ok?' A concerned voice whispered from outside the bedroom.

'Come in, Peter, please,' replied a relieved, but shaken Molly.

Peter slowly opened the bedroom door, revealing her sat shaking, in a foetal position on the bed.

'What is it? I heard you crying out as I was drifting off. Are you okay?' asked Peter as he sat on the side of the bed.

'I thought it was just a nightmare, but it seemed so real. I've never experienced anything like it. It was as real as I'm talking to you right now.'

'It's something to do with that bracelet Molly. I'm telling you now, you need to get rid of it or at least bring it to someone who may know a little more about its origin. You've not been yourself since the old man gave it to you.'

'What do you mean?' Snapped Molly defensively. 'I'm no different now to who I've always been. I just want to find out what happened to my dad. Surely you can understand that, can't you?'

'I don't know Molly. I can and, I can't. Sure, I can understand you wanting to find out the truth, but at what expense? It's obviously dangerous. We don't know what it's capable of. What if, it was the reason for your dad's disappearance? What do you think it would do to your mum if you went missing as well? Peter lowered his head as he continued. 'I don't know what I'd do if anything bad happened to you.'

Molly smiled as she moved closer to him. 'Nothing bad is going to happen to me, Peter. If anything, I feel even more determined to go through with this, knowing you'll be with me. I couldn't do it without you Peter.'

Peter looked up that those big blue doe eyes. He knew how determined she was. He knew he couldn't let her do this on her own. And he knew, she knew it also. He couldn't deny her anything. His feelings were too strong. Wherever she went, he went. 'Okay, you win,' he replied, jumping off the bed, realising he was revealing a bit more than he'd like. 'I'm off to sleep. It's going to be another long day tomorrow. Will you be okay now if I go?'

'I'll be fine.' She answered, a little surprised by his sudden urge to leave. 'I'd feel more comfortable if you would leave the door open though. Oh, and could you turn on the landing light as well please?' She continued, as she climbed back into bed.

Molly lay there, with bated breath listening for the sound of his bedroom-door, hoping she wouldn't hear the sound of it click shut. She began to breathe easy once more, knowing he'd deliberately left it open, able to hear if she needed him.

Exhausted from the night's events, Molly's eyes could remain open no longer. Comforted by Peter's concern for her, she drifted into a deep sleep.

Chapter Eight

The early morning call of the cockerel resonated around the room. Molly blinked whilst shielding her eyes against the invasion of daylight that poured into the bedroom as she drew back the curtains. Lifting up the sliding-sash window, she filled her lungs with gallons of fresh country air, that reminded her of times past. Times when she was a small child, on holiday with her parents.

She remembered as she stood gazing from the window, of the times her father would sit her on, Charlies back. The donkey her aunt took in, after he'd been used, taking young children for rides on Douglas beach in the summers. After many years of service, he'd gotten too old to continue, so Olivia, other than see him live out the rest of his life alone in a field, bought him, so, Bailey and Molly, when she visited, could sit on his back from time to time and look after him in his old age.

Many, fun filled summers were spent on the farm. Helping with the chores, (that never seemed like chores to her) helping her mum and dad milk the cows. Collecting the egg's, the chickens had laid. Feeding the various animals that kept the farm sustainable.

After Olivia's, degenerate of a husband decided to try his luck elsewhere, (not that he was of any use when present) most of the farms live-stock had to be sold off due to the heavy workload, as well as a large portion of the surrounding land.

Olivia had enough money to make sure, she and Bailey were comfortable enough, without the need of a fully functional farm, but kept enough livestock to ensure it maintained its purpose.

A dull ache nagged at her left shoulder as she pulled down the window. Suddenly, memories of last night's lucid dream came flooding back. 'Surely that's impossible.' She muttered to herself, remembering the hideous creature that grabbed her shoulder moments before she woke. Slowly lifting her t-shirt over her left shoulder, Molly gasped with shock to see four red marks, grazes, that had slightly penetrated the skin. 'What the hell!' She swore, trying to make sense of it.

Molly dismissed the idea. Convincing herself she must have banged it against the headboard as she was thrashing around, remembering the winged creatures that were tormenting her as she tried to evade their sharp talons. 'That must have been it' She tried to assure herself, deep down knowing, it was less likely, but satisfied there maybe a number of reasons for her injury, considering all that's happened so far. Determined to put it to the back of her mind, Molly grabbed her wash bag and headed for the bathroom.

'Which one of you two idiots put food colouring in the toothpaste!' Screamed Molly, as she burst through the kitchen door, looking like she'd just eaten a punnet of blueberries.

Gina, Olivia, Bailey and Peter, took one look at her and burst out laughing. 'Was that you Bailey?' asked Olivia, biting hard down on her lip, trying to suppress her amusement.

'Guilty as charged,' roared Bailey, as he almost choked on a piece of bacon.

'I'll kill him!' Molly slammed the kitchen door shut as she made a beeline for the condemned tormentor.

'Hold it right there,' ordered Gina, grabbing hold of the angry girl before she could throttle him. 'It's way too early for this nonsense. You've barely been in each other's company five minutes.'

'He's an idiot!'

'Hang on. Have you forgotten about the time you put, gum-numbing gel into my toothpaste a few years ago? I couldn't feel them for hours after. I did warn you I'd get my own back,' said Bailey as he received a high-five from Peter, sat opposite.

'Don't you congratulate him you, Judas! You're supposed to be my friend!'

'You can't have a go at, Peter after the amount of practical jokes you've subjected him too,' interrupted her mum.

'That's different.' She replied, pulling her arm away from the loosening grip. 'He gives back his fair share.'

'Can we all just have a nice breakfast, without you two trying to get one up on each other. Why can't you both call a truce?' Pleaded Olivia.

'Never!' Snapped Molly, eyes fixed on the smirking, Bailey as she sat down at the table. 'This isn't over. Just you wait. I'd sleep with one I open if I were you.'

'Bring it on blueberry chops,' taunted Bailey, sending a cocky wink her way.

'That's enough! If there's any more of this, nobody will be going anywhere today. You will all stay inside and do chores,' warned Gina as she slammed her knife and fork onto her plate.

Everyone jumped with the shock of metal hitting crockery. Molly and Peter looked at each other, worried their plans would be scuppered if they were grounded. Molly began to relax, knowing there was plenty of time to plot her revenge. She could wait. The best practical jokes took time. Unfortunately, this wasn't the time. She had more important things to do today. Things that couldn't wait.

'We're off now mum,' announced Molly, taking the rucksack packed with food and drink for the day.

'Have you both made your beds and tidied away your clothes?' asked her mum as she dried the last of the breakfast dishes.

'Yep, all done.' She replied, handing Peter the bag of refreshments.

Molly opened the backdoor as her mum placed a hand on her shoulder. Causing her to wince slightly from the sudden touch, remembering the marks on her shoulder she couldn't explain.

'What's the matter sweetheart? Have you hurt yourself?'

'I'm fine mum. I just banged my shoulder on the door handle as I was picking something up off the floor. It's no big deal.' She reassured, giving her a hug to keep her from examining what damage was done. 'Bye mum, we'll see you later. I love you.'

Molly looked into her mum's eyes. Eyes that had aged too much over the last couple of years. Many tears and sleepless nights had taken their toll. Crying herself to sleep. Night after night. Listening to the same song, over and over again. Their favourite song. 'Love bites, by Def Leppard' The song they danced to on their wedding day.

Was she doing the right thing? Could she let her mother go through this all over again? The answer was, absolutely not, but she had to know. She had to find out what happened to dad. Was it realistic? No, but too many things had happened. Too much evidence to suggest that things were not as they seemed. It was a chance she had to take. Besides, Peter would be with her. There was no way she would do it on her own. She was confident he would keep her safe.

He always had her back. The time Callum James attacked her…like prince charming coming to the rescue. How did he know where to find us? The question was never asked. They'd made a promise to never speak of it. Never mention it again. To be honest, she didn't want to know. The idea that he appeared out of nowhere just to save her, was far more heroic than the truth.

'I love you too my darling,' replied her mum. Surprised at the sudden show of affection. 'Please take care won't you. And remember, stay away from, Port Soderick.' She insisted, her tone more serious.

'Okay mum. We'll be home for tea.' Molly replied, waving, as they marched across the courtyard, disappearing through the tall oak trees.

The walk to Port Soderick was a tense one. Neither of them knew what to expect or what they would do when they got there. What did they expect to find that the emergency services hadn't already discovered? There were no clues. No signs of a struggle. Nothing. The only thing they had that the police didn't, was this bracelet. That was strange enough in itself. The power that came from it was magnetic. It was out of this world. There had to be some sort of connection. It was the only answer left.

'Don't put it on until the time is right.' The explicit warning from, Mr Wittleworth, repeating over and over in her head. Why would he say that unless he felt something too? He'd kept the bracelet for two years. Why hadn't he put it on? Had he ever felt the urge? The pull of it was incredible. Ever since she possessed it, she felt drawn to it, like a moth to the light. She was sure it was calling to her. Not in the literal sense, but psychically. Willing her to put it on. Be one with it. The other night when, Peter startled her as she was about to put it on, she felt its magnetic pull. Forcing itself onto her wrist.

There was too much unknown and yet so much to discover. Her dad was alive. Somewhere, someplace and she was certain she had a part to play.

'Do you have the bracelet?' asked Peter as they approached the top of the winding road that lead to the beach.

'Yeah, it's still wrapped inside the handkerchief in my jeans pocket.' She replied, placing a hand over her pocket to check it was still there.

Port Soderick beach was deserted as usual. This once vibrant, bustling tourist attraction was now an eerie, morbid, desolate place. Even the dog walkers, that frequently enjoyed its lush headlands had abandoned this now, forgotten coastal resort.

Reality began to sink in for Molly and Peter. Was this really a good idea? Would anyone come to their aid if anything were to go wrong? (Which was highly likely) The nearest house was a mile away. Even the signal on their phones were hit and miss.

'I can't believe how different this place feels to when I was last here,' said Molly, remembering the happy memory, of when her dad brought her here, when she was about seven years old, skimming stones into the sea and listening to him tell stories of when he played here as a child.

Molly wrapped her arms tightly around herself, sensing the unusual chill in the air, considering the time of year. 'Don't you feel that?'

Peter was far too concerned with getting this over with as quickly as possible, to worry about the temperature. 'Can we just get on with it please? I'd like to leave this place asap!' He pleaded as he pointed to a large crack in the cliff-face.

'Yeah, that looks like it might be the one,' acknowledged Molly. 'I can't see anything else that resembles a cave. Okay, let's do this.'

They both made their way slowly towards the cave, holding on to one another as they negotiated their way across the awkward slippery rocks, covered in slimy green algae. Molly's heart rate began to increase as she heard a faint sound, coming from the cave. She stopped in her tracks, remembering the story the old man told her.

'Can you hear that?' She asked, grabbing tight hold of, Peter's arm.

The young man jumped, almost losing his footing. 'Don't do that! You nearly gave me a heart attack!' He gasped, clutching his chest, 'I don't hear anything.'

As they approached the mouth of the cave, the noise started to grow louder. Molly's anxiety started to kick in as she felt a tingling sensation on the top of her leg. 'The time is now Peter.' She announced, taking the wrapped trinket from her pocket.

Molly carefully unwrapped the, bracelet as they entered the cave. 'Surely I can hear it now!' Shouted Molly, barely able to hear herself above the deafening foghorn type below.

'Why are you shouting?' asked Peter, plugging his ear with his index finger. 'I still can't hear anything. Put the bracelet on now,' he continued as he guided Molly's attention towards the now, illuminated trinket.

Realising there was no going back, Molly slipped the antique over her hand. This time, the bracelet was not going to be denied and in one swift movement, shot quickly onto her wrist.

Watching on in disbelief, Peter gawped at the glowing object as it began to shrink, fitting comfortably around her wrist. Molly's feet slowly began to move without her moving them. A bright light at the other end of the cave caught her eye as she felt a strong pulling sensation, she was helpless to resist.

'Peter! What's happening? Grab my hand! Please!'

Peter, caught a little off guard, mesmerised by what he was witnessing, sprang into action, grabbing a firm hold of her hand. The second he made contact with her; the deep, loud foghorn echoed around his ears. 'I hear it Molly! I hear it!' He screamed as he held on tight, the force of the pull becoming more difficult by the second.

The light at the other end of the cave began to take on a peculiar form. Growing larger and larger. Swirling like a spiral, bright lights shooting from its vortex, drawing them closer and closer into its void.

'Don't let go Peter! Whatever happens, don't let go!' Pleaded Molly terrified, knowing there was only one way she was going.

'Never!' Shouted Peter, desperately clinging on to her hand, as if her life depended on it.

Just as they were about to be sucked into the nothingness beyond, the bracelet began to grow, spreading up her arm. Link by link, it quickly transformed into a kind of armour. First covering her hand, then, her shoulder. She was about to scream once more, before the links swiftly locking into place, moved swiftly up her neck, eventually drowning out her cries as it encased her head.

Peter watched in horror as it continued quickly towards him. The force, sucking them harder, so that it lifted them horizontal in the air, the golden armour covering Molly's body, like she was being entombed. Peter contemplated letting go for a second, realising if he didn't, he would suffer the same fate.

Remembering his promise, he held on tight, determined they would see it through together. Peter gritted his teeth as the armour continued down her arm, then, picking up speed, it swiftly covered both of their hands as it spread, encasing his whole body, before sucking them deep, into the unknown.

Beams of light streamed past them. Arced Horizon's came and went. Billions of stars glittered in the darkness. Every second, different patterns emerged as they seemed to pass through holes in space.

Molly began to drift in and out of consciousness, capturing a new constellation each time she woke. She felt strangely calm as the uncertainty of their destination ran rampant through her mind. Maybe the thought she might see her father was keeping her sane. He must have endured the same experience. He had the other bracelet; Had gone into the same cave and had not returned.

The touch of Peter's hand. Knowing he was with her, comforted her further, as she drifted away once more.

Strange visions; Memories, but not her own. Memories of another's life invaded her mind. It looked like her mother, but younger, much younger, dancing with a young man. Was it her father? It must have been. Another memory. A wedding. A beautiful bride with her groom, face to face. Her parents walking arm in arm down the aisle. They looked so young, so happily in love.

How could she be seeing her mother's memories? It was impossible.

Then another. Lying on a hillside, looking up at the sky. Kissing, laughing, a little older this time. Her mother, wearing a floral summer dress that she recognised. She remembered her mother kept it as a reminder, of what she said was, one of the happiest days of her life. Other visions took over. This time they felt different. A vague recollection pricked her memory. Her mother sitting on her father's lap. His hand stroking her swollen belly. Was that her? Was she witnessing her mother carrying her? The next one. Her mother, smiling down on her. Again, a sense of familiarity as she mouthed words she couldn't understand.

Memories skipped from one to the next, like an old film-real, jumping to the next scene. Captions of someone's life. Her mothers, invading her mind, as though they were her own, one giving way to the next. A small girl, about three or four, holding hands with her parents. Laughing with delight as they swung her high into the air as they strolled through the park. She remembered this one. Not vividly, but moments of it felt familiar. But still, the memories were not her own. How could they be? She was seeing them through the eyes of another.

Galaxy's seemed to disappear in an instant, one after the other. Their format different each time, yet the void they were passing through seemed separate, like they were travelling through their own space. Hole after hole, folded over itself, momentarily allowing them to see a new spectre.

More visions pierced her mind. Each one becoming more lucid. The memory clearer, although not her own. A little girl, with long golden hair. A sad look on her face as her mother fixed her clip-on tie. She recognised the school, Maelgwyn primary school. Her first day of school. Not a memory she cared to remember. But she wasn't seeing her own. These were her mother's precious memories. There must be some sort of psychic connection between them. How else could she be having these visions.

She wondered if Peter could be having a similar experience. The touch of his hand, the only comfort she had he was still with her. The rigid armour restricting any movement. Communication useless, although the occasional movement of his hand realising, like her, he was drifting in and out of consciousness, a comfort he was still alive.

The memories began to fade, becoming blurred as they drifted from her mind. Blackness again took over. Until there was nothing.

Chapter Nine

A speck of light. Then another. Molly blinked as she tried to shield her eyes against the brilliant daylight. She could move. The armour had gone. Checking her wrist, she noticed the bracelet had returned to its natural form, but still clung tightly to her wrist. The ground felt peculiar. It felt like grass, but softer, the texture of rabbit fur. And the colour; Although green, was a vibrant, lighter green that consistently looked the same wherever she found it.

Molly suddenly thought of Peter. Where was he? Quickly, she turned her head right, then left. Overcome with relief, she spotted him lying face-down, no more than three feet behind her. Thank you, God, she said to herself as she crawled over to check he was okay.

'Peter. Peter. Wake up' She whispered, gently shaking him, trying not to startle him.

Molly guessed, by the gradual rise and fall of his body, he was still breathing at least. Peter let out a grunt in complaint. 'Just another ten minutes, mum.'

Molly shook him even harder this time. 'Peter, wake up! It's me, Molly, you idiot! We're here.'

Peter raised his head spitting out a tuft of grass. 'What! Here! Where's here?'

Molly slowly got to her feet, staring in awe as she surveyed her surroundings. 'I'm not quite sure. We're certainly not in Kansas, I can assure you of that.'

Peter too, quicker and far easier than he expected, considering he'd just opened his eyes, jumped up to see what was so strange. 'Oh my God! Look at this place!'

The scene was like a setting from, the wizard of Oz, in technicolour. Fields as far as the eye could see, filled with flowers, the likes they'd never seen before. Colours of, reds, yellows, blues, pinks, whites, deeper in colour and more vibrant than anything that was normal. A few hundred yards to the east, (what they assumed was the east) a lake, the lightest, clearest blue, that was as transparent as a pain of glass, full of marine life, all of which they failed to identify. Trees as big as skyscrapers and as thick as a castle's turret, with branches that stretched out far and wide, home to hundreds and thousands of leaves as big as Frisbees.

Then, as they both looked beyond the canopies; The sky; The almost white sky that only hinted a shade of blue, hosting a multitude of moons. Some larger than others. Some closer than their neighbours. There must have been at least a dozen of them spread across the sky, lit up by the sun, a star that seemed twice as large as their own. Either that or it was much closer. It was difficult to tell. The air was sweet. Every breath, a euphoric feeling that coursed through them, giving them a high that was intoxicating. Even the temperature was surprisingly perfect, considering the closeness of the sun.

'Look at that!' Shrieked Peter, pointing excitedly at a pair of peculiar looking birds as they floated by in close proximity. Their wings spun like helicopter blades as they bobbed up and down like a carousel, singing the most harmonious chorus as they passed over-head.

'Where on earth are, we?' asked Molly, struggling to take it all in.

'I think earth is the last place we are.' Joked Peter, still watching the strange birds as they disappeared into the distance.

'Peter!' Screeched Molly surprised she hadn't noticed sooner. 'What's happened to your hair? It looks like it's grown another two inches.'

Peter immediately ran his fingers through his hair, realising it had almost covered the back of his neck. His fringe, no longer curtains, but more like drapes. 'This is so weird! Yours looks longer too.' He laughed noticing although her hair was quite long anyway; it was almost halfway down her back.

'How long did it take us to get here?' asked Molly, becoming increasingly worried at this point. 'I'm so sorry I dragged you into this Peter. My mum and your parents must be going out of their minds by now. God knows how long we've been out there.'

Molly covered her face. Her eyes filling up with tears, the magnitude of their predicament dawning on her. Peter gently put his arm around her, slowly moving her hands away. 'Molly. It's not your fault. It was my decision to follow you. Do you seriously think I could let you do this on your own? I'd never be able to live with myself. Besides, we're still alive. Try to look on the bright side. We must be here for a reason. Your dad must be here too. Think about it. He was never found. According to, Mr Wittleworth, he had an identical bracelet to yours, so, he must be here. Let's keep moving. Hopefully, we can find someone who can help.

Molly took a deep breath as she looked up at Peter. His eyes said everything. The way he looked at her melted her heart. What was this new feeling?

'Come on, let's go.' She said, dismissing her emotions, putting them down to their situation.

'Wait. Is that someone over there?' asked Peter, pointing to a small figure sat fishing by the side of the lake in the distance. 'I didn't notice anyone there earlier. Did you?'

Molly narrowed her eyes, as she looked to where he was pointing. 'It is someone. Come on, let's see if they can help.' She said cautiously, making her way towards the tiny figure, unsure if it were man or beast.

'Wait! We don't know what it is,' said Peter, stopping her in her tracks.

'What choice do we have? We need help Peter. We'll get nowhere if we stay here,' replied Molly, convincing him they had little choice.

'Excuse me sir,' said Molly as they approached the peculiar looking little man, sat whistling a joyful tune, momentarily damming his luck as he let another one get away.

'Can never catch one of the blighters,' he cursed, lifting up the empty line that was tied to the end of a long stick.

Molly and Peter stared at the strange looking old man as he awkwardly got to his feet, tossing the handmade fishing rod to the ground.

The strange being was no more than three feet tall. He wore an old, tatty, hooded robe, that stretched the full length of his tiny frame. A thin, frayed piece of rope tied tightly around his waist. His bony little hands barely visible as they poked through his unnecessary wide cuffs. The little man's eyes were narrow but, looked pleasantly friendly as he opened and closed them like a camera lens shutter. A pointed, upturned nose with nostrils that flared slightly each time he smiled. His lips, non-existent. Just an opening for a mouth that revealed softly pointed teeth. His long flowing white hair that began at the back of his head, that was completely bald on top, almost covering his tiny, shell like ears.

'Good day to you both,' greeted the elf type creature, his voice, deep and gravely, like he'd smoked twenty cigarettes a day. 'Allow me to introduce myself. My name is Shiftervorgoethryn. And I am the gate keeper and wish master. But you may call me Shifter.'

'Very pleased to meet you, Shifter. My name is…'

'Molly Miggins,' interrupted the little man, grinning with satisfaction.'

Molly, stunned into silence, wheeled around to look at Peter before bringing her attention back to the strange man.

'How could you possibly know who I am?' asked a shocked Molly Miggins, not quite believing what she heard.

'We have been expecting you,' he announced, linking his spindly fingers together. 'A little later than expected, but you're here now,' he continued.

'I don't understand. What do you mean, you've been expecting me?'

Shifter paused for a moment as he scratched his perfectly round head. 'You should have been here days ago.'

'I still don't understand. How could you know who I am? Where am I? What is this place? What do you mean, days ago?'

'One question at a time, young lady. First, allow me to welcome you both to the planet, Kaplon.'

'Kaplon! I've never heard of a planet called, Kaplon in our galaxy.'

The old man laughed. 'Nor would you. Our planet does not reside in your galaxy. Nor does it exist in your universe.'

Molly clung tight to Peter, trying not to faint. 'What? Not our universe. How many are there? I wasn't aware there was any more than one.'

Shifter sighed, the expression on his face saying he'd made this speech countless times too many. 'There are multitudes, young lady. Yours is but just one of many. I'm afraid you would be unable to comprehend the number if I told you. In the simplest terms, there are, $10^{10^{10^7}}$.'

'You're right,' said Molly, not even pretending to understand. 'Then how did we get here so quickly? Surely it would take billions of light years.'

Shifter smiled again, pondering on his answer, trying to think of the easiest way to explain it without blowing her mind.

'There are things far too incomprehensible for the human mind to understand. The simplest way to explain it to you is, gravity. Multiple wormholes, folded upon each other, coupled with the force of gravity, means we can transport any being from anywhere in the multiverse. And of course, your bracelet. The bracelet protects you from imploding, as you travel through them.'

Molly's head was spinning by this time. The information, too much to take in.

'I will be happy to answer all of your questions on the way. We must go now, before we are too late,' urged Shifter, as he invited Molly and Peter to walk on.

'Go. Go where? Late for what?' asked Molly, becoming more confused by the second.

'All will be revealed soon enough, Miss, Miggins,' said the old man, leading the way.

He moved surprisingly fast for someone that looked so old. Gliding along the ground like he was on a hover board or something. Maybe that's why he was called Shifter, thought Molly, transfixed by the strange old man.

'One thing is bothering me though,' he continued. 'Who is the human male that accompanies you? I was made aware there would only be you, young lady.'

With everything going on, Molly forgot all about, Peter. It hadn't occurred to her that, her friend wasn't supposed to be there.

'I'm assuming your friend was somehow connected to you as the bracelet began to take its protective form?' asked Shifter rhetorically.

'You assume correct,' replied Molly. 'Please, excuse me for being so rude. This is Peter. He was holding my hand as, like you say, the bracelet covered me.'

'Ah.... I see. It is extremely rare for two beings to travel together. You are very fortunate indeed. With two of you, the chances of completing the realms are slightly increased,' explained the dwarf.

It was, Peter's turn to question the little man. 'Excuse me,' he interrupted. 'I'm pleased to meet you, by the way, but where are you taking us? The only reason we're here, is, because Molly's father disappeared through, what we believe the same wormhole, type thing, two years ago. He wore the same bracelet that brought us here. Have you seen him? Is he here?'

Molly waited with bated breath. Praying the old man would have the answers she craved.

'Norman Miggins,' replied Shifter.

Molly's face lit up in pure delight at the sound of his name. 'Yes! That's my father! Where is he? Is he okay?'

'Yes, he is on Kaplon.' The old man confirmed. 'But I have to explain something you may find difficult to understand. 'Time moves differently between our two worlds. Although it has been, two years and three months in your world. Here, it has only been, nine days.'

The colour from both, Molly and Peter visibly drained from their faces. The reason for their sudden hair growth, slowly beginning to make a little more sense.

Molly, tried to do the maths in her head, before figuring out which question to ask first. 'Are you saying, it took us about, three months to get from our world, to yours?'

'Not precisely, Miss, Miggins,' replied Shifter, deciding there was no need to be exact. 'But you are not far from being correct. Time is relevant, my young friends. To explain relativity, would take time you don't have. Time is moving somewhat faster on your planet. So, may I suggest that we waste as little of it here, as necessary?'

Molly and, Peter agreed to make haste, worried as they contemplated the consequences from the amount of time they might lose.

'Where is my father, Shifter?' asked, a now angry, Molly.

'Your father, Miss, Miggins, is trapped,' answered the dwarf. At least that's what species she assumed he was, not curious enough to enquire his origin, considering their situation.

'Trapped! Trapped where?' asked Molly, the worried look on her face evident.

'He is being held prisoner in the last of the three realms. He fought bravely, Miss, Miggins. Almost completing the realm of spells. Further than most humans. Unfortunately, he was taken by the, tree of souls and will remain there for all time, until freed by his kin. Please, we must make haste. I will answer all of your questions in good time.'

Molly and Peter fell silent as they tried to absorb the horrible revelation, apprehensive of the truth that was yet to transpire.

Chapter Ten

Molly had so many questions running through her head. Only one of them mattered at this time. 'How do I find him? Take me to him now!' She demanded.

The old man suddenly stopped, a serious look on his ancient face, resigned to explain the perils they faced. 'Unfortunately, that is impossible, Miss, Miggins. You must complete the very same tasks your father endured,' replied the dwarf.

Three realms stand in the way of you and your father's freedom. Only by completing all three realms, will you be able to free your father and return to your world,' he continued. 'Very few beings, especially humans, have conquered the realms of, Kaplon. Many trials will test you. Test your courage, sanity and strength. Many beings from this and other worlds, will try to stop you from reaching the gate that will take you to the next realm. Most are deadly. Some are there to help. Some are there to deceive. But the one that controls all is THE ORIGIN. The Origin is the creator of all that is! This is his game. His test.'

Molly was about to reply before Peter interrupted. 'Wait, what are you trying to say? That there is this almighty, Origin, creator, playing god with lives, just for his own amusement.'

Shifters eye's opened wide, exposing his fear. 'Please Peter. The Origin sees everything. He has no mercy for those who oppose him. He is all powerful and rules this universe. For over ten thousand of your years, he has had the power to access other's, which has enabled him to transport beings from other worlds once beyond his reach. He draws his power from those that have fallen. The more powerful he becomes; the more worlds he is able to find. The only way to save your father, is to accept the challenge. There is, no other choice.

'Please, we must press on,' he continued, as they followed the old man. 'Time, for you is valuable. Others are not so fortunate I'm afraid. As I explained earlier, time is relevant. Many beings, even those that have conquered the realms, have remained in, Kaplon to serve the Origin, as time, in their own worlds, has past years beyond what they once knew. Their world, changed by time and their reward for remaining to serve the Origin, too great to refuse. Your kind are fortunate in comparison, as the time difference in both our worlds means you, have the chance to return to a time you belong. Humans are precious to the Origin. He will do anything in his power to keep you from succeeding. The few who have succeeded, rarely accept his invitation for that reason. The power he receives from your kind is greater than any other. The energy the human mind possesses, is irresistible to the Origin.'

Molly and Peter were beginning to realise, after hearing the daunting task that lay in wait for them, there was little chance of success. 'I need to get home to my mother, Shifter. She probably thinks I'm dead. I shouldn't have put her through that again. What was I thinking Peter? Why didn't I listen to you?'

Molly turned her attention back to the dwarf. 'I had these weird memories as we were traveling to your world. I'm sure they were my mother's memories, but how could that be?'

Shifter paused for a moment, contemplating the easiest way to explain it to her. 'It all stems from the strong connection you have with your kin, Miss, Miggins. The psychic link you share means you were able to share her memories as she was having them. It is rare, but when a being yearns for a lost one, the signal they send can connect with your psyche, enabling you to share in their memories.'

'Wow! You mean I was actually connected to my mother as she was actually having those memories?' asked a surprised Molly as she looked to Peter, wondering if he'd had the same experience.

'Don't look at me,' said the confused young man. 'I haven't a clue what you're taking about. Maybe I don't have the same connection with my parents.'

'The universe connects through unseen power, young Peter,' interrupted the little old man. 'Mrs, Miggins previous loss meant, the yearning for her kin, combined with that loss, sent a strong signal to the young lady's psyche, which allowed her to share memories. The bracelet she was wearing, acted like a beacon, enhancing the signal. It is unusual for travellers to have these experiences.'

Molly took Peters hand noticing; he too was hurting. 'You know your parents love you Peter. Your mum is always on the phone, checking up on you. They'll be in so much pain right now. We need to get back to them, no matter what it takes.'

Peter squeezed Molly's hand, appreciating her kind words. 'I know Molly. I was just jealous is all. You're right, we have to get out of here.'

Peter turned to the dwarf, remembering something he said when they first met. 'Didn't you say you were the wish master? Are you able to grant wishes?'

Shifter smiled at Peter, knowing exactly where he was going with the question. 'I am bound by laws, young Peter. I am only able to grant wishes after the test is complete and only then under exceptional circumstances. It has been thousands of your earth years since I was last able to grant a wish.'

'Thousands of years?' asked Molly. 'Well, I'm guessing that's unlikely to happen anytime soon then.'

Peter laughed sarcastically, trying hard not to show his disappointment.

'There is but one way and one way only my friends. You must complete the realms in order to free your father and return home.'

'How will we know where we're going? Are we to do this alone?' asked Molly, worried they would stand little chance of survival in this strange world without help.

'I will be your guide, young lady. I am able to lead you through the gate of each realm, point you in the right direction and answer any questions you may have. But I cannot offer any help that aids your success in conquering the realms. As I have already mentioned, I am governed by laws written by the Origin. There are severe consequences for those that disobey the laws of our world.'

Molly felt a little more at ease knowing there was, at least someone to guide them, even if it did seem impossible. 'So, is that the only help we have. A guide?' she asked, hoping it wasn't just down to the two of them to get through this hellhole.

Shifter pointed to the trinket on Molly's wrist. 'Your trinket, young lady. You have everything you need to help you through to the end from the golden band. The emblems you see around it, are there to help you advance. They will change with each realm you are able to enter. All you need to do when danger presents itself is, tap the emblem you need. It will come to your aid instantly.'

Molly stared at the trinket. Feeling much different towards it than she used to. It was their lifeline. Their only protection. 'How will I know what emblem to touch and when to use it?'

'You won't,' replied Shifter bluntly. 'That will determine on how good or bad your judgement is. Choosing the correct emblem, could be the difference between success or failure. I know what you're going to ask, Miss, Miggins,' he continued, stopping Molly as she opened her mouth. 'And no, I cannot advise you on which emblem to choose. I am there to guide you and that is all.'

Peter suddenly stopped in his tracks. 'Well I'll be dammed,' he said, eyes as wide as saucers, staring at the magnificent fortress, looming up even higher and more impressive than the huge trees that surrounded it.

All three stood in awe at its grandeur. Even the little old man took in a deep breath, drinking in its splendour as he had many times before. It looked like something out of the king Author legend, Camelot. The bright silver castle, with its imposing turrets dominated the landscape.

'I'm assuming that's where you're taking us,' said Peter, still transfixed on the imposing structure ahead.

'The gateway to the, realms and fortress of the Origin, young Peter.' Shifter stretched out his arms, as he presented their fate, their destiny.

'The Origin? You mean he lives here?' asked Molly as they continued on their way.

'You will both, be presented to the Origin before your quest begins, Miss, Miggins,' replied Shifter as the sky above began to fill with strange species of birds, the likes of which they'd never seen before. The fortress sparkled, as colours from the suns aluminous rays bounced off its perfectly smooth surface. The trio watched as the birds played and danced in between the flecks of light. Intertwining with each other as if they put on a show just for them, narrowly missing one another as they majestically swooped and soured, high above the fortress, before making way for the next wave.

'That is beautiful!' Said Molly, clapping her hands in appreciation. 'Their timing and symmetry are flawless.'

'They are the, Sagitta. Their arrow shaped bodies mean, they can move effortlessly, using the air to their will. Their wings can move so fast, that they become invisible to the naked eye. They are here to welcome you,' said Shifter as they approached the citadel.

Their reflections greet them as they got closer. No marks or imperfections were to be seen. It was like looking into a perfect glass mirror.

Chapter Eleven

'How do we get inside?' asked Peter as he scanned the fortress for a way in.

Shifter held up a hand, before pointing to Molly's bracelet. 'Look for the emblem of the door, Miss, Miggins. Touch it and the door will appear.'

Molly lifted her arm as she tried to identify the emblem the little man described. 'This must be it,' said Molly as she touched the one that resembled a door.

The markings lit up as she lifted her finger. The same image immediately began to take shape on the fortress. Beams of light, escaping from the cracks of the giant door that cut into its, perfect surface, as if someone were using a blowtorch on the other side.

Shifter stretched out his arms once more, as if prompting the door to open. Without warning, the giant door began to move, slowly at first, then effortlessly swinging wide open to reveal a spectacle which immediately took their breath away.

The vast entrance gave way to a never-ending hallway, decorated with creatures that were carved out of all sorts of precious stones. Diamonds, Emeralds, Sapphires, Ruby's and other gems they couldn't identify.

Amaroks, Bonnacon, Gargoyles, Imps. All types of gothic creatures littered the length of the hallway, as if they were guarding the way. The time and skill it must have taken to carve them out of such hard material, should have been impossible, lighting the way ahead, penetrated by the sun as it beamed through the long-arched windows that separated each one.

Molly and Peter, astonished by the magnificence of it all, followed the old man as he flowed, like a gondolier across the glass parquet floor, that reflected the ceiling above, enhancing its size even more than necessary.

The hallway seemed to go on forever. No end in sight. 'How much longer, Shifter?' asked Peter, wondering if everything in this world was exaggerated.

'We Will be there shorty, master Peter.'

'Really?' Remarked the young man, not quite so sure.

'One thing you should both remember. Not everything in this world, is, what it seems.'

'Then how will we know the difference, between what is real and, what is not?' asked Molly, somewhat confused.

'Instinct, young lady. A sense you humans possess, but rarely take much notice of. You will find, many of your senses will be more affective in this world.'

'Yeah! My sense of smell is definitely working better. My BS barometer is going off,' joked Peter, as a door, suddenly appeared in front of them from nowhere.

'Wow! Where did that come from?' He asked. Slightly embarrassed by his last remark.

'You will get used to things, you're not quite accustomed to here, young man,' replied the dwarf as he prepared to open the door.

Both Molly and Peter, stood up straight as if they were waiting, ready to enter the headmaster's office at school.

The old man gave the double doors a shove. Without any effort, the doors swung gracefully open, revealing a sight that turned their legs to jelly.

Crowds of creatures, some recognisable from storybooks, some never seen before, packed the gigantic throne room, cheering and clapping as, Molly and Peter stood there, rooted to the spot, almost losing control of their bodily functions.

It seemed like, good and evil had congregated in one place, deliberately separated on either side of the throne room to welcome them. On their left, were, Cyclops, Fenrir, Golems, Grendel, Ogre's and many more they could not identify. On the opposite side were more friendly types, like, Unicorns, fairies, some with, some without wings. The ones with, hovering above the crowd. Elves, gryphons, pixies, along with others too many to mention.

How is this possible? Thought Molly. Surely these creatures belonged in story books and fairy tales. There was no such thing as Goblins and Unicorns. Centaurs and Manticores were from Greek mythology, not real life. Not standing there, clapping and cheering in front of them.

Shifter beaconed them onward. Leading the way towards a dark figure at the end of the room. Creatures parted ways, making room so they could continue. The imposing figure getting closer, larger, more sinister with every step.

The room fell silent as the intimidating ruler raised his hand. 'Your majesty. Please allow me to introduce, Molly Miggins and her friend, Peter Hughes,' announced Shifter as he bowed his head in respect. 'Molly, Peter. This, is the Origin.'

The creature was almost human like. His features certainly resembled something you would call human. But that was where the similarity ended. Molly guessed he must have been at least eight feet tall as he rose from his golden throne. A long, black satin robe hung from neck to feet, covering his body. His pale hands were extraordinarily long. Sharp, hook like, black nails protruded from his, even longer fingers. His skin was smooth. No age lines visible on his white ashen face. His teeth sharp to the point. Both incisors longer than the rest, threatening when visible. Lips as blood red as his eyes. Two black curved horns flowed from his bulbous head, each one finishing at his hunched shoulders.

The ghastly, ghostly looking figure walked slowly, one step at a time towards the two terrified humans at the bottom of the steps. 'Let me get a closer look at them,' said the intimidating ruler, the authority in his voice enough to send the congregation a few steps back, wary of his wrath should any of them offend him. 'Two for the price of one. We have done well, haven't we?' He continued, demanding approval from his subjects. The creatures all made agreeable gestures, nodding and whispering comments of praise towards him.

The Origin stalked Molly and Peter. Looking them up and down, nodding his head as he reached out a long finger examining Molly's hair.

'Don't touch me!' screamed the angry young lady, causing the creature to stagger back for a moment unexpectedly. The crown gasped in horror, waiting for certain retribution.

The Origin laughed out loud, throwing back his head as he clapped his hands. 'I'll enjoy consuming your life force. I can see it all around you. Strong and bright. More power than most of your kind I see,' he said, licking his lips as he rubbed his hands in anticipation.

'Over my dead body!' interrupted Peter, standing in between them.

Once more, the assembly of creatures took in a sharp gasp, surprised at the human's boldness.

Again, the Origin began to laugh, circling the two confused humans. 'All in good time my friend. All in good time... Silence!' He roared towards the audience as they tried to mimic his mockery with fake humour.

The tall creature turned, leaving the humans in shock as he slowly made his way back up the steps, towards his throne. 'Has the Galpherin explained the rules to you both?' asked the Origin as he sat down, gesturing at Shifter.

So that's what species he was. Thought Molly, wondering if there were more of them.

'I have, your Majesty,' replied Shifter, lowering his head again.

'Good. Take them to the holding chambers and ready them for the realm of Legends.'

Molly and Peter looked at each other, trying hard to hide their fear. 'Wait!' cried Molly as two Centaurs approached, holding spears. 'Where is my father? What have you done with him?'

The Origin focused his gaze on the angry young girl, a cruel grin on his face. 'Hasn't the Galpherin told you? Your kin is a prisoner of the tree of souls and will remain there waiting to either be freed or condemned. After you fail to rescue him, all of your life force will belong to me.'

Peter quickly made a bee line for the gothic creature, barely progressing a few steps when, the ruler stopped him in his tracks, holding out his arm as he lifted the boy, high in the air with a mere gesture of his hand.

Peter kicked and flayed in mid-air as the crowd cheered and applauded at their leader's magnificence. 'Put him down now or I will never play your stupid game,' insisted Molly, trying to reach Peter. 'You're all insane. What kind of place is this? I'm not afraid of you! I will get my father back and you'll get nothing.'

The Origin smiled at Molly, almost pleased at her impudence as he released the young man from his levitating state. 'Good! Remarked the evil ruler. 'I look forward to your challenge. Your life force will taste all the sweeter when you are defeated. Shiftervorgoethryn, take them away. The games will begin in Unus hora.' With a wave of his hand, the wind instruments sounded as the Centaurs lead the young humans and Shifter away.

'That was a foolish thing to do, young lady,' said Shifter as they entered their dressing chambers. 'It is not a wise decision to challenge the Origin.'

'I was angry, Shifter. He's a bully. We don't back down to bullies where I come from,' replied Molly as they looked around the dome shaped room.

Wall-to-ceiling mirrors covered the entire dressing room, making it seem bigger than it actually was.

Just then, one, no two then three, four fairies came out of the liquid glass, floating just above the ground, their tiny wings a blur as they hovered around the young girl and boy. Their delicate bodies dressed in twinkling silk threads. Long white wispy hair that gently lifted as they rushed around, gathering what they needed to work.

'Hello,' said one of the fairy folk as she stroked Molly's hair with her pale exquisitely elegant hands. 'We are Fairdressers and we'll be readying you for your journey. Please, take a seat while we take care of you.'

Her voice was intoxicating, her hypnotic tone reassuring, like there was nothing to worry about. Molly sat down and relaxed into the comfortable armchair as two of the angelic creatures busied themselves with her hair. Darting to and fro, tossing her hair around elegantly as they worked. Peter too sat tentatively as the other two Fairdressers snipped away at his curtains.

'I could get used to this,' purred Peter, relaxing into the soft reclining chair.

'Me too,' agreed Molly.

The Fairdressers finished by tying off Molly's beautifully platted ponytail, before Shifter entered the room. 'There is some last-minute information I need to give you while you are in a relaxed state of mind,' announced the Galpherin, closing the door behind him. 'Once we are finished here, we will make our way to the first realm. The Realm of Legends. It is my duty to make sure you are prepared before you enter. You will encounter many mysterious creatures on your journey. Some you have already seen.'

Molly sat upright remembering the creatures from the throne room. 'Most of the creatures we saw, I thought, were either mythological or from fairy tale books. How could it be possible they actually exist?'

The old man folded his scrawny arms as he prepared to explain. 'They are all very real, Miss Miggins. How do you think they got into your story books and mythology tales?' He asked rhetorically. 'Because those of your kind that have conquered the realms thousands of years ago, wrote about what they had seen. Most people at that time, thought they were mad. Soon, those stories became fairy tales and myths.'

'So, what your telling me is, any creature, beast, spirit, witch or demon I've ever read about is real and lying in wait for us,' asked Molly, more than a little concerned as she watched Peter checking out his new hairstyle in one of the many mirrors. 'Oi! Hair flick. Stop faffing with your hair and pay attention!'

'Don't worry, I'm listening,' said Peter, calmly running his fingers through his hair. 'The way I look at it, is this. If we want to free your dad and get home, then we've got no other option than, complete these realms. At least you've a bracelet to protect you. What do I have? Nothing.'

The little old man floated quietly to the centre of the room and opened up his arms. Molly and Peter watched, as two torpedo shaped pods rose up from the floor at his command.

'Please, step inside,' instructed Shifter as they watched the pods open. 'Inside, you will be changed into your armour. It will protect you to a certain point, but beware. It will not protect you from the more powerful beings.'

'Well that's a weight off my mind,' joked Peter. 'Who needs a magic bracelet.'

Molly shook her head as she returned his wink with a wry smile. 'Get in there, you fool.' She said, pushing him into one of the pods.

The doors closed, the moment they entered. Steam seeped from the pressure valves, startling the fairy folk with the sudden hiss of escaping air. Everything went silent as the doors slid open to reveal, first Molly, dressed in a full length cat suit. The material was thin but tough, like it was made of snakeskin but, soft to the touch. It had a hint of maroon in its, black shade as the light caught it from a certain angle. Peter's armour was much the same, the only difference being, it was in two parts.

'Wow! You look…. Erm, cool,' said Peter as he looked Molly up and down, hoping she couldn't tell what he was thinking.

'Thanks. So, do you.' She replied, thinking exactly the same thing. 'What's it made of?' She asked, turning her attention to the old man.

'It is spun from Arachnida thread,' answered the Galpherin. 'It is one of the strongest materials known to us.'

Molly looked puzzled. The name sounded familiar, closer to Latin. 'Arachnida? You mean, Spider thread? I've noticed, some of your words sound Latin.' She queried.

'You are quite correct Molly Miggins,' replied Shifter, looking surprised, impressed that the young lady had such knowledge. 'Again, where do you think, Latin originated from? You may find many languages you hear sound familiar. Latin is the most popular language on this planet. As I mentioned earlier, those of your kind that made it back to their world, took some of our languages and used them. Does it not seem strange to you that there are so many different speaking tongues on your world? I can speak thousands of languages. Many of them from your world but originated from this one. This Universe is infinitely older than yours, therefor you will find, a lot of what you know from your planet, will have begun here many years ago.'

Was it all so difficult to believe, Molly thought to herself? Things the old man said, made some sense. Little things he explained were, beginning to click into place.

The world they had found themselves in was, undeniably beautiful. The air they breathed was intoxicating and refreshing. Even simple things like, moving around, seemed effortless. Was it down to differences in Earth's and Kaplon's atmosphere? Was it the amount of oxygen that circulated around the planet, the reason everything was so much bigger? Molly could understand why some beings decided to remain in this world. Especially if there was little left for them to return home to. Whatever the Origin was offering them, it was certainly more appealing for them to stay.

To Molly, it made no difference what he was offering, even if they were to succeed. The only thing that was important was, freeing her father. What would he look like? How will he react to seeing her? Would he even recognise her, considering she was almost three years older now?

'Okay. Where to now?' asked Molly, drinking in a long deep breath.

Shifter glided to the centre of the room as he began to wave his arms in different directions. The room seemed to move. The comfortable seats disappeared, replaced by a huge dining table, accompanied with two matching chairs. The mirrors turned, 180 degrees, displaying pictures that came to life of creatures in battle. It was like, multiple cinema shows, playing around the room for their pleasure.

'Now, you eat,' replied the Galpherin as he double clapped his hands.

Suddenly, the door flew open as half a dozen fairies scurried in, carrying dishes filled with treats. Gigantic pieces of fruit lay, sliced on silver trays. Sweet meets accompanied a, variety of vegetables. Glass jugs filled with, what looked like water, ladened with multiple specks of light dancing around its contents.

'Please, sit down and eat your fill. It may be some time before you eat again,' said Shifter as he drifted towards the door.

'I am starving,' said Molly, pulling her chair out to sit down. 'I could eat a horse. But I'm not so sure it was a good idea to have us eat, after we got changed.

I mean, this thing is tight enough. I'm not sure I'll be able to breath after I've eaten.'

'I don't care,' said Peter as he proceeded to do battle with a grape the size of an egg. 'I'm famished. If you think about it, we haven't eaten for three months.'

Molly screwed up her face, realising he was right. 'How is that possible?' She asked, turning to find the old man halfway out the door.

'A question for another time. I will be back to collect you when you are finished.' The old man closed the door before Molly could challenge him. Leaving them to reflect, on what was an extraordinary day.

'What's the matter?' asked Molly as Peter suddenly stopped chewing, like he'd remembered something he wished he hadn't.

'Do you realise, our birthdays have come and gone? While we were stuck in that bloody armour, travelling through space, our sixteenth birthdays had passed us by.'

Molly sat back in her chair. The realisation of it sinking in. 'Oh my god! I didn't even think about that. We were unconscious most of the time, so, it probably seemed quicker than it was.'

Peter nodded his head in agreement as he poured the, (literally) sparkling water into his glass, oddly wondering if it were safe to drink. 'I know. Do you realise, if we ever do get back, we will have missed our seventeenth, even though we haven't? And. This is really gonna do ya nut in. Bailey will be older than both of us!'

Molly suddenly let go of her glass, just as Peter was about to pour. 'What? What do you mean? This is so confusing. Don't say anymore. The only thing I want to think about at the moment is, getting to dad. Hopefully in one piece.'

Molly took a small bite out of a piece of apple. At first, the juices tingling her taste buds, before they exploded in her mouth, sensing her body being nourished with every swallow. 'What's in this fruit?' She commented, reaching for another piece.

'I know yeah,' answered Peter as he bit into an oversized blackberry. 'And I'm not a big fan of fruit. I'd prefer chocolate any day, but this tastes amazing.'

Molly and Peter sat there, stuffed. A strange feeling of fulfilment swept over them. Maybe she could smuggle some of this fruit home with her. She thought, if they were lucky enough to make it, that is.

The fairies buzzed around, their wings making a tuneful whistle as they went about clearing the table.

'What is your name?' asked Molly as one of the winged wonders hovered next to her.

'I am Kimi,' replied the beautiful creature as it gracefully moved left and right.

'Nice to meet you, Kimi. My name is, Molly and this is, Peter,' replied the young girl as Peter acknowledged the, sprite with a nod. 'Are you from this world?'

The delicate creature continued to busy itself before answering. 'We are very pleased to meet you, Molly. Yes, the Fairy folk have inhabited this world for thousands of our years. Unfortunately, there are very few of us left. Our habitats destroyed by creatures who have come from other worlds over time. Fire breathing Dragons have, burnt down most of our territory. Now, we are used to serve the Origin. In return he keeps, what woodlands and inhabit lakes that are left, safe from destruction.'

'Fire breathing what?' Exclaimed Peter, nearly toppling back off his chair. 'Are you kidding me? How the hell are we going to fight fire breathing Dragons?'

The fairy cupped a delicate hand over her mouth as she let out a pleasant giggle. 'What's so funny?' asked Molly, a little smile of confusion on her face.

'You have the bracelet,' replied the sprite. 'It has everything you need to protect you from danger. Most beings forget to use it when they are in danger. They begin to panic and allow fear to take over. Then of course, it's too late.'

'What about me?' Interrupted Peter, a sense of panic stirring inside him. 'I don't have a bracelet. What do I do when a, Dragon breathes fire down on me?'

'It is unusual for two beings to enter the realms together. You are at a disadvantage Although your suit will offer you some protection, Molly will need to protect you as well as herself, with only one bracelet. On the other hand, it usually makes the wearer more aware they have it, knowing another being's life is in their hands.'

Peter put his head in his hands, muttering something under his breath. 'What's that?' asked Molly, not quite able to catch his comment.

Peter looked up at her, a hot flush evident in his cheeks. 'I said, Great, that's all I need.'

'That's all you need!' Molly snapped. 'That's all I need you mean! I not only have to worry about, my life. I've got to keep you safe as well.'

Peter let out a sarcastic huff as he leant on the table, his anxiety easy to sense. 'Don't worry too much,' interrupted the chirpily sprite. 'I'm sure you will both work very well together. It is all about teamwork and trust.'

Molly jumped, as the door opened, interrupting their conversation as shifter entered the room, causing, Kimi and her companions to quickly disappear as the old man abruptly clapped his hands, prompting a comforting smile from the fairy as she waved farewell.

Chapter Twelve

'Are you both ready?' asked the old man as the crowds gathered again, booing and hissing as they walked towards the great door that loomed towards them. Molly grabbed tight hold of Peter's arm as the creatures got closer.

'Get back!' Demanded Shifter, stretching his arms out wide, trying to keep them at bay.

Peter pulled his friend close as the door drew ever nearer, revealing the grand tormentor, stood, arms ominously open wide to welcome them.

'At last! The time has come!' Announced the devil like creature, whipping the crowd into a frenzy, some of them salivating at the mouth, leering at the humans with sinister intent. 'Come forth and enter the first of three realms. The realm of legends. Your task is to find and recover the key that will open the door to, the second realm, the realm of, Hopes and Fears. The key however is guarded by the Dragon Glycon. You must do battle with and defeat Glycon, retrieve the key that hangs around his neck, before opening the door. Failure to succeed will end in defeat and your life force will belong to me.'

Realisation began to sink in. Molly looked at Peter in desperation. Wondering if they would ever see home again. See her mum again.

'Before you sign,' said, the Origin, handing the quill to the Galpherin. 'There is an alternative.'

The two humans looked curiously at the evil ruler. 'What alternative?' asked Molly cynically, before taking the quill.

The Origin lifted his long finger, pondering for a moment as he tapped the corner of his mouth. 'If you agree to stay here for the rest of your lives, there will be no need for you to endure this, hopeless task. I will take, most of your life force, leaving you with enough to live, so you are able to serve me. Your kin will be released, free from the tree of souls.'

The crowd went silent, waiting with bated breath. Wondering what decision, the humans would make.

Peter turned to Molly. The look on her face said all he needed to know. There was no way she was going to give in. Although it seemed hopeless, if there was the slightest chance of making it home, then they would never surrender.

'Never!' Shouted Molly, throwing her shoulders back in defiance.

The Origin clapped his hands together with delight. His sinister teeth exposed as he laughed out loud. His subjects, joining him in rapturous applause, relieved at the human's defiance. 'Good. We do so hate it when they surrender so quickly,' said the smug ruler, playing to the crowd. 'Sign here!' He continued, instructing the little old man to hand her the quill.

Shifter quickly did what he was bid as he pointed to the open book, lying in wait, open on top of a plinth. 'Your signatures bind both you and I to the rules and laws of this world.'

Molly was understandably hesitant, as translating the contract was impossible, being as it was in a foreign language. 'If you refuse to sign, you will not be able to enter the realms, therefor conceding defeat,' he continued.

Molly looked at shifter as the old man gave her a nod of reassurance. Taking the quill from the old man, she signed her name to the contract. Shifter took the quill from, Molly and handed it to Peter.

'What, me too?' He asked, hoping they'd forgotten about him.

'Kill him!' Came a command from the crowd.

'Who said that?' Demanded the Origin, baring his teeth as he searched for the offender.

The hall went silent as the creatures looked at each other, licking their lips in anticipation, knowing what consequences lay in store for the offender.

'You! It was you!' He shrieked, singling out a terrified Goblin type creature, who stood trembling, mumbling some sort of an apology. 'How dare you demand the life of the challenger! If his life is taken before he enters the realm, I will lose his life force forever!'

The crowed quickly began to part. Exposing the trembling perpetrator, to his inevitable fate. Before the creature could protest, the evil ruler thrust his hand, pointing his finger at the Goblin. A blinding flash of lightning shot out from his finger, instantly incinerating the creature, leaving only a pile of ash, where it once stood.

The crowd cheered once more as the Origin basked in his glory. 'This place is a lunatic asylum,' said Peter, finding it difficult to comprehend what he had witnessed. 'Give me the pen, quill, whatever it is. I'll sign your damn contract.'

Peter signed the book, dropping the quill on the floor in defiance as he stepped away. 'Now, can we get on with it? I'd like to get home. We've got belated birthdays to celebrate.'

Molly looked at Peter, a little impressed with him as he puffed out his chest, sending her a cheeky wink.

'Enough!' Snapped the devil-like creature, unimpressed with the young human's false bravery. 'It's time! Shiftervorgoethryn. Lead them into the realm of legends.'

The congregation cheered once more as the old man ushered, Molly and Peter in front of the huge arched doorway.

'Good luck,' said the Origin sarcastically, whirling round and round, whipping the crowd up into a frenzy.

'Are you ready?' asked Shifter as he pointed to the trinket on Molly's wrist. 'Press the door emblem young lady, whenever you are ready.'

Peter put his hand on Molly's shoulder, smiling at her as he gently squeezed it, reassuring her he was there with her.

Molly took a deep breath, as she raised her arm, finding the emblem resembling a door. Light sprung from the cracks that, once sealed its entrance. The door, slowly opened as the crowd held its breath, waiting for the two humans to disappear through its portal.

The entrance looked like a wall of liquid, rippling as it held fast its stay. 'Don't be afraid,' said the old man, reassuring them it was safe to follow him through. The old man walked straight into the fluid entrance, disappearing instantly. Peter grabbed tight hold of Molly's hand as he took a few short sharp breaths. 'We ready to do this?' asked the young man, readying himself before the plunge.

'As ready as I'll ever be. Don't let go,' replied Molly, squeezing his hand, extra tight, worried she may lose him on the way through. After giving themselves a count of three, they closed their eyes and held their breath as they walked slowly through the abyss.

It seemed like an eternity to pass through door, but eventually they came through to the other side.

The scenery was spectacular. Lush, bright green grass covered the uneven landscape. Dense forests in the distance came alive as the wind picked up. Curious looking birds disturbed from their shelter, took to the sky. A sky whose colour was a mixture of red and yellow, a sign that maybe it was dusk, although there was no sign of a setting sun. Derelict ruins lay in waste, further ahead in the distance. An eerie stillness from them, sending a shiver down Molly's spine as she noticed a broken pathway showing the only way ahead.

'I'm guessing that's the way to go?' asked Molly, pointing towards the uneven road.

'It is, indeed, Miss, Miggins,' replied the old man. 'But I'm afraid this is where I must leave you.'

Molly and Peter wheeled around to confront the, Galpherin as he turned to leave. 'Leaving us! What the hell! I thought you were supposed to be our guide?'

The little man slipped his hands through his wide sleeves, standing still, before returning through the open doorway. 'And that I am, young lady,' assured Shifter. 'I will be waiting for you both, each time you make it to the door, to the next realm. If you need to ask any questions whilst on your journey then, all you have to do is, call my name. I will appear in the form of a hologram and I will try to answer any queries you may have.'

Molly and Peter felt lost. They had very little chance of succeeding before this announcement. Now they were on their own, a feeling of hopelessness washed over them. 'Believe me my friends,' said Shifter, before allowing them to protest. 'You will have a better chance of success, without my physical presence. The least amount of distractions there are, the better your chances. As I have just said, I will answer when called upon. Just call my name and I will appear. One last thing before I leave you. The Origin has the power to appear in each realm, as friend or foe. Changing shape in order to deceive you. So, as I warned you earlier. Remember, things are not always what they seem.'

'Great, that's all we need,' said Peter, throwing his arms in the air in resignation. 'Not only do we have, monsters and whatever else is out there, to deal with. Now, the master of doom, is able to throw another spanner in the works by, changing into whatever he wants to. Do you get the feeling he doesn't want us to succeed?'

Molly would have laughed if she weren't so terrified. 'Do not forget,' interrupted the old man. 'You have something he doesn't have, that is far more valuable. You have the bracelet. Listen to it. Bind your mind with it. It has everything you need to succeed. Don't succumb to your own fears or it will be useless. Master Peter, you have a vital role to play. The young maiden will need you more than ever before.'

Peter looked baffled by the description. 'Young maiden?' He asked, looking for someone else. 'He means me, dopey,' joked Molly, shaking her head.

'You will have to make sure she stays focused and calm,' continued the old man. 'Fat chance of that,' scoffed Molly, giving Peter a despairing look. 'I can be responsible and switched on when I want to be,' replied Peter defensively. Dismissing Molly's insult, with a wave of the hand. 'Remember, I'm a boxer, so, I have to be focused when I'm in the ring and this situation is like being in the ring.'

The old man nodded his head in approval. 'Indeed, you do young man. Indeed, you do.'

With that the, Galpherin turned and disappeared back through the translucent door. 'Well, it's just the two of us now,' said Molly as the door sealed behind them, any thoughts of going back diminished.

'Come on, let's go,' said Peter, making his way towards the pathway. 'We're getting nowhere fast at the moment.'

Molly duly followed, her thoughts drifting towards her father. Did they really stand a chance of rescuing him? Only time will tell. But they would certainly do everything in their power to succeed.

Was it a change in temperature or was it something else? Whatever it was, an uneasy feeling came over, Molly just before they reached the brow of a hill. 'Wait,' whispered Molly as she halted Peter, suddenly grabbing his arm. 'Do you here that?' She continued.

Peter harked, crouching down as they peered over the brow to see where the strange sound was coming from. 'What are they?' He gasped as two creatures did battle with each other at the bottom of a valley.

The first creature had the body of a man, with its other half resembling that of a horse. The second was more agile, with wings to help it manoeuvre better to its advantage. It had the head of a man, as well as the head of a goat that sprouted out of the rear end of its body. A sinister looking, scorpion like tail, thrashed around, searching its prey. Molly thought she recognised one of them from the throne room but, couldn't be sure. The two creatures stalked each other. One, waiting for the other to make a move.

'What should we do?' asked Peter, trying to be as quiet as possible.

'We've got to talk to Shifter,' replied Molly all the while, watching the creatures circling each other with intent. Peter nodded in agreement as the girl called out his name.

'Shifter. We need your help. Are you there?' Called the young girl, as loudly as she dared, without alerting the other beings to their presence.

Suddenly, the old man appeared, flickering in and out of focus as his signal tried to establish itself between realms.

'Shifter?' asked Molly, unsure if she were speaking with the real thing.

'What can I do for you, Miss, Miggins?' Came the broken-up reply, the old man, at times fading in and out of focus.

'What are those creatures down there and why are they fighting each other?'

The Galpherin flickered even faster as his hologram drifted towards the brow of the hill. 'Creatures will always fight young lady. They will fight for territory. They will fight for food. But most of all, they will fight for the Origins favour. The one on your left is a Centaur. Half man, half horse. It is a very maligned creature. Once given a reputation for doing bad. Representing barbarism and unbridled chaos. But contrary to popular belief they are, in general a good species. The other one is a Chimera. This is, especially one to avoid. It has the power to absorb its victim's life cells. You can see it has the head of a goat on its back, as well as a human face, and if you look at its tail, it will tell you it has encountered an arachnid at some point in time. Be careful my friends.'

'But what if…' began Molly, before the, Galpherin began to fade, eventually vanishing from sight.

'Molly. We have got to do something,' pleaded Peter as the Chimera advanced towards the Centaur. 'Otherwise, that horse man, type creature will be just another part of that multi beast. Besides, they're blocking our pathway, so, we have no choice if we want to continue on our journey.'

The two beasts suddenly flew at each other. The Centaur, stumbling as he came under attack from the scorpion tail. 'Okay,' replied Molly, looking at the bracelet for inspiration. 'You distract it, while I find something to fight it with.'

Peter looked at her, a little confused. 'Distract it? Distract it how?'

'I don't know. Throw rocks at it or something. I'll check the bracelet for a weapon.'

Molly searched the trinket for anything she thought might help her. That'll do, she whispered to herself as she spotted a symbol resembling a bow and arrow. Peter, by this time, had done as he was asked and, began launching bricks at the multi beast, ensuring at the same time he wasn't too close. Molly tapped the emblem on the bracelet. Instantly, a beam of golden light shot out from the trinket, etching the weapon out of thin air.

'Wow!' She exclaimed as the bow and arrow gleamed, before she quickly grabbed it out of thin air. 'Keep it busy, Peter!' She screamed, before running down the hill, plucking an arrow from the quiver.

'Hurry up and do something Molly!' Shouted an anxious, Peter as the, Chimera, after being struck on the head by a boulder, launched itself towards the retreating young human.

The, Centaur kicked out its hind legs. Hurling the beast ten feet in the air. A sudden cry of pain came from the stunned creature as it eventually gathered itself, spreading its wings, ready to launch another assault.

Molly released the bow, just as the, Chimera was about to land on its intended victim. The arrow swiftly flew through the air. Molly punched the air as the arrow hit its target, piercing straight through the eye of the beast. An almighty shriek of pain filled the air as the assailant writhed around in agony. The life, slowly draining from its body, until eventually, its time was up.

Molly sat there, exhausted. Her chest heaving as the, bow and arrows, slowly disappeared before her eyes. 'Is it dead?' She asked.

The Centaur looked curiously at the human, cocking its head to one side as if translating in his own mind what language she was speaking. 'I bloody well hope so,' replied Peter. Watching the, half horse half human creature, walk over to where his nemesis was lying lifeless on the soft grass.

'It appears so,' said the Centaur, kicking the beast with one of his hooves, checking for any signs of life.

Molly and Peter stared at each other, surprised the creature spoke, let alone spoke the same language. 'How do you know our language?' asked Molly, standing up to acknowledge the, Centaur.

'I know many languages young human,' replied the beast as he pivoted around to face his rescuers, confident his opponent was dead. 'Please, let me introduce myself. I am, Chiron and I am at your service.

The name sounded familiar to Molly. She took a keen interest in mythology and was sure she had come across that name in one of the books she'd read. 'Thank you, both of you, for your assistance. I was certain I was all but finished until you showed up. I owe you my life. The Chimera is a formidable opponent. If he had of got hold of me and drew blood, he would have absorbed my cells into his, ending my life.'

The Centaur was a handsome beast. He stood at least eight feet tall, from mount to head. Its body stood strong and proud as its tail swished gracefully, from side to side. The human half was, decorated with tribal tattoos, signifying either its species or tribe. Its thick set, muscular arms and shoulders flexed when it moved. His face was bold, exaggerating his features. The jaw line looked chiselled, as did the nose that dominated the rest of his face. His eyes were soft and warm, the corners slightly turned up, in the same direction as its pointed ears. The Centaurs hair was as black as coal, matching its lower body, flowing elegantly down its back. A gold band with some sort of tribal emblem, mounted in the middle, sat proudly around his head, holding his magnificent hair in place.

'You are more than welcome, Chiron,' replied Molly, fascinated by this grand looking creature. 'My name is Molly Miggins. And this is my friend, Peter.'

Peter brushed himself down, before waving his hand to acknowledge the beast. 'Why was that thing trying to kill you?' asked the young human, curios to learn why they were fighting each other. 'It was here to kill you,' revealed the beast.

Molly and Peter, stunned, both responded at the same time. 'What!' They screamed. 'How the hell do you know that? The creature was attacking you when we got here,' continued Molly.

'That is true,' agreed Chiron. 'But it was sent to intercept you! I merely got here before you did, to try and stop it.'

Peter looked confused, shaking his head in disbelief. 'But how did you know we__.'

'The Origin,' interrupted the beast, knowing exactly what the young man was about to ask. 'The Origin sends these creatures to try and prevent you from reaching the next realm.'

Molly held a hand up, halting Peter from continuing his interrogation. 'Wait.' She demanded. 'So why are you helping us? Why do you not serve the Origin? I thought he controlled everything in this universe. This could be a trap for all we know.'

'You are correct,' replied the Centaur. 'The Origin does rule the universe. But even he has to abide by our laws. Those that are native to this world, must sign a contract that is mutually beneficial to both parties, before the Origin can command our services. The decision is more difficult for those that are brought here from other worlds. For them, there is little other choice. The benefits, out way the alternative. There is nothing, the Origin has to offer that would convince me to serve him. We are a proud species. The Origin is desperate to recruit us.

But we will never succumb to temptation. Many of us have been killed over time. Trying to pick us off, one by one, because we will not give in to his demands.'

Both Molly and Peter listened intently, feeling sorry for the beast, especially as he was about to sacrifice himself for beings he didn't even know, just to stand up for what he believed was right. 'That is awful Chiron! Isn't it Peter?' Sympathised Molly, hoping Peter would agree.

Peter nodded as the Centaur turned towards him. 'Traditionally, we fight in herds,' continued the beast. 'But so many of us are gone. We are lucky if we come across another. Also, my lance was broken in battle, many of our moons ago, so, all I have to protect you, is, what you see.'

Molly walked towards the brave creature as he knelt down to meet her. 'We thank you Chiron, for your bravery. We are as much in your debt, as you are in ours.'

The Centaur smiled softly at the young girl, before rising up high on his hind legs, sending Molly back on her heels a little. 'If you would do me the honour, I would like to accompany you both to the door, that will take you to the realm of hopes and fears.'

Molly's eyes lit up with excitement as she noticed, Peter nodding his head in agreement. A friend is exactly what they needed at this moment. 'Thank you, Chiron. We would be delighted and equally honoured if you would accompany us on our journey.

The three friends, all excited by their new acquaintance, continued on their quest, buoyed by thought that they now had each other.

Chapter Thirteen

The light was beginning to fade as the three companions approached a small stream. The water itself, was not very deep, but the speed at which it travelled would make it difficult for the humans to cross safely.

'Here,' said the beast as he knelt down as low as he was able. 'Climb on my back. I will take you across.'

Molly and, Peter straddled the Centaur as he quickly stood up as steadily as he could. 'Hold on to my hair, Peter, and Molly, you wrap your arms around Peter,' advised the Centaur as he slowly stepped into the water.

Molly slipped forward, nestling tight into Peter, before the Centaur straightened his gait. 'Get any closer, Molly?' Joked Peter, moving back himself a little, so that their bodies were tight against one another.

Molly edged back an inch or two, but not confident enough to let go of his waist, a little embarrassed by his mocking tone. 'Ha-ha, very funny,' replied Molly, a hot flush warming her cheeks. 'I didn't do that on purpose,' she protested.

Peter laughed to himself, knowing she was aware, he had got one over on her, secretly enjoying their brief close encounter all the same.

All of a sudden, Chiron lurched forward. Suddenly, something had curled around one of his legs, preventing him from climbing the riverbank on the other side. 'I can't move, something has grabbed hold of my leg!' cried the Centaur, struggling to free himself from whatever was holding him. 'Quick, climb off or we will all end up in the river.

Molly and Peter quickly jumped from the beasts back, onto the riverbank. Peter grabbed Molly's shoulder, dragging her back.

Out from the river, sprang a creature so sinister, they feared for their friend. Its legs were long, broad like tentacles that wrapped tight around the, Centaurs whole body as he tried to escape its grasp. The river monsters body was, as dark as coal, its muscles defined, by the water it used to hide, waiting patiently for its victims.

Chiron tried desperately to grab hold of its large bulky, bull like head as the creature opened its jaws. Teeth, long and sharp glistened as spittle dripped from its Scythe like fangs. Bright amber eyes, sunk deep into its head, intent on finishing off its prey, before they had a chance to retaliate.

The two beasts flayed about so much, it was difficult to know which was getting the better of the other, as the disturbed white foaming waters, made it difficult to distinguish which body part belonged to who.

'What the hell is that thing?' asked Peter as Molly checked her bracelet.

'I don't know, but we better do something quick. I don't think, Chiron will last much longer. That thing has put him under the water twice already. If he goes under again, I'm afraid he'll be done for.

'Try that,' said Peter, pointing at an emblem on the bracelet, resembling what looked like a lance.

'It'll have to do. We have no time to use anything else,' said the desperate young girl.

Molly quickly tapped the symbol, hoping it wasn't too late. Immediately, a beam of light sprang from the bracelet, etching out a long golden lance, right in front of their eyes. Molly reached out and grabbed the weapon before it dropped to the ground. 'There's only one way to do this.' She said readying herself.

'Wait,' said Peter as he snatched the lance from Molly, just as she was about to jump.

Molly was about to protest when Peter leaped high into the air, holding the weapon above his head as he aimed for the beast who had managed to get on top of the Centaur holding his head under water (probably for the last time) and plunged the lance straight through the creature's body.

An ear-piercing shriek gurgled from the beast as its back arched and writhed in agony. Peter quickly withdrew the weapon, jumping headfirst into the river, getting as far from the fatally wounded monster as possible. Chiron suddenly scrambled to his hooves, taking in a huge gulp of air, freeing himself from his assailant at the same time.

'Quick, give me your hand Peter!' Screamed Molly as she reached out to grab him.

Peter grabbed hold of his friend's hand as she dragged him onto the riverbank exhausted, his chest heaving as he lay there. Chiron too, scrambled himself to safety as they watched the lifeless monster, float down the river, out of sight.

All three sat there, silent for a few moments, exhausted as they Watched the lance vanish, as quickly as it appeared.

'What, in god's name was that?' asked Molly, plonking herself down on the wet grass.

'That was a, Bunyip,' replied the spent Centaur, collapsing onto his hind legs.

'A Bunyip?' Interrupted Peter. 'It looked more like a sea dog, with teeth and flippers.'

The Centaur gently lowered the rest of himself down until he was comfortable. 'A Bunyip is a river monster. It usually lurks in swamps or billabongs. Sometimes hiding in, creeks and riverbeds waiting for its prey. It has a craving for human flesh, preferably the female kind. I think it was trying to pull me over to get to you, Molly. Another one of the Origins traps I'm afraid.'

Molly fell back on the ground, tired, wet, confused, upset, but more than anything else, she was angry. Angry that she'd brought, not only her best friend to this hell hole, but had been the reason this poor being had risked his life twice, trying to defend hers. 'I'm so sorry, Chiron. It's all my fault. I should never have accepted your offer of help. I can't be responsible for you risking your life for ours.'

The Centaur looked at Molly. A sadness came across his face as he gently held her hand. 'Please, do not apologise, Molly. I have nothing left to live for,' said Chiron, his eyes showing the pain of so much loss. 'The Origin has left me with nothing. All I have left is my honour. And it would be an honour, to escort you and, Peter to the realms end.'

Chiron stood up and walked over to the recovering human, lying flat out on the ground. 'Thank you, Peter,' he continued, offering the young man his hand. 'Again, you have saved my life.'

Peter stood up, taking a firm grip of the beast's hand. 'No, thank you, Chiron. If it weren't for you, we'd have died in that river for sure, so you, saved our lives by risking your own.

Molly looked at Peter and smiled, a little surprised at his response. Peter wasn't usually this thoughtful. Maybe after all they had been through, his heart had softened a little. Whatever it was, it caused her to see him in a different light.

'Come on, we need to keep going. It looks like it'll be dark soon and we need to find somewhere to sleep,' said Molly, dragging herself up off the floor.

'Follow me,' replied Chiron. 'I think there's an old wooden fort, not far from here. We can rest there for the evening.'

The three dishevelled friends brushed themselves down, before setting off on, one last push.

The light was fading fast as the trio found themselves in dense woodland, the path becoming more difficult to follow. The sky above looked spectacular as the moons that littered the night sky, showed the way with the light they borrowed from the setting sun.

All sorts of strange and wonderful noises seemed to come to life as the night, hastily woke them from their daytime slumber.

Molly jumped, as a freakish cry came from above, hiding high in the trees. 'What was that!' She asked as she clung to Peter.

'That sounds like Vespertilio,' replied the Centaur as the unnerving noise continued. 'We'll be okay, as long as we stick together. They will only attack solitary beings, so, try not to stray. A single Vespertilio, will drain a being your size of its blood, in only a few minutes.

Peter's hackles stood upright on hearing the Centaurs warning. 'Blood!' Cried Peter, his head on a swivel, more aware of his surroundings. 'What are they, Vampires? This place is freaking me out. We need to hurry up and find shelter. I don't fancy having the life sucked out of me.'

Chiron stopped, interrupting the human as he noticed the silhouette of a building a short distance away. 'That looks like it,' said the beast, pointing towards the derelict fort. 'We should be safe there for the night, but we have to stay together. Please, no one should wander off on their own. The woods are not the place you want to be once night falls.'

Molly and Peter both nodded, still a little preoccupied by the blood sucking, Vampire creatures lurking, worryingly above their heads. 'Yeah, whatever you say,' responded Peter, his only thoughts now, on getting to something that had a roof on it.

The fort looked anything but a shelter, that would protect them from anything, let alone creatures that came from above. The large wooden structure seemed as though it was thousands of years old. The thick beams that made up its structure seemed rotten and decayed. The door or what was left of it, was hanging off, unable to stop a small child from braking in, never mind someone determined to cause them harm.

'How is this meant to keep us safe?' asked Peter as they walked cautiously through the, non-existent door which, Chiron knocked off on his way through. 'Great,' he continued as it fell to pieces. 'Might as well knock the whole thing down. We'd probably be safer if we built it by scratch.'

Molly turned and gave Peter one of her hard stares. 'Stop moaning will you. It's not Chiron's fault. He's only trying to help us.'

Peter looked at the Centaur, a little embarrassed, realising she was right. 'Please accept my apologies, Chiron. I'm just a little tired is all. Just ignore me. Molly's right, I shouldn't blame you.'

The Centaur held up a hand, as if to stop Peter from going any further. 'Don't apologise young Peter. I completely understand. It has been a long day for us all. The best thing to do now, is build a fire and get some sleep.'

The young man felt even worse as he turned back at Molly, the look of disgust on her face, like a knife through his heart. 'I know! I know!' He said, realising he'd been an idiot.

'Go and grab the remains of that door,' said Molly abruptly. 'It's about all it's good for now. By the way, how are you planning to start a fire?' She continued, realising they had nothing to light it with.

'With these,' replied the Centaur, picking up a couple of flints from the ground. 'These are everywhere around these types of buildings. Left by those, needing shelter for the same reasons. This fortress has stood for many years and sheltered many beings on their quest. If you notice the straw beds, the table and chairs, the ring of stones, laid for the fireplace. All the basics you would need to survive.'

Peter dropped the wood in the fireplace, before interrupting. 'Not everything,' he said, pointing to the table and chairs. 'There's something missing from the table.'

Molly looked over at the uneven legged table, wondering what he was on about. 'I don't see any food on it. I'm not sure about anyone else, but I'm famished.'

The Centaur looked around, wondering if there were any scraps left by the previous occupants. 'I'm afraid it looks like we're out of luck young Peter. Unfortunately, it's unsafe to go outside at night, looking for food. We'll have to wait until the morning.' Peter grumbled, along with his stomach as he contemplated a night with an empty belly.

Lying down on the soft straw beds, they drifting off into a deep sleep as they watched the flames dance around the pit, too tired to worry about food any longer, hoping when they woke, it was all a dream.

Molly's eyes, suddenly sprang open, woken by a familiar voice coming from somewhere outside the fort. The fire was almost out by this time. Hot smouldering embers was all that remained.

'Molly…. Molly,' repeated the voice once again, more urgent this time.

'Who was that? Why does that voice sound familiar?' She whispered to herself, wondering if she were dreaming.

Intoxicated by its sound, feeling neither, fully awake, nor asleep, Molly followed the hypnotic voice. It can't be, she thought to herself. It was impossible.

Molly eyes searched the darkness as she crept through the open doorway. Nothing. No sign of anyone. But where was it coming from? The forest ahead was densely thick, trees mingled into one, swallowed up by the darkness. Trees that she knew were hiding the bloodsucking, Vespertilio, waiting to ambush their unsuspecting victims.

Again, that voice. It can't be her, she thought, as the hairs on her arms pushed against her suit.

'Mum?' She whispered, knowing how foolish she'd feel if the others woke to hear her calling out for her mother.

'I'm in here Molly. I'm lost, please help me.'

Molly came over all cold. Like someone had walked, no, danced all over her grave. 'What the hell.'

Molly slowly crept towards forest. 'Mum. Is that you?' She asked again, adamant, there was no way she was going into that black hole.

'Please help me Molly! I can't move. I'm stuck!'

The cries were becoming louder. Molly began to panic. Irrational thoughts, now taking over her mind. All logic abandoned. What if it really was her mum. It was possible. She may have gone looking for her in the cave, sucked into the vortex just like her and, Peter. Was there another bracelet she didn't know about? It was possible.

The cries now, even more distressing. Sounds of someone struggling, began to coincide with the cries for help.

Molly couldn't bare it any longer. Fear or no fear. If her mum was in trouble, then it was up to her do what she could to get to her as soon as she could. 'I'm coming mum! Hold on!' She shouted as she ran into the trees, all thoughts of self-preservation abandoned.

'Where are you?' cried Molly as she searched deeper into the woods. 'Please, I can't see you.'

The light was now non-existent as the tree canopies above, ganged up against the moonlight struggling to gain entry. Different sounds echoed around the woods, sending Molly's head on a swivel, twisting left and right at the slightest sound.

She turned, trying to find her bearings, unsure which way to go as It slowly began to dawn on her, that this, was just another trick. She had been lured into these woods by, him.

Molly had no choice. She knew what she had to do but was too frightened to make a sound. If she wanted to get out of there alive, it had to be done.

'Peter...! Chiron...! Screamed the girl at the top of her lungs.

The canopies burst into life. Leaves, twigs and debris rained down from above as, Molly suddenly felt a hand, grab her by the shoulder.

The hideous creature loomed over the human. Its wolf type snout snarled at her, as its razor sharp teeth, glistening from spittle, dripped from its fangs. Its eyes narrowed as they glowed in the dark, like two infer red beams, that seemed unable to focus on anything. Maybe it too, was struggling to see through the pitch blackness.

The creature growled menacingly as it moved closer towards the terrified girl. Molly could just make out two, deer like antlers sticking out of its head. Wondering if it were some sort of cross bread, between a, deer and a, wolf.

All of a sudden, a noise startled the beast, causing it to wheel around distracting its attention. Without thinking, Molly quickly picked up a rock and smashed it, as hard as she could into its face, allowing her to brake free. The stunned creature let out an almighty howl. Reeling back from the force of the blow. Molly wasted no time as she ran as fast as she could, caring less what direction she was going.

'Shifter!' Shouted Molly, desperately looking for somewhere to hide 'Please Shifter, I need you!' She continued, ducking behind a tree, too scared to look back to see if the beast was following.

Just like before, the old man flickered in and out of focus as he appeared before her. 'Yes, Miss, Miggins. How can I help you?' asked the Galpherin, his hologram signal a little clearer than the last time they made contact.

'Shifter, thank god!' Exclaimed Molly, relieved to see the old man. 'What is that thing? What am I going to do? I'm lost.'

The small old man moved closer looking over his shoulder as if someone were watching him, from wherever he was. 'I can't talk for long. His spies are watching,' he whispered, looking back at the young girl. 'The creature pursuing you, is, a Wendigo. They are beasts that are easily manipulated to committing gruesome acts that I care not to tell you. There's not much time. All I will say is, this one is not what it seems. His eyes will tell you everything. Remember Molly Miggins. Use the bracelet. There is a symbol to protect you from every beast.'

The Galpherin vanished as quickly as he appeared. Molly tried to steady her breathing as she searched the emblems on the bracelet, looking for one that could help her.

'Which one can it be?' She asked herself, scanning the trinket.

All sorts of strange objects jumped out at her, each one, seemingly as ineffective as the next. A net, a strange looking head with things sticking out of it, a sword. The lance, Peter used earlier.

'Wait, a sword! That might work.'

Without hesitation, Molly tapped the symbol. The trinket began to glow as it shot out a beam of golden light, forging the weapon into the night air.

Molly froze, rooted to the spot, unable to move as a blob of sticky liquid dripped onto her head, feeling the warmness of its breath moving through her hair. The sound of jaws snapping shut, eager and ready to devour its prey.

Molly dropped to the floor as fast as she could, hoping to get to the sword, before the, Wendigo could get to her. The beast was too fast, leaping on top of the girl, clawing at her back with its sharp talons as it landed. The suit tore open as a sharp pain seared through her like hot knives through her flesh.

Molly screamed in agony as the beast stood over her, poised to attack.

This is the end, Molly thought to herself as she gazed into the Wendigos blood red eyes.

Molly suddenly remembered the old man's warning. 'This beast, is not what it seems.'

The realisation hit her. It was the Origin. The Origin was controlling the beast.

It was too late. Molly covered her eyes, waiting for the end as the creature readied himself to pounce.

Suddenly, surprised by a pained howl, the girl snapped open her eyes to see the, Wendigo flying through the air, before smashing hard against a tree.

Her two friends had appeared from nowhere, undetected through all the commotion, surprising the Wendigo as the, Centaur raised its hind legs, kicking the beast, as it was about to tear the young girl to pieces.

'Peter, be careful!' Cried Molly as the young man quickly picked up the sword.

The creature, still dazed, began to climb to its feet. With one swift blow, Peter swung the samurai-like sword slicing clean through the Wendigos neck sending its head hurtling deep into the forest.

The trio watched, relieved as the beast dropped to its knees, all life draining from its body.

A strange green mist began to seep from its neck, like some kind of entity were being released, floating into the night air as the beast lay there, still, lifeless.

Molly tried to get to her feet. The pain from her shoulder suddenly returning, reminding her of the Wendigos attack.

'Quick Molly, we need to leave,' urged the Centaur, quickly scanning the area. 'There's no time to waste. We're not safe here. There's a smell of blood in the air. It won't be long before the, Vespertilio catch the scent. Although there are a few of us, the urge to attack will be too strong to resist.'

The Centaur gently picked up the wounded young girl, helping her onto its back. 'Quick Peter, jump on, I can hear them coming,' demanded Chiron, noticing the canopies above were moving far too much considering there was only a light breeze that evening.

Peter quickly climbed onto the Centaurs back, keeping tight hold of the samurai sword, careful not to inflict more pain on the injured girl.

The flesh on her shoulder, open and exposed, was looking worse by the second as the Centaur took off at high speed. 'Faster!' Screamed Peter, watching in horror as he turned around to see a mass of winged monsters flying towards them, some of which, he noticed were fighting amongst themselves, gauging up on the unfortunate Wendigo, lying lifeless, food for the Vespertilio. 'They're catching us!' He warned, slapping the hind leg of the Centaur, urging him to go faster as the winged flesh eaters began to gain on them.

Their grotesque heads, at least three times the size of their bodies. Long snouts exposed razor like teeth, with two of protruding incisors, capable of making short work of someone his size.

Peter swung his sword at the blood sucking horrors, whilst struggling to hold onto a very week, Molly at the same time. 'Get away from us!' He screamed, as he chopped one down (with luck, rather than precision) at a time.

The young man suddenly yelped in pain as one of the vile creatures managed to bite into his flailing arm. 'Chiron! Try to wrap your arms around, Molly. I can't hold onto her.'

The Centaur grabbed hold of the unconscious girls as, Peter released her, taking the sword with his other hand.

With one swift movement, Peter cut off the Vespertilio's head's. 'We're almost there, Peter! Keep them off a little longer!' Shouted the Centaur, catching a glimpse of the moonlight through a gap in the woods up ahead.

Peter swung the golden Samurai randomly aloft, hitting anything and everything that came near him.

The young man, feeling the last bit of energy drain from his body, breathed a huge sigh of relief as the, Vespertilio suddenly stopped, afraid to break through the barrier separating them from the moonlight and darkness, retreating back into the forest, screaming with frustration.

'Quickly, we need to get her into the fort,' said Peter, lifting Molly from Chiron's back.

The young girl seemed deathly pail as Peter, carefully carried her into the fort, laying her gently down on the straw bed.

'Molly….! Molly….! Can you hear me?' asked Peter looking helplessly at Chiron, hoping the Centaur would know what to do.

'I'm sorry Peter. The only one who can help her now is, the Galpherin,' said Chiron, looking somewhat concerned for his friend.

'But I can't call him. Only the wearer of the bracelet can summon, Shifter. Hang on a second,' said Peter, remembering what the old man said. 'Didn't Shifter say, something like: The bracelet has everything you need to help you?'

The Centaur looked concerned, noticing Peter's arm could also use some attention. 'It looks like you may need the Galpherin's assistance very soon too Peter.' The young man stared at his arm, shocked that it had deteriorated considerably.

'I'm okay for now. We need to help, Molly. She doesn't look like she's going to last much longer.

Peter, gently lifted Moll's arm as he looked intently at the trinket, trying to find something. Anything, that might help. 'That looks like it might be useful,' said Peter, spotting, what looked like the symbol of a, jar on the trinket.

Peter tapped the emblem and waited. 'Nothing is happening!' He said, frustrated. 'May be it's only Molly that can use it,' he continued.

Suddenly, he had an idea. Gently taking her index finger, Peter tapped it on the symbol, secretly praying to himself, for some divine help.

Instantly, the trinket began to glow as a beam of gold light shot out from its surface, carving the item into thin air.

Peter quickly grabbed hold of the jar as soon as he felt it was safe to do so. 'I hope this has what we need,' said the young man, twisting the lid off the jar, revealing a clear gel type liquid inside. 'It looks like some sort of ointment,' he queried, smelling the gooey substance. 'It smells awful too.'

Peter hesitated, not sure if he should take a chance and apply it to Molly's shoulder. 'What if this makes it worse.'

The Centaur looked anxiously at the ashen faced human. 'We don't have much time Peter. She is fading fast.'

Peter pulled up his sleeve, exposing the wound on his arm. 'I'll try it on me first. If something goes wrong, then you will have to take her quickly to someone who could help.'

Before Chiron could protest, Peter scooped up a blob of the foul-smelling gel and spread it onto his wound.

Both, Peter and, Chiron watched in awe as the bite marks slowly began to heal, eventually disappearing, as if never there.

With no time to marvel at its healing powers, Peter sat his friend upright as carefully as he could, scooping a large portion of the magic healing cream from the jar and, as gently as he could, evenly spread it over Molly's, rapidly deteriorating wounds.

Peter winced, noticing her flesh tremble, trying hard not to cause her anymore discomfort.

Just like with him, the wounds immediately began to heal. Closing swiftly, like someone were zipping up each wound, until eventually. They were gone. Not a single mark left.

'Molly,' called Peter as he watched the colour returning to her face.

The young girl's eye lids, slowly began to flicker, before opening wide as she looked up to see two familiar faces staring down at her. 'Where am I? What happened?' asked a confused Molly as she tried to sit up, before realising how weak she was. 'Never mind, I remember now.' She continued, laying back down, her head pounding as the memory of the Wendigo flashed through her mind, those blood red eyes revealing who it really was. 'Where is it? How did I__?'

Peter stopped her before she could finish the sentence. 'Quiet now Molly. You've been through enough for one day. I'll tell you everything in the morning, I promise. No doubt, it'll be another long and difficult day tomorrow, so you'll, we'll need all the rest we can get.'

Chiron nodded his head in agreement, still amazed by his friend's dramatic recovery. 'Don't you two worry. I will be on guard for the rest of the night, keeping watch.'

'We can't expect you to do that,' protested Peter. 'You need your rest too.'

Chiron smiled as he picked up wood, before setting the fire once more. 'Centaurs don't need a lot of sleep my friend. I've already had more than I need. I'll wake you early, so, sleep now, both of you.'

Peter began to breathe easy, secretly pleased with his friends generous offer, far too tired to argue with the Centaur as he attempted to return to his bed of straw.

Suddenly, he felt a hand on his arm, stopping him from getting to his feet. 'Would you stay with me?' asked Molly, an air of vulnerability detected in her voice.

'Err, okay,' replied Peter, a little surprised by the request as he lay down beside her, sensing her relax, knowing he was there.

Peter watched the flames begin to dance once more as the Centaur Stood guard at the entrance of the fort, like a centurion at its post, Statuesque like.

The young man strangely wondered if the Centaur would be in the same position when he woke in the morning as his eyes began to close, flecks of fire light hypnotising him as Molly's warm breath lightly tickled his neck, drifting off into a deep sleep, too exhausted to be concerned about what the day ahead had install for them.

Chapter Fourteen

Molly slowly opened her eyes. The sight of Peter, facing her, less than an inch away, confused her slightly. How on earth did that happen? She thought to herself. The night before, somewhat of a blur.

Little snippets gradually sneaked their way into her head as Peter, half a smile on his face, opened his eyes.

Molly curiously observed her friend, confused as the satisfied grin on his face told her, he knew something she didn't. 'Good morning,' said Peter, the smug grin, a reminder of how much he got on her nerves.

'Good morning,' she replied. 'What are you grinning at?'

'Don't you remember?' He asked, uncertain if she were able to recall the previous evenings strange events. 'You asked me to sleep beside you last night. You looked a little scared. I'm not taking the mickey out of you. It was nice to know you needed me,' he continued, careful not to sound too cocky.

Molly seemed a little baffled by his confession, slightly embarrassed she couldn't remember, although relieved it gave her a plausible excuse for denying it ever happened.

'Rubbish!' She snapped, dismissing the whole statement as utter nonsense.

Peter shook his head in acceptance. He knew damn well she would never admit it, even if she was pretending not to remember. He'd known her far too long. Molly was stubborn, as well as head strong. The only way he could prove he wasn't lying, was to ask the Centaur to confirm his story. But Peter already knew that, Molly already suspected the same. And although he would like nothing more than to get one more over on her, he suspected that now was not the right time.

'I'm starving,' said Molly, quickly changing the subject. 'Where's Chiron?'

'Over there,' replied Peter, pointing to the Centaur, who was busy placing the rest of the food he'd foraged on the table.

A large selection of oversized fruit adorned the table. Jugs, filled with fresh water, sat waiting for them as they quickly made a bee line for the welcomed feast.

'Oh my god! Thank you! I could eat a scabby horse,' blurted Peter, before he realised what he'd said. 'Ooooops! Sorry Chiron. I meant, a scabby dog.'

The Centaur smiled as he poured the clear liquid into the wooden cups that, by the looks of them, been used countless times before them.

Molly and Peter, caring little for the hygiene of their predecessors, gulped down the invigorating substance without stopping for air, before reaching for the jug once more.

'Why is your fruit so big?' Questioned Molly, biting into what looked like a blueberry the size of an apple.

'Big?' Replied the Centaur. 'Is this not the size of all types of fruit?'

'God no!' Laughed Molly. 'Our blueberries are only about this big.' She continued, picking up a small stone, giving a rough example.

'How do you all survive on such meagre portions?' asked Chiron, helping himself to a selection of the banquet he'd supplied.

'We eat a lot of it,' mumbled Peter, before he could finish what was in his mouth.

Molly's expression began to change as small details of the previous night's events began to invade her head once more. 'What exactly happened last night.' She asked, reaching over her shoulder, feeling for something that she knew was once there.

'You tell us,' replied Peter. 'I was woken by a scream that scared the living hell out of me, only to find there was no sign of you anywhere. What the hell Molly! What on earth possessed you to go out there by yourself?'

Molly closed her eyes tightly, trying to piece everything together. 'A voice!' She recalled suddenly. 'I heard a voice. I must have been half asleep at the time, but the closer I got, the clearer it became. By the time I got close to the woods, I was certain it was my mum calling me. She was calling my name, Peter.'

'Don't talk nonsense!' laughed Peter, dismissing the notion with a wave of his hand. 'What made you think it was your mum calling you? Do you remember where we are for goodness sake?'

'I know! I know! It doesn't make any sense, but I know what I heard.'

'The Origin,' interrupted Chiron. 'This sounds like the work of, the Origin.'

Molly paused for moment as the memory came flooding back to her. 'That's it!' She exclaimed. 'I called Shifter as I was being chased by this monster. What was it? Oh yeah, a Wendigo. He told me; the beast was not who it seemed to be. I remember, the last thing I saw was its blood red eyes staring down at me before I blacked out. I remember thinking at the time. It's him, It's the Origin. He's controlling the beast. But there was nothing I could do about it. I was so weak. It clawed my shoulder, sending me crashing to the ground. The next thing I remember, is when I woke up this morning. What happened after I blacked out?'

Molly listened intently while Peter and the Centaur began to reveal the horror that befell them. And how they battled to defeat the Wendigo as it was about to tear her to pieces. As well as their race to escape the swarms of Vespertilio, who chased them through the forest, desperate to drink their blood.

The young girl gasped as, Peter told stories of magic creams and fast healing wounds. All of which, to him, strangely seemed to pale into insignificance from the pleasure he got, as he told her of her need for him to be closer to her while she slept.

The table went silent for a few moments, all pretty exhausted from Peter's enthusiastic rendition of the night's events. 'Well. You two obviously had a lot of fun,' said Molly flippantly, taking a deep breath as she reached for a well needed drink of water.

'Peter was right though Molly,' said the Centaur, getting back to the point. 'You should never venture off on your own. There are too many dangers in this realm. If you want to find your way out, then we have to stick together.'

'I couldn't help it Chiron. It was like I was being hypnotised. All sense of fear had gone. All I could think, was following the voice of my mother,' said the young girl, feeling her explanation was more than understandable considering.

'Most definitely the power of the Origin,' confirmed the Centaur. 'He will do anything in his power to defeat you my friends. You have to be wise. And at all costs, work together if you are to prevail.'

'That's easier said than done if he's going to play dirty tricks like that,' protested Molly, before finishing the last of the, sweet refreshing liquid.

Thought of another day like the previous one, filled the two humans with dread as, Chiron called for the humans to ready themselves for one final push towards the end of the realm, that would take them to the realm of hopes and fears. 'Remember my brave friends, expect the unexpected, stay vigilant at all times. The Origin is clever. He has played this game many, many times before.

And has prevailed more often than not. The only way you will defeat him, is, by using your head.'

They left the fort, unsure of what lay ahead. The only thing certain was, nothing was certain. Surprisingly revitalised from the hearty breakfast, Molly and Peter, took comfort from the fact, they were at least one day closer to their goal. Rescuing Molly's father.

The forest seemed different in the morning light than it did the night before. The sky-scraping trees looked magnificent as they reached high into the translucent white skyline. It was difficult to believe that no more than a few hours ago, they gave shelter to a host of blood sucking creatures, baying for their lives. The pathway ahead was clearer, the forest, more inviting, more welcoming in the daylight. The sounds of, more cheerful wildlife lifted their spirits a little, although the words of, Shifter and Chiron never too far from their minds. Things are never quite what they seem. They could never lower their guard. Not for a second. He would be waiting, ready to strike.

The pathway began to narrow the further into the woods they ventured. Shorter, stout trees and bracken bullied their way onto the track. Making it more difficult to stay on course. Every step becoming harder to find, until eventually, the road ended, the forest denying them access.

'What are we going to do now?' asked Peter, pulling his foot from a thicket of brambles he'd got caught in.

Molly looked at Chiron, hoping he had the answer. 'I'm sorry my friends, but I've not been to this part of the woods before. Maybe we will have to go back and find another way.

'What do you mean, you've never been here before? I thought you knew the way,' said Peter, his tone a little on the curt side.

'I know in which direction we need to go. But the pathway changes each time. I Have told you before. Things are different here. Things are never what__.'

'They seem,' interrupted Peter, getting more agitated by the second.

'We don't stand a chance really, do we?' asked Molly, beginning to get disheartened.

'Please, my friends, try and stay positive. He will feed off your despair. The more disillusioned you are, the stronger he will become. I've told you before, no matter what, you have to remain positive. There will be many more obstacles ahead before this is over.'

Molly took a deep breath, trying hard not to show her emotions. 'You're right. I know you're right. It's just sometimes, I wish we'd never come to this place. I mean, what are our chances of succeeding anyway? I've put other people's lives at risk, as well as my own. And for what? The chance that I, might be able to find my father?'

Realising how worked up she was becoming; Peter gently placed his hand on her shoulder. 'I've told you before Molls. Where you go, I go. I'm a big boy now. I'm sixteen,' he joked, trying to lighten her mood. 'So please, don't feel responsible for me. I'm big enough and, ugly enough to make my own cock-ups.'

Molly glanced up at her cheeky companion. He always knew what to say to snap her out of slump. Ever since they were kids, Peter thought of her first, before himself. What were these strange feelings she was having all of a sudden? She'd tried to block them out several times since arriving here. They were just friends, she kept telling herself, time and time again. But something was different. Something had changed. Was it this place? Yes, that was it. She tried to convince herself. It must be this place. Her emotions were going off in all sorts of different directions, as well as her hormones. Yes, her hormones. She could definitely use those as an excuse. The answer to a thousand questions, we couldn't explain.

'We have no choice,' said the Centaur, resigned to defeat. 'We have to find another way. The longer we wait, the more dangerous it will be.'

'Then let's go.' Molly quickly agreed, eager to get started before something else bad happened.

No sooner had the words left her lips, something prickly grabbed hold of her ankle. Then the other one. Suddenly, the forest came alive. Long vines came out of the woods, wrapping themselves around the trio as they tried in vain to escape.

'What the hell is happening!' Screamed Peter, as another one curled around his waist.

'Yateveo!' Shouted the Centaur, as more of the poisonous branches reached out from the forest restraining them, each one wrapping tightly around their limbs.

'Watch out for their poisonous spines!' cried Chiron. 'If they cut you, they will feed on your blood until every last drop is drained!'

'Great!' Exclaimed Peter, snapping one of the vines in two, a black slimy sap squirting out of its stem, hissing as if it were in pain. 'Something else wanting to drain our blood!' Quick Molly, we need some help from your bracelet!'

Molly tried to find something, anything as the vines seemed to sense what she was up too, grabbing tight hold of both arms. 'I'm trying!' She screamed as they quickly wound around her arm, trying to prevent her from reaching the trinket.

'Hit anything! Before they get hold of your other arm!' Pleaded Peter, his body now covered in foliage.

Meanwhile, the Centaur had managed to free one of his limbs as he reached out towards the girl, struggling to move. 'Quickly Molly, now!' He demanded, ripping a cluster of bramble, before they could grab the young girls free hand, ripping his own to shreds in the process.

Before it was too late, Molly quickly tapped the bracelet, just as the animated vines broke loose, wrapping themselves around her wrist.

Suddenly, dozens of dazzling rays of light, shot out from the bracelet, revealing a host of tiny creatures, dancing erratically all around them.

Vivid illuminous colours filled the sky. Reds, greens, purples, blues, gold, all leaving comet like trails in their wake. 'Not more fairies!' Screamed Peter, blood dripping from his wrists. 'How are they going to help us?'

The tiny creatures were hard to describe, as they moved so quickly. Their tiny naked bodies seemed transparent. A little flicker of light coming from inside, indicating a beating heart. Their faces appeared endearing, yet serious at the same time. High cheekbones, lifted the corners of their mouths, exposing razor like teeth that when wielded, would do serious damage.

'Wait! Look!' Said Molly as she watched in awe at the tiny wonders, swooping like fighter planes shearing through the vines and brambles with their teeth, like knives through butter. One by one, they took turns, a light humming noise echoing around the woods as they dipped gracefully in formation, cutting free each limb, the blood sucking foliage retreating back into the forest, defeated by these micro assassins.

Peter dropped to the ground, his limbs ripped to pieces, by the savage creepers. Molly and Chiron had sustained some injury, but the young human had bared the brunt of the assault.

'Peter! Are you okay?' Molly looked anxious as Peter lay there still. 'Chiron, what are we going to do? I can't find the symbol for the jar of ointment, Peter used on our wounds.'

'Maybe you're only able to use a symbol just once, Molly,' guessed the Centaur, kneeling to lift the boy onto his back.

'Wait, what are they doing?' Molly jumped as their tiny rescuers hovered closely over the injured human, before quickly darting to and fro above his damaged body. Their delicate wings, lightly brushing his broken flesh. Faster and faster they went, until they seemed like a blur of light. A gentle humming filled the air as they surrounded the human, busy, mending his ravaged body.

The two shocked observers flinched as some of the flying healers darted over to them. Surveying their wounds, before repeating the process, standing there, stunned as they fixed their broken frames.

Peter slowly opened his eyes while the fairy folk hovered in the air. Satisfied smiles seemed to appear on their faces, as if pleased with their work.

Molly looked at her arms, checking her companions mended wounds as she did. 'Wow! That's incredible!' She said in disbelief as she marvelled at her friend's miraculous recovery.

'Well, I guess you did hit the right symbol then,' he joked, checking himself over in the process.

The Centaur seemed distracted as they watched their tiny saviours, still buzzing around, as if readying themselves for another task. 'What are they up to?' Queried the Centaur, watching them hover majestically, switching places with the other, as if getting into formation.

'Never mind them,' said Peter dismissively. 'We still need to find a way out of here. I don't think going all the way back, is the best idea.'

As if they understood, the tiny aerobatic creatures began to make a strange noise. It was like a hissing sound, instead taking in a huge gulps of air. Suddenly, their cheeks bulged as they showered the three companions with clouds of sparkling dust. Micro particles of golden like glitter, showered down on them, making them light on their feet.

Peter gasped as he watched both Molly and the Centaur lift slowly off the ground. 'Oh my god!' He shouted as the young man followed his two friends.

The fairies quickly split into three groups. The majority gathering around the Centaur for obvious reasons. Their tiny hands (aided by the fairy dust) lifted the trio high into the sky, leaving the forest, from which it seemed, there was no escape, far behind.

The sweet fresh air felt wonderful as they sailed like birds through the sky, like it was something out of a Peter Pan novel, the forest, now far behind them. Spectacular views dominated the horizon as they surveyed their surroundings.

Strange birds, like those they observed when first arriving, flew passed without a second glance.

Suddenly, Molly yelped, the ground beneath getting closer and closer as she noticed their tiny saviours disappear one by one, popping like bubbles, lowering them closer to the ground, until the last ones, making sure their charges were safely on firm ground, disappeared.

'I don't know what to say,' said Peter, finally having the opportunity to check his once, lacerated body. 'I thought we were done for, for sure.'

Molly was too busy looking at something in the distance to concentrate on what her friend was saying. 'They don't look too friendly.' She said as she noticed four menacing winged creatures approaching, making the most horrendous noise she'd ever heard.

The trio covered their ears as a loud, high pitched screech, pierced through the air. 'Maybe we should have stayed where we were,' said Peter sarcastically as he searched for an easy escape route.

'Harpies!' Shouted the Centaur, scooping the young girl up off the ground while Peter leapfrogged onto Chiron's back.

'I've seen them somewhere before,' insisted Molly, holding tight hold of the Centaur. 'My dream. They were in my dream. But how is that possible?'

Chiron galloped as fast as he could, zigzagging from side to side whilst trying to evade the, Harpies as they swooped down, clawing at the two humans.

The Creatures features seemed demonic, with bat like wings that spanned at least the size of a small aircraft, supporting their thin skeletal bodies. The constant noise they were creating, made it difficult for the Centaur to hear anything the humans were saying. Teeth like needles filled their gaping mouths, with two small horns poking out from their heads. Their legs were just as intimidating, heavy set and muscular, built for carrying heavy cargo.

'Get off me!' screamed Peter as one of the creatures attempted to grab hold of his arms, before the young human snatched it away, temporarily evading its clutches.

Desperate to hold on, Molly tried to wrap her arms around the Centaur. Any symbol would be better than none, but his barrel like chest prevented her from reaching the trinket.

'I'll head towards that mountain!' Exclaimed Chiron, hoping the mountain face may hinder the Harpies large wingspan.

Suddenly, the Centaur stumbled, falling into a dip in the ground, unsteadying his companions as Peter, trying to keep his balance, flung his arms into the air.

Two of the Harpies screeched excitedly as they saw their chance. With precise accuracy, they swooped in low, each grabbing an arm as they lifted the screaming human off the Centaur's back, cackling triumphantly between themselves.

'Help me, please!' he screamed as Molly attempted to grab hold of his legs.

'No!' Bellowed Chiron as the other two demons capitalised on the young girl's mistake, quickly snatching her whilst attempting to rescue her friend.

Molly looked down in horror, watching her friend and protector get smaller and smaller as the Centaur reached out in vain, shouting something she was unable to understand, above the magnanimous cries of the Harpies.

There was nothing they could do but wait and ride it out. The bracelet was useless as long as her arms were shackled by the winged devils. But wait for what? Was this the end? Was this another trick by the Origin? Where were they taking them?

The Harpies flew high up into the sky. Ascending the face of the mountain, shrieking as they chastised each other, wings clashing each time they did.

As they approached the summit, a deep rumbling began reverberating everywhere around them. The irregular boom, getting louder, the closer they got. Molly's heart began to beat faster. Somehow, she knew what it was. She'd remembered what the Galpherin had said. She'd remembered his name.

An expletive cry came from Peter directly above her. Molly understood what it meant, without hearing the words as she caught her first glimpse of the monster that dominated the landscape.

The colossal dragon must have been, at least a fifty-foot-tall as it was wide, blocking out the sun with its magnificent wings. Its burgundy, dark red mass glistened as the sun reflected off its scales. His eyes, yellow, like two roaring bonfires narrowed, observing its insignificant opponents before it. The ground shuddered beneath its feet, as it prowled and stalked his prey. Large clouds of smoke blew from its nostrils as it, readied itself for battle.

The Harpies spun out of control, before bursting into flames as the beast, irritated by their presence, lit its almighty pipes and blew out from its mouth the fires from hell, incinerating the winged devils, turning them to ash.

The creatures barbed spine quivered in delight, pleased with itself as it snapped its jaws together, before turning its attention back towards the unfortunate duo.

'Look,' whispered Molly as she grabbed Peter's arm, turning his attention an object dangling from a chain around the dragons neck.

'Is that what I think it is?' asked the young human, his eyes fixed firmly on the golden key.

Suddenly, the fire breathing monster, beat his majestic wings as it rose high enough to reveal, Shifter was standing there, waiting for them.

'Is this what the Origin calls competition?' Roared Glycon.

The dragons voice, reverberated around the mountain, sending both Molly and, Peter staggering backwards. 'You insult me with these morsels. They are merely offerings. I have waited centuries to do battle. And this is what he sends me. Maybe he should add you, into the bargain, Galpherin,' threatened the beast, trying to intimidate the old man.

'Shifter bravely took a step closer to the dragon, clearly unimpressed by his warning. 'Believe me Glycon, they are more than worthy adversaries. If I were you, I would not be so confident. These are humans. Do you remember the last time you faced a human?'

The beast hissed as his long-forked tongue vibrated wildly, inches away from the Galpherin.

The old man stood firm, clearly unmoved by the monsters threatening gestures.

'Yes. I roasted it,' he replied smugly as his sly eyes turned towards the humans.

'Yes, but not before it cut a piece from your wing,' said the Galpherin, a satisfied smile creeping across his face.

The monster loomed up, clearly angry with the old man's mocking words.

'Molly check your bracelet quickly. That flying lizard thing, is about to kick off,' insisted Peter, anticipating Shifter may have goaded the dragon one time too many.

Molly quickly looked at the trinket, unsure what to look for. What could possibly be of use against a fire breathing dragon?

'Look!' Said Peter excitedly, pointing to the symbol of a shield.

'We're going to need more than that to defeat a dragon,' said a worried Molly as she looked for an alternative.

'Yes, but we'll need something to protect us from the fire that thing spits out, if we're going to stand any chance of surviving. We can worry about a weapon after we prevent it from barbecuing us.'

'You're right, good thinking.'

Molly quickly hit the symbol as a beam of golden light shot out from the bracelet hitting the dragon full in the chest. The beast wheeled back, shocked by the phenomenon as the beam carved out pieces of the dragons scales, sending the creature into a frenzy. Glycon, furiously beat his magnificent wings, trying to free itself from the hostile invasion.

After extracting what was needed, the beam ceased its assault, whirling around like a disco laser light, fusing the pieces together, guiding the dragon scale shield into the arms of the young girl.

Glycon leaped high into the air, roaring and thrashing around. The sky seemed to darken as the beast's huge stature eclipsed the sun.

'Quick! He's coming around!' Screamed Peter, noticing the dragon falling from the sky, gliding as Its wings used the air to guide its course.

'He's heading for Shifter,' said Molly, running to the old man's aid.

The dragon picked up speed before craning its long neck, taking in a massive gulp of air. The young girl hurled herself towards the old man, just as the dragon breathed out a flame thrower, hotter than hell itself.

'Stay behind me, Shifter!' Said Molly, standing in front of the Galpherin, the flames beating against the dragon scale shield.

The old man crouched behind her as the flames seemed to bounce off the shield, engulfing everything around them, while they remained untouched by the inferno.

In the meantime, Peter had managed to make his way, undetected towards the rear end of the beast.

This is a bad idea. He thought to himself as he climbed on top of the dragon's tail.

Using the teeth which ran down its spine, Peter carefully placed one foot in front of the other, all the time praying the overgrown lizard wouldn't feel his presence. Clouds of smoke filled the air, sending a mass of dust and ash, raining down all around him.

The heat was becoming unbearable. The dragons fire seemed to have no end as the young girl began to struggle the longer it went on. 'I can't hold on for much longer,' complained Molly as the heat began to penetrate through the shield.

Suddenly, the dragon stopped, as if something had interrupted its assault. Glycon Began to move his head from side to side. Craning his neck, like he was looking for someone.

Molly gasped with shock, looking at a figure she recognised clinging up the back of the dragon. 'What the hell does he think he's doing up there? He's going to get himself killed.'

The young girl looked at the old man in desperation. Hoping he would do something, before the beast turned him into toast. 'I'm sorry, Miss, Miggins. I am forbidden to help you,' said Shifter, before the young girl could ask.

'But he's going to die if you don't help him! Please!'

Before the Galpherin could answer, Molly heard a desperate cry for help, turning to see the beast launching itself into the air. Peter clung on for dear life, the dragon twisting and turning as it tried to dislodge the human, clinging to its neck. The young boy held a tight hold of the chain hanging around Glycon's neck, the look on his face one of terror and desperation.

'Who is that?' She said to herself, noticing a familiar figure coming up over the mountain side.

'Chiron!' Molly cried, relieved to see her friend.

'Hurry, jump on, there's no time to loose!' Demanded Chiron, reaching out an arm, scooping her up on his back.

'I knew you'd come for us,' said Molly, clinging tight hold of the Centaur.

Chiron galloped towards the shield which the young human had left lying on the ground. 'Quickly, look to your bracelet. We need something fast; Peter won't hold on for much longer,' said the Centaur, scooping up the dragon scale shield. 'The Galpherin can't help you,' he continued, as if reading her mind.

Another scream from Peter, jolted Molly into more haste as she quickly scanned the bracelet, desperate something would jump out at her. 'Nothings calling out to me.' She said, frustrated with herself. 'A lance? No, that won't even pierce the skin. A gun? That'll just bounce off its tough scales. Sword? No, again, that won't make a mark. All these weapons are useless! Wait, calm down. Remember what Shifter said. Everything I need, is on this bracelet.'

Suddenly, Molly's eyes lit up as she recognised something. She'd noticed it once before but hadn't taken much notice of it. 'I know what this is.' She said excitedly to herself as she tapped the symbol without hesitation.

'Peter needs to get off before I use it!' Shouted Molly as the beam shot out from the bracelet, etching out the head.

'The only way he'll be able to get off the dragon, is, if it gets closer to the ground,' said the Centaur, stopping as the young girl jumped to the ground.

Molly grabbed the head as soon as the trinket had completed the process. 'Chiron cover your eyes. Don't look at it!' Ordered Molly, covering her eyes as she raised the head in the air.

'Peter! Jump!' Bellowed the Centaur, just as the giant lizard landed, readying itself for one last attack.

Peter saw his opportunity as soon as he recognised what Molly was holding. Turning his head from its gaze, Peter leaped from the dragon's neck. Glycon was too busy clearing his windpipe, to see what the young human was holding. Just as he was about to let loose, one final almighty flame thrower, the beast locked eyes with the gorgon. Medusa's eyes lit up, just as the dragon lent forward, catching her gaze full on. The snakes that made up her hair, slithered and hissed as Glycon suddenly froze, with fear at first, unable to move, slowly turning to stone.

'Don't make eye contact with her!' Ordered Chiron as the dragon roared in agony, every part of its body solidifying. Until suddenly, silence.

Medusa's head, instantly disappeared as the three exhausted companions stared in disbelief at the once mighty dragon, standing there, still, like a statue. The almighty, invincible Glycon, now a monument.

The three friends looked at each other, not knowing quite what to say. The magnitude of what they had done, rendering them speechless.

'Congratulations, Molly Miggins,' said the old man. 'And may I take this opportunity to thank you for your help,' he continued, humbly bowing his head. 'If not for your quick reactions, I would have been burnt alive.'

Molly smiled at the Galpherin, a little embarrassed by the old man's praise. 'Please, Shifter. I only did what anyone would do in that situation.'

Suddenly, a thunderous noise erupted around them as they looked up shocked to see, the statue beginning to crack under the strain of its own mass.

Quickly, hairline cracks began to spread from the bottom up. Huge pieces of the beast began to break from the pressure.

All four beings moved swiftly from the area as the remains of the great dragon came crashing to the ground. The once feared colossus, now rubble at their feet.

The old man gestured towards a shiny object lying amongst the debris. 'This now belongs to you, young lady.'

Molly, carefully stepped through the wreckage, out of respect for her worthy adversary. Bending down, the young girl picked up the golden key, dusting off its previous owners remains.

'Is this it? Have we done it?' She asked, not quite believing what they'd achieved.

The old man smiled as he clasped his bony fingers together. 'You have conquered the realm of legends, Miss. Miggins. Just as your father before you.'

Molly stared longingly at the key, clenching it tightly in her hand. The thought that her dad had passed through here not that long ago, as well as the sense of achievement she felt, brought a lump to her throat, as she looked proudly, at the friends that had helped her.

The Centaur slowly approached his young friends. A look of sadness appearing on his face.

'What's the matter, Chiron? Why so glum?' asked Molly.

'I'm afraid this is goodbye my friends,' said Chiron as he held out his hand.

'But you can come with us! He can come with us, can't he Shifter?'

The Galpherin slowly shook his head, knowing all too well it was impossible.

'I cannot pass through realms I'm afraid, Molly,' interrupted the Centaur. 'I am an independent being who belongs in this realm. The Origin controls which beings belong in which realms. If I were to pass through to the realm of hopes and fears, I would not come out of the other side and would be trapped there, in limbo. The only possible way I could do that, would be to swear my allegiance to the Origin. Meaning, I would be his to control. So, for me, it is far better that I stay in this realm and help those beings try and make it through to the next.

'You've been a good friend, Chiron,' said Peter, sensing his friend was fighting to find the words. 'Thank you for everything. We won't forget you.'

The Centaur extended his arm, shaking the young man's hand. 'The pleasure was all mine, Peter. Look after Molly, won't you? I have great faith in both of you and I know you will make it home.'

Molly suddenly reached up, grabbing hold of her friend, squeezing him tightly, unable to let go. 'I'm going to miss you.' She said, her voice beginning to break, clearly showing how emotional it was for her to leave him behind.

'Look after each other and good luck. Remember, trust your instincts.'

The Galpherin cleared his throat, indicating it was time to leave. 'This way, Miss, Miggins,' said the old man as he gestured towards the door.

Peter reached over and gently took hold of his friend's hand. 'Come on Moll's, it's time to go.'

Molly squeezed his hand in return, the look she gave, telling him she was grateful he was there.

'Goodbye my friends,' said Chiron, as the pair waved, before turning towards the door that would lead them one step closer to freedom.

'Place the key in the lock and twist it one turn to the right,' instructed the Galpherin.

Molly let go of Peters hand as she examined the key, before gently sliding it into the lock as requested.

Instantly, a blinding light burst through the outer edge of the door as it gradually began to creek open. Just as before, the door opened to reveal an entrance that seemed liquid like, slowly rippling as it held its solidity.

'After you,' said Shifter, stretching out his arm cordially.

Molly grabbed tight hold of Peters hand once more as they both held their breath, stepping through once again, to the unknown.

Chapter Fifteen

Six iron doors adorned the oval room. Each one, a gateway towards the unknown, yet one step closer to her father. One step nearer to home.

What had become of mum? Had she survived the pain of so much loss? How much time had passed? How much time would they lose before returning home? Would they ever see home again? Dasher! What had become of her dog? So many things were going through Molly's mind.

You need to focus, she thought to herself. She could worry about home when all this was over. 'One down, two to go.' She whispered to herself.

'Welcome to the realm of hopes and fears,' said the old man as he presented the selection of doors.

'Okay,' replied Peter, shrugging his shoulders.

The Galpherin paused as he surveyed the great oval room, before explaining their fate. 'As you were travelling to this world. This universe. Your thoughts and dreams were recorded and stored for this very realm. If indeed you were successful enough to get this far that is. The Origin extracted a selection of your hopes and fears from the memories collected from your minds and devised a series of trials. As we were only expecting, Miss Miggins, there was a little confusion as to why there were such a contrast in thoughts, memories and dreams. All of which became clear on meeting your young friend. Behind each door, is one of your hopes or fears. You will need to do battle with your fears or, be worthy of your hopes, to complete the trial. At the end of one of these doors, is the door that will lead you to the final realm. The realm of spells.'

Molly's head snapped around on recognising the name. 'That's the realm my father is being held prisoner, isn't it?'

The old man nodded, before responding. 'Your father is suspended in the tree of souls, young Molly. If you fail, his life force along with yours, will belong to the Origin. But we're getting ahead of ourselves. Firstly, you must concentrate on making it through, the realm of hopes and fears. The key to completing this realm, is to remember, these are your hopes and your dreams. Conquer them and you will prevail. Succumb to them and you will fail.'

'How do we know whose hopes and fears are whose?' asked Peter, weighing up each door.

'You don't,' replied the old man. 'That will only be revealed once you have chosen the first door.'

'So, let me get this straight,' said Peter, struggling to understand all the rules. 'There are six doors. Correct?' The Galpherin nodded. 'Each door has behind it, something you have taken from our minds,' he continued.

'Something the Origin has taken,' corrected the old man.

'Whatever,' dismissed Peter. 'Anyway. We are only permitted to choose three of the six doors. But the door that leads to the realm of spells could be behind any of the six. Is that what you're telling us?'

'That is correct,' answered the Galpherin, taking a minute to make sure the young man was right, before answering.

'Well that doesn't seem very fair! We have to not only, battle through our hopes and fears, but will only have a fifty-fifty chance of being able to continue?' asked Peter, getting more annoyed the more he thought about it.

'The realms are not designed for you to succeed, young Peter,' replied Shifter, sympathetically. 'The Origin wants your life force and will do what he can, as long as it is within the law to get it. The only advice I can give you, is what I have always given you. The young lady's bracelet is all you will need. It is your lifeline. That is all I can tell you.'

Molly looked at her wrist, clenching her fist, as she studied the trinket. 'Well, it's not let us down yet.' She said, taking a deep breath, readying herself for the uncertain journey that lay ahead of them.

The old man made his way to the centre of the room as he turned to face the humans, resigned to whatever lay ahead of them. 'Please, choose your first room,' he instructed.

The two friends looked at each other, shrugging their shoulders, unsure who should choose. 'Err! Let's try…' began Molly, before something interrupted her choice.

'What was that?' She queried, feeling a single vibration coming from the bracelet.

'What was what,' replied Peter.

Was it a sign? She thought to herself.

'The first door!' Exclaimed Molly, wondering if the trinket were sending her a sign.

'As you wish,' responded the Galpherin as the door lock snapped open, revealing the liquid type entrance that seemed to pave the way to every door that opened. 'Welcome to your first challenge. This is called, the Enigma.'

'Not again!' Protested Peter, looking menacing towards the old man. 'I hate having to hold my breath, every time I go through these doors.'

The little man gave a slight chortle, amused by the human's ignorance. 'There is no need to hold your breath young, Peter. You are not passing through liquid.'

Peter sent a defiant glance towards the old man, wondering if he should hold it anyway.

'Good luck to you both. And remember, things are not always what they seem.'

Molly, more for comfort than safety, grabbed Peter's hand as they slowly stepped through the translucent entrance.

The place seemed unnatural. Like it was part real life, part animated. The ground beneath their feet felt hard, like they were standing on solid ground, but seemed cushioned under foot, like grass.

Slowly, things began to make more sense, as if someone somewhere were making alterations to the place around them. Making it more realistic by the second, until everything seemed strangely real.

'What's going on here?' asked Peter, a little freaked out by his surroundings.

'I'm not sure,' replied Molly. 'But I don't like the look of that maze over there.'

Stretching out in front of them, as far as the eye could see, was a magnificent maze. A thousand different twists and turns littered the way, that would confuse the most avid puzzle solver, never mind two teenagers with no idea where they were going.

'Look, over there,' said Molly, noticing two strange looking individuals, arguing amongst themselves. 'Let's go see if they can help.' She continued.

'Okay, but we need to be careful. We've been stung more than once already,' warned Peter as they slowly made their way towards the two oddities.

'Excuse me,' said Molly, making sure they kept a safe distance. 'I wonder; can you help us?'

The smaller individual stopped what he was saying and looked curiously at the young lady. 'And what may I ask, can we be helpin you wiv?' replied the funny looking elf like creature.

Standing no higher than four feet tall. His chirpy pink face seemed like it was stuck on smile. His unusually high cheek bones, giving the impression his mood was permanently jovial. His matchstick arms and legs looked lost, in the moth-eaten lime green hessian all in one suit. A tall crooked top hat of the same colour, with a red band wrapped around the rim, seemed to set the whole Irish, Elf thing off perfectly. Even the brown pointed moccasins, looked traditional.

'Err, I was wondering if you knew the way out of here,' replied Molly as she tried to take in his extremely tall companion.

'Please excuse me manners, lil miss, and allow me to introduce us. My name be Tweedy and this be me compatriot, Buckhammer. But you can call him Buck.'

Buck was at least eight feet tall. A stiff breeze looked as if it might blow him over, given how thin and unstable he looked. Half-mast pants, held up by bracers, looked as if they'd seen better days. His weather warn face looked as tough as old boots as he chewed on a piece of straw, he'd plucked from the hat that flopped down over his ears.

'Allow,' said Buck as he touched the rim of his hat, acknowledging the two strangers.

'I'm sorry, what were you two arguing about?' asked Peter, rubbing the back of his neck, worried he might have whiplash if he looked up at Buck much longer.

'Oh, don't you be worrying about such fings, me old matey. Me and Buck are always avin a good old debate of some sort or other. We was debating if the next victims, oops, sorry my mistake, challengers.'

The two oddballs burst out laughing. The joke, obviously as old as the two of them. 'We was wonderin if ya would make it to the end. Lookin at ya's, I said no. But Buck here has a bit more faith in ya.'

Molly and Peter looked at each other, each wondering if this were truly real or just a bad dream they'd wake from instantly.

'Well I'm glad that we're the source of your entertainment, but we'd really like to get out of here as soon as possible, if that's okay with you two jokers? Said Peter, more than a bit miffed by this point.

'Please, don't take offence youngster. Me and Buck are just pullin ya leg. We don't get much time wiv the challengers, so we like to av a bit of fun wiv em, Ya know, just to break up the day.'

The elf's large gormless companion began to snigger like a child, amused by his friends teasing.

'Wait, don't be like that,' pleaded the elf as the two unimpressed humans began to walk away. 'What can we do for ya?'

Molly sighed, before letting go of her friend's arm. 'We need to know which direction we're going if you don't mind?'

'That's easy,' replied the elf.

'Yeah, easy,' repeated Buck.

'Ya just have to get from this end of the maze to the other. Without gettin dead,' continued Tweedy.

Molly and Peter stared at the impossible puzzle, the daunting task that lay ahead, evident on their faces.

'There'll be many fings you'll need to defeat, before ya get to the end.'

'Yeah, defeat,' confirmed his dopey friend.

'But be quick mind. Coz if ya not there in time, the door will lock itself, and yawl be stuck here, entertainin me an ol Buck here.'

The two oddities laughed out loud once more as they suddenly wandered off, Buck slapping his friend on the back, causing them to bicker once more.

'Wait!' Shouted Molly. 'Is that it? What do you mean the door will lock?'

Molly raised her hands in the air in frustration as the wannabe comedians ignored her protests, bickering as they continued on their way.

'What the hell,' said Peter as he turned to his friend, wondering how they were gonna get through this. 'We're fighting a losing battle here Moll's. The rules seem to change by the second in this world. No one said anything about a time limit.'

Molly looked towards the entrance of the maze as she held up a hand, gesturing for him to be quiet.

'Shh! Do you hear that? She asked, a faint clicking noise grabbing her attention.

Peter craned his neck as he listened intently. 'I don't hear anything. Listen, we've got to get going. The longer we wait, the more likely we'll get stuck in this mad place. Besides, I don't know if you've noticed, but that is a maze. And if we come to a dead end, we'll have to go back, meaning less time.'

'Come on, let's go,' agreed Molly as they cautiously made their way through the entrance of the maze.

Memories began to come flooding back to when they were in the forest. The vines grabbing and tearing at his flesh. Smothering his whole body, before blacking out.

'I don't like this Molly. Did you notice the bushes moving?' asked Peter, jumping at the slightest movement.

'Relax will you, it's nothing!' Snapped Molly, a little jumpy herself.

'Don't tell me to relax. There's no way we're getting through this unscathed. Just be ready to tap on that bracelet.'

Molly suddenly stopped. That clicking sound again. 'Can you here that?' She asked as she noticed movement from the far end of the path.

Peter froze with fear as the freakish creatures came scurrying towards them in their thousands.

Unsure which way to turn, the humans backed off as the creatures began to expel their weapons. The red-hot silk thread, scorching the ground as it landed.

'Spiders!' Screamed Peter, the colour in his face turning a shade of grey. 'I hate spiders! They're my worst nightmare.'

Molly grabbed hold of his hand, pulling him along with her as they tried to outrun the disgusting army of arachnids. 'So, it looks like we've jumped into your fears,' guessed Molly as the creatures began to multiply.

The gruesome spiders varied in size. Their large hairy abdomens hovered low to the ground as their legs readied themselves to launch their attack.

'I hate all creepy crawlies!' Cried Peter, tripping over his own legs as he tried to get away. 'Spiders are my worst fear.'

The two friends ran as fast as they could as the creatures gathered pace, gaining on them with every second.

'Quick Molly, tap your bracelet, we're not going to be able to outrun them,' pleaded Peter, the spiders webs now catching his heel, burning through the soul of his shoe like butter.

Molly looked at the trinket, frantically searching for the right symbol to use. Nothing was jumping out to her. 'I don't know which one will help us!' She screamed, as one of the silk threads landed on her arm.

The young girl cried out in pain, the hot web cutting through her suit burning her as the eight-legged freaks began to climb the back of her leg. Most of them falling off as she slammed her feet to the ground with every hurried step.

'Just hit anything!' Insisted Peter. 'It worked last time.'

One of the creatures had almost reached the top of her leg, spitting out its fiery web, cutting her like a laser beam, criss-crossing over her thigh.

'I've got no choice.' she said to herself, the agony from the hot silk thread like someone were cutting her with a sword.

Molly poked the bracelet, unsure which symbol she touched, praying it would help. Anything would do at this moment. Time was up. The spiders were upon them.

A light, shot from the trinket, etching out their aid. 'What the hell is that!' Screamed Peter in agony, energy sapping from him like a cheap battery.

'It looks like a jar,' said Molly, unable to hide her disappointment. 'We're done for.' She continued, her body becoming numb with the constant abuse it was taking.

Suddenly a voice came out of nowhere. 'Open the lid! Open the lid now, before it's too late!'

'Do it! Open the bloody lid!' Cursed Peter, about ready to collapse as the spiders began to overwhelm the two humans.

Molly quickly grabbed hold of the jar as it was about to fall to the ground and with the little energy she had left, twisted off the lid.

A sudden vacuum caused Molly to drop the strange object to the ground. One by one, the terrifying creatures began to disappear, sucked into its cavern. Even the larger of the beasts were helpless against its relentless pull. Thousands of them, unbelievably vanishing into its void. Molly and Peter, continued to stare, open mouthed, unable to comprehend how so many of them were able to fit into such a small container.

'Quickly, close the lid,' came the voice once more. Hurry or they'll be back,' it continued.

Unconcerned to see who was making the demands, Molly grabbed the lid, quickly twisting it tightly shut.

Peter checked his suit, wincing as he touched the paper-thin cuts all over his flesh. 'You ok?' He asked as he noticed the two oddballs appearing out of nowhere.

'Tweedy and Buck?' asked Molly rhetorically as the two oddballs stood, arms folded in front of them.

'Yip,' said the little elf, grinning like Cheshire cat. ''Tis us. And not a moment too soon if ya ask me.'

'Yeah, a moment too soon,' repeated his clueless companion.

'Them arachnids would o melted ya down in no time, if ya had o waited much longer,' continued the elf as he elbowed his annoying friend in the knee.

'But how did you know where to find us?' asked a confused Molly as the pain began to set in, the adrenaline beginning to wear off.

'Well, we felt a bit bad, leavin ya all on ya own without any words of advice to help ya on ya way. Ya can blame ol Buck here if ya like. It was his fault. He's always distractin me,' said the elf, causing his companion folded his arms in a huff. 'We knows the maze like the backs of our hands. We knows all the hidden doors an entrances.'

Molly and Peter watched as the jar suddenly vanished as quickly as it appeared.

'You've got a good eye for knowin which symbol to choose little miss,' said Tweedy, turning his attention towards the trinket.

'I didn't consciously choose anything,' replied Molly. 'I've simply guessed the last couple of times that I've used it.'

The elf laughed as he nudged his dumb companion once more, initiating a delayed chortle. 'There's no guessing with the golden band,' said Tweedy. 'You choose, what ya suppose ta choose. Ya brain makes a decision in the moment. Maybe ya don't realise it, but the decision is a conscious one.'

Molly tentatively rose to her feet as she checked her bracelet, wincing from the sudden reminder of her injuries.

'Ya won't need the healing liquid lil miss,' said Tweedy, knowing exactly what she was looking for. 'They will heal in no time at all. Anyway, if there's nothin else, me n ol Buck here will be on our way.'

'Wait!' Said Molly, causing the two oddballs to stop in their tracks. 'What did you mean earlier when you said, we needed to hurry before the door locks?'

'Did I?' asked the elf as he shifted his hat, trying to remember. 'Oh yeah. Don't worry you'll be fine, as long as you make it to the door before the sun goes down. Plenty of time, lil miss.'

With that, the two strange beings turned and went on their merry way, whistling in harmony as they went.

'Come on Molly, let's get out of here. I don't want to get stuck in this place,' urged Peter as he headed off in the same direction as little and large, eager not to lose them.

'Peter, look!' Exclaimed Molly, noticing her suit was beginning to mend itself.

Peter stopped as he checked his suit, surprised that his own wounds were starting to heal. 'Wow! These suits really are impressive,' he said, realising that the pain was beginning to dissipate. 'I can't believe my injuries are gone.'

Molly carefully patted her waist and legs, surprised that she too was feeling no pain. 'I wonder why our suits didn't heal as fast when we were attacked in the realm of legends?' She queried, her suit now looking as good as new.

'Maybe the damage was too much,' replied Peter.

The two friends remained alert as they continued their journey. The hedges that made up the structure of the maze, seemed to change with each turn they took, like they were going back on themselves, as if it were taking them back to the start.

'Somethings not right here Molly,' said Peter, totally disorientated by this time. 'We've been walking for ages. Surely, we must be close to the end by now.'

'Shh. Did you hear that?' Whispered Molly, spooked on hearing a rumble coming from the other end of the path.

'That doesn't sound friendly,' replied her friend as the unnerving noise grew louder.

Suddenly, the humans gasped as a dark sinister figure loomed out from the shadows, its large menacing fangs, snapping angrily as it slowly stalked its prey.

'What the bloody heel is that thing!' Screeched Peter as his blood turned cold.

'Oh my god!' Said Molly, frozen to the spot, recognising the beast. 'That's Dioskilos!'

'What on earth is a Dioskilos?' asked Peter, surprised at her recollection.

'I used to watch old films with my dad when I was younger. Dioskilos, is a two-headed dog from Greek mythology if I remember correctly. He gave me nightmares as a child. That's why I remember it.'

The beast must have been at least the size of a small horse. Large sinister white fangs stood out from each of its black heads, snapping at each other as they sparred for the right to draw first blood. Its thick rough black coat gave it a more intimidating demeanour. Razor like claws dug huge clumps of turf from the ground as it stalked like a bull, ready to strike. Drool and spittle dripped from its open jaws as Its wrinkled snout twitched with anticipation.

Peter grabbed hold of Molly, helping her out of her frozen like state, slowly edging away from the beast, who's two sets of blackened eyes were watching their every movement, waiting for the right moment to pounce. Its two bulbous heads complained at the other, each one desperate to be the first to strike.

'Molly, this thing is about to attack. You need to find something on that bracelet or we're dog food,' insisted the young man, never taking his eyes from the beast. (Either of them)

Molly, carefully looked over the trinket, desperately checking for something she thought might dispose of the two headed creature. A net? She thought. No, no good. It'd eat through that with ease. The jar? There's no way it's getting into that small space, magical or not.

Just then, she spotted two cutlets, one crossed over the other. 'They'll have to do.' She said, noticing Dioskilos was crouching even lower, his attack imminent.

The golden beam shot out like a bullet from the trinket, carving out the weapons in perfect symmetry. Both Molly and Peter each grabbed hold of a sword as soon as the bracelet had finished its job as the beast's heads howled in unison. (Annoyed with itself for allowing their prey to arm themselves).

'We need to separate,' said Peter as he coaxed the creature away from his young friend.

'Be careful!' Warned Molly, moving in the opposite direction.

The confused dog, seemed in conflict with itself as it tussled one way and then the other, not knowing which human to attack first.

Suddenly, the beast lunged at molly, its huge bulk sending her crashing to the ground, knocking her unconscious.

Satisfied the girl was no threat, Dioskilos quickly hurled itself towards the boy. The monsters both sets of teeth, snapped menacingly as Peter narrowly missed one of its heads with a swing of his sword. The beast, enraged by his opponent's retaliation, quickly took advantage of the young human's error, using its own sharp instruments, slashing at his chest with one almighty swipe of its talons.

The young human cried out in pain as the suit of armour opened up like paper, instantly exposing his wounds.

Sensing its prey was immobilised, Dioskilos began to inch closer to the human, confident he was there for the taking.

Peter lay there, dazed by the assault as the creature loomed over him, salivating, each head eager to devour the spoils.

A strange look came across one of the creatures faces, as if it were smiling, mocking the other. The beasts other head, suddenly lunged towards the boy, causing its neighbour to spring into action, as both heads began to fight amongst each other, snapping furiously between themselves as to which one deserved the reward.

A stomach curdling yelp pierced the air, so high pitched, it would have broken a thousand glasses. Peter stared up at the hell hounds, its heads writhing in agony as the young man felt a type of liquid dripping on his torso that seemed to be coming from the monster.

Peter gasped with fear as the hound, a deathly look on its faces, came crashing down on top of him, just as Molly withdrew her sword.

The young girl stood there, chest heaving, bloody sword in hand. 'Are you okay, Peter?' She asked, a desperate look on her face.

'Help me get this thing off,' said Peter, the dead weight of the beast too much for him alone.

Molly dropped her sword, reluctantly grabbed a clump of the monster's fur as she helped roll it off his injured body. 'Look at your chest!' Yelped Molly, noticing the open wounds. 'We definitely need the ointment for this one.' She continued as she scanned the bracelet for the magic cream.

'I'm afraid ya won't find ya healin' slime on the golden band, lil miss,' came the now familiar voice from behind them.

Molly and Peter wheeled around to see the odd couple standing before them. Tweedy, tapping his foot, arms folded. His gormless friend, pointing at the lifeless body of the beast lying on the ground.

'Ya can't use the golden bracelet while it's already in use. Besides, ya wounds l be fine in a lil while. Ya only really need it if ya life is threatened.'

Molly scowled at the pair, beginning to feel a little miffed by the two oddballs by this time. 'Why do you two always seem to turn up at the last second? We could have done with your help about five minutes ago.'

Tweedy stamped his foot firmly on the ground, annoyed at the young girls chastising. 'We come, exactly when we supposed to come lil miss. And not a moment before! Come on Buck, we know when we not wanted,' moaned the elf, both of them storming off in a huff.

'Wait! I didn't mean t__!' Shouted Molly as she reached out to help her friend off the ground. 'Come on, let's follow them.' She continued, hurrying after the odd beings.

'I don't believe this!' Exclaimed Peter as he surveyed the familiar surroundings. 'We're back where we started!'

Tweedy and Buck, stood there, the smaller man nodding, confirming Peter's observation. 'Yip! That ya are young sir. This is where me n Buck hangs out. Where else would it be?'

Peter looked exasperated, about to explode, before his friend interrupted. 'Why have you brought us back to the start?' asked Molly, a little more diplomatically.

'We didn't bring ya back anywhere, lil miss. You followed us two,' replied Tweedy, correcting the young girl.

'Yeah but!' Shouted Peter.

'But nothing,' interrupted Molly. 'He's right. We did follow them. Let's face it, we're stuck here.'

'Not stuck,' interrupted Buck.

The two humans looked at the tall dopey character, wondering if he were just rambling away to himself.

'Me friend is right,' said Tweedy, patting his companion on the hand. 'Remember what the Galpherin has always told you.'

'I know. There's always something on the bracelet that will help us,' said Molly, before the elf could reply.

'Ye, that too. But he also said things are not always what they seem,' he replied, a smug smile appearing on his face.

'Yes, we know!' Said Peter, getting even more irritated. 'I wish people would stop talking in riddles.'

'Wait!' Said Molly, as if a light bulb went off in her head. 'Maybe there is no maze.'

The elf stood there silent, the smile lingering on his face.

'What are you saying? It looks like a maze to me,' insisted Peter, pointing out the obvious.

'I know, but Shifter keeps on reminding us that things are not always what they seem. Maybe the maze is simply that.'

Molly and Peter looked at the duo, hoping for a response. Tweedy and Buck remained tight lipped. A strange smile on each of their faces, their only response.

'Come on, let's go. It's worth a try,' said Molly, eager to test her theory.

'Go where!' Asked peter, throwing his arms out in front of himself. 'There's no time Molly. The sun is going down. Look!'

Molly looked to the sky, noticing her friend was right. With everything that was going on, they'd failed to notice, the day was almost over. 'Quick! There's no time to loose. Follow me.' She demanded, as she ran towards the entrance of the maze.

'What are we doing here?' asked the young man, wondering if his friend were going mad. 'The sun is almost gone.'

'Don't ask me how, but there is something about this bracelet,' said Molly, excitedly.

'You're only now discovering this?'

'Don't interrupt me.' She said scolding her friend. 'It's like, it's somehow communicating with me. I can't explain it but sometimes I do things without thinking, but it always seems to be the correct decision. It was something Tweedy said earlier. He said, I didn't touch the symbols randomly. That I always knew which one I wanted to use, even though I didn't think I did.'

'What? You're not making any sense,' said Peter, shaking his head.

'I know what I mean. Anyway, like you say, we're almost out of time.'

Molly looked at the entrance of the maze, as she manoeuvred Peter on one side of the entrance, whilst making her way over to the other side.

The young girl quickly raised her arm as she tapped the symbol. The golden trinket suddenly sprang into action, etching out a perfectly symmetric cube that spun on its axel, before slowly coming to a halt.

Molly plucked the cube out of the air as Peter watched in awe. As if she knew exactly what to do, the young girl twisted the golden box, like a Rubik's cube, trying to solve the problem. Suddenly, the walls of the maze began to move, twisting and turning in different directions until they lined up perfectly in front of them. Presenting them with the pathway to their door.

'Hurry! There can't be much time left,' said Molly as she waved goodbye to their two odd friends.

Buck raised an arm, waving enthusiastically as tweedy cupped both hands around his mouth. 'Good luck lil miss! Ya both gonna need it!' Shouted the elf as he waved farewell.

Molly took her friends hand, squeezing tightly as they ran as fast as they could, hoping the door would lead them to the realm of spells.

The suns last speck of daylight began to disappear as they lunged for the door, pushing it open just in time as they fell onto the floor of the room. Back where they started.

Chapter Sixteen

'Well done to you both,' congratulated the Galpherin. 'Unfortunately, you did not succeed in finding the door to the realm of spells.'

Molly and her friend remained flat on the floor. Exhausted, unable to complain or move.

Peter slowly sat upright, shocked by the rapid improvement of his wound. 'Look! The damage on my suit has almost repaired itself. And I feel no more pain.'

The old man smiled, peering down as Peter prodded a finger at his chest, checking for any weakness in the suit. 'As I have said young Peter. The suits will protect you up to a certain point. They will heal insignificant lacerations, as well as small tears in the flesh. Deeper wounds will need significantly stronger intervention.'

'You mean, magic healing cream,' said Peter, interrupting the Galpherin.

'Even the, saccharum crepito would cease to be affective if not used swiftly enough,' replied Shifter.

'The what?' asked Peter.

'It's Latin,' replied Molly, tentatively climbing to her feet. 'It means, synthetic cream.'

Peter looked at Molly, a little shocked by her sudden knowledge of a language she'd never studied. 'How did you know that?' He asked.

'I have got no idea. Maybe it's the bracelet. Strange things are happening to me, I mean, the way I suddenly knew how to escape the, Enigma. How did I know what to do? Enigma means puzzle by the way. Very apt if you consider the maze.'

Peter's head began to spin with all the information. 'Wait, wait. Take a breath will you. That's all well and good, but it didn't take us to the realm of tricks, did it?'

'Realm of spells,' corrected Molly.

'Whatever! What I mean is, it didn't take us to where we needed to be. If you are supposed to be in sync with it, why has it lead us straight back to the start?'

'I don't know,' she replied. 'Maybe it takes time. If you think about it, it's taken a while and I'm only just beginning to sense things, like knowing what symbol to use and interpreting the language.'

The old man nodded as the girl tried to make sense of it all. 'The golden bracelet is part of you,' he interrupted. 'You have to allow yourself to be at one with it. You are beginning to believe in its power, Miss Miggins. If you trust it completely, it can take you home.'

Molly beamed as the Galpherin continued to emphasise the importance of the trinkets part in their journey.

'Subconsciously, you are already starting to listen. Not in the literal sense, but if you are at one with your aid, it will direct your decisions. Helping you to make the correct ones.'

Peter scratched his head in confusion as he watched Molly and the old man getting carried away.

'Okay! Enough with it all. I'm glad you two are all excited with how this is all going. But can I remind you that we have more pressing matters at hand.'

Molly and Shifter stopped their conversation in mid flow, a little surprised by the interruption.

'What's up Peter? You're not jealous, are you? Are we not paying you enough attention?' Teased Molly, a mischievous smile appearing on her face.'

'Jealous, me? Are you mad?' Replied her friend, a little embarrassed at the accusation. 'It may have escaped your attention, but we are being chased by monsters and a god that wants to drain our life force. So, if you've finished patting yourself on the back, can we press on with the mission at hand?'

The old man's demeanour turned serious as he cleared his throat. 'You are quite correct young Peter, but equally, I must explain what it means to understand the power of the bracelet. It will prepare you for the dangers ahead.'

The Galpherin walked back to the centre of the room as they surveyed the doors around them. 'It's time to select your second door, Miss Miggins.'

Molly took a deep breath as she waited for the bracelet to give the signal.

'Please, what is your choice?' asked the old man for the second time.

Why won't the bracelet vibrate? She thought to herself, sensing that Shifter was getting a little impatient. 'Err, I'm not sure,' she replied as the trinket finally began to vibrate. One, two, three, four times. 'Door number four!' She exclaimed, after the bracelet had settled.

'The choice has been made,' said the old man as he stretched his arms out wide, prompting the door to swing wide open. 'Please enter, os navale.'

Molly's head wheeled around at the Galpherin, suddenly understanding the meaning. 'The bone yard?' She asked, her palms beginning to sweat.

'Very good, Miss Miggins,' answered the old man, pointing and nodding his head towards the all too familiar fluid entrance.

'Bone yard?' Repeated Peter, alerted by what Molly had said, being preoccupied with the entrance. 'Oh, wonderful Moll's. Great choice. Let me know when you're fully in sync with that thing will you,' he said sarcastically.

Going with tradition, Molly snatched hold of Peter's hand, letting him know his attempt at humour wasn't appreciated.

Peter pulled his face in discussed as he held on to Molly's sweaty palm.

Molly returned the look with one of her own. One that said, don't even think about saying what your about too. And with that, they both, as usual held their breath and walked through the translucent door.

Peter's eyes bulged as he tried to take in what he was seeing.

Molly sensed he was trembling as he continued to cling tight hold of her hand. 'Easy there, tiger,' said Molly, as she pulled her hand away, flexing her fingers as she tried to get the circulation back into them.

'Could you have picked a worse door than this Moll's?' asked Peter, his head on a swivel, looking for anything creeping out of the dark.

Molly, for once was lost for words, unable to take her eyes off their inevitable pathway ahead. 'Unless you can see another way,' said the young girl. 'It looks like we're going through that.' She continued, pointing at the largest cemetery she'd ever seen.

Peter's jaw hit the floor as he pulled focus. The cemetery was like something out of a Stephen King novel. Looming out from the darkness, the cemetery boasted all the characteristics of your worst nightmare. Old crooked headstones adorned the decrepit resting place. Mausoleums with doors half open, their occupants resting, waiting for their calling. Ancient crypts who's stone lids lay broken on the ground, gave Molly the creeps as she noticed someone or something moving in the graveyard.

'Look. Over there.' She said, nudging Peter. 'Is that someone digging?'

Peter peered through the tall rusty iron fence, noticing an old man digging, what looked like a new grave. 'Do you really think we should approach him?' asked Peter reluctantly.

'He looks harmless enough,' replied Molly, trying to get a better look at him.

'You know as well as I do by now, looks can be deceiving. Especially in this place,' he said, reminding her of rule number one.

'You're right,' said Molly, cursing her stupidity. 'But we need some direction, and my guess is, if you're going to attack someone, you're not going to present yourself in plain sight in a graveyard.'

Peter screwed up his face, trying to understand her logic. 'Hmm, not sure about that, but let's be on our guard. Remember, we have no weapons until you summon one.'

The two humans opened the large double gates as they cautiously made their way over to the gravedigger.

'Excuse me sir,' said Molly, sensibly keeping at a safe distance. 'Can you help us?'

The stranger stopped as he straightened up, before slowly turning around to face the two friends.

Molly and Peter both took in a sharp gulp of stale air, their eyes springing wide open as they looked at the gnarled figure in front of them.

'What can I do for you?' Replied the freakishly strange character.

His voice was gravely and interrupted, like its larynx were all messed up. The man, creature, thing, whatever it was, stood tall at around six and a half feet. It's thin, flesh eaten face looked grotesque. Most of it eaten away, like it had been lying in its own grave for the past two hundred years. His lips, non-existent, exposing what few teeth remained. A tatty old dirty Stetson, sat loosely on his head, covering the, little white mattered hair that was left.

The two friends cringed, as an extremely long centipede attempted to scuttle from its hiding place, under one of the gravediggers' lapels, into his exposed jaw that quickly chomped down on the overgrown insect, sending its gooey insides dribbling down the creatures face.

'Oh my god!' baulked Molly as she covered her mouth. 'I think I'm gonna be sick.'

The ancient figure plunged his spade into the dirt, finishing his delicious treat, before whipping his flaky hands on his moth-eaten jacket. 'Pleased to meet you both,' said the curious character. 'I'm Bones.'

Molly and Peter looked at each other. Not knowing whether to laugh or cry, the sense of irony not lost on either of them.

'Lovely to meet you, Bones. I'm Molly and this is Peter.' She replied, whilst trying to control her laughter by clearing her throat.

Sensing their deride, Bones offered his hand to greet the young girl, whipping the smile of their faces in the process.

Molly, a little embarrassed by her obvious mocking, gritted her teeth as she gave the man's hand a quick shake, before discreetly wiping off any rotten flesh.

The gravedigger gave a satisfied chuckle as he continued with his work.

'We're looking for the door out of here. Can you help us sir?' asked Molly, keeping her wits about her.

Bones smiled as he dropped a shovel full of earth into the hole. 'Follow the largest moon,' replied the gravedigger. 'But be careful mind. I've only just started burying this one.'

The two humans looked down into the freshly dug grave, noticing a partially buried body lying still at the bottom.

'This is what happened to the last challenger. All I seem to do these days, is dig hole after hole.'

Molly and Peter quickly stepped back from the grave, as Bones dropped another shovel full of soil into the ground.

'Molly, what are we going to do? There's no way we're going to make it out of here alive. I've got a bad feeling about this one.'

Peter was visibly shaking as he began to pace up and down, all the time, his senses on high alert.

'Peter, calm down. The last thing we need right now, is for you to freak out. Take a deep breath.'

Molly placed both hands on her friend's shoulders, mimicking deep and controlled breaths as she attempted to calm him down.

'I can't help it Moll's. I hate cemeteries. I can't even look at them. I don't know if you've ever noticed but, even when I pass one, I turn my head away.'

Molly looked at him, sensing this was real for him. That she would have to approach this one sensitively. 'I didn't notice if I'm being honest with you but listen. We're gonna get through this, but the only way we'll succeed, is if you and I work together. We've made it this far and I'm not about to give up on us now.'

Peter slowly nodded his head, taking in one deep breath at a time. 'Okay, this is working. I can do this,' he said, trying to convince himself it was possible.

Molly looked into his eyes as they softened. If it weren't for him, she would surely be dead by now. Why had he sacrificed himself to protect her? Was it purely for friendship? And why was she having these feelings? It felt like his eyes were looking into her very soul. Molly looked away; afraid he might see into her heart. Sense the same feelings that had been stirring, unknown by her, inside him for years.

Bones threw down his shovel, breaking the silence. 'There is one being you must avoid if you are going to make it out of here,' interrupted the gravedigger.

Molly stepped back from Peter, noticing the hot flush in her cheeks. 'Err, what was that.' She replied, not quite concentrating on what Bones was saying. Peter, on the other hand, was more than alert, although just as curios to know why his friend looked flustered. Was she having the same feelings? Was that connection more than friendship? Those questions would have to wait.

'Who is it? What monstrosity are we up against now?' asked Peter anxiously.

The decrepit gravedigger walked ahead, staring into the abyss of the unsettled resting place. 'Mikaeus,' replied Bones. 'Mikaeus and his minions. They are the guardians of the underworld; they guard this realm.'

Molly and Peter stood staring into the darkness, reluctant to ask the question. 'Who is Mikaeus?' asked Molly eventually, knowing the answer wasn't going to be good.

'He is Mikaeus the unhallowed. He controls those who lye resting in this cemetery. If he senses your presence, then there will be only one outcome.'

Peter gulped as he dared to ask the question. 'And what outcome is that?'

Bones turned towards Peter. His unnerving smile sending a chill down his spine. Without saying a word, the gravedigger looked at the freshly dug hole in the ground and gestured a nod in its direction.

'Is there any way we could pass through undetected?' asked Molly, before Peter could say a word.

'What has the Galpherin told you?' Replied Bones, this time gesturing towards the trinket around her wrist.

'I know, but I'm not sure I'm completely at one with the bracelet as yet. What if I get it wrong?'

The gravedigger shrugged his shoulders, an inevitability of the gesture about it. 'I'm sure you know the answer to that, don't you?'

Peter looked towards the largest moon, shining bright in the night sky. 'That way?' He asked, thinking that if he listened to any more of the gravedigger's warnings, he'd surely have a nervous breakdown.

Bones nodded as he picked up the shovel again, leaving the two humans to the daunting task ahead.

Strange sounds filled the air as Molly and Peter slowly made their way through the cemetery. The ground felt soft and slimy under foot, making it difficult to walk without making a noise.

'This squelching sound is enough to wake the dead,' joked Peter, trying to be light-hearted, considering the situation they were in.

'Very funny,' replied Molly, her head twitching, alert to every sound.

Suddenly, a loud shriek pierced the air. 'Oh my god! What the hell was that?' asked Peter, trying hard not scream.

Molly pointed, her hand trembling as she noticed the ground beginning to open up in front of them. 'Look!' She said, grabbing tight hold of her friend.

Peter gasped as dirt began to pour out from the earth. The ground started to tremble beneath their feet as the frightened young man took hold of Molly's wrist, beckoning her to use the trinket before it was too late.

'I'm not getting any signs.' She said, panicking as she noticed something rising out of the ground.

'What's that?' asked Peter, pointing at the symbol of what looked like a cloak.

'That's it!' She said, somehow knowing exactly what it was.

Molly immediately tapped the symbol as the bracelet sprang into action once more, magically creating their aid. 'Quick, wrap it around us,' urged the girl as they grabbed the cloak, covering themselves completely.

Out from the foul earth, rose the imposing figure of the most devilish creature. Mikaeus the unhallowed, seemed somewhat human in some respects. His ghostly white appearance gave him the look of death itself. Wearing a white robe with golden trim, he stood high above, even the tallest of mausoleums. Strange symbols adorned his long sleeves as he opened up his arm, as if summoning what was lying beneath.

Molly and Peter could only stand and stare as the creature surveyed his surroundings, looking for his prey.

'He can't see us,' whispered Peter as they held on tight to the cloak of invisibility.

140

The creature of death growled as he searched in vain, wondering for what reason he was unable to see who had disturbed his sleep.

Molly quickly put a finger on Peters lips, urging him to be silent as they carefully began to walk forward.

The slimy earth not only hindered their progress with the noise it made from their footsteps, but the impressions they made were clearly visible for anyone to see.

Mikaeus began to get more frustrated as he wielded his long staff high into the air, whirling it around, like he was calling for some kind of assistance.

Suddenly, the two humans stopped, sensing a slight breeze stirring through the air around them. Peter froze as the cloak began to ripple, the breeze growing stronger with every wave of the creature's staff.

Molly and Peter tried hard to hold on tight as the wind became stronger and stronger. The cloak now lifting, exposing their lower limbs as they battled to keep the garment from blowing clean away, revealing their presence.

'I can't hold on much longer,' said Molly, desperately clinging on to their lifeline.

Mikaeus wheeled around as he spotted something moving a short distance away. The creature roared, swinging his staff furiously, the wind grew stronger, swirling into a storm that sent the cloak flying into the air revealing the two humans as the elements left them exposed to the mercy of the graveyard.

Mikaeus's sinister dark eyes opened wide, revealing the horror behind them as he grinned, relaying his intentions.

Molly and Peter stood rooted to the spot, fighting against the ever-increasing storm that seemed to be forcing them towards the monster.

'Molly, we need to run now or we're dead!' Screamed Peter, holding on to his friend as he watched their camouflage disappear.

The two humans held tight hold of each other, mustering all of their strength as they battled against the wind.

Mikaeus reacted swiftly by raising his staff, slamming it hard into the earth, causing the ground to tremble.

Peter looked horrified as he noticed things beginning to break through from beneath the earth. Hands thrusting out of the ground, fighting their way to the surface. 'He's calling the dead! Look, over there. And another one there!'

Two, three, four, soon dozens of them, crawling out from their resting places. The unholy cries of the undead filled the air as the lord of the underworld pointed his staff in the direction of the terrified humans. 'Take them!' Bellowed Mikaeus ordering his minions to do his bidding.

'Where's the door? I can't see it!' Cried Molly as she searched through the darkness, hoping the light from the moon would show the way before it was too late.

Peter suddenly spotted a dim light struggling to break through the night. 'It's too far away!' He replied. 'We'll never make it!'

The two friends ran as hard as they could, battling against the storm as the zombie like creatures quickly began to gain on them, somehow unaffected by the strong winds.

Suddenly a hand grabbed hold of Molly's ankle, halting her progress. 'Peter, help me!' She cried as the creature refused to let go.

The young man kicked out as hard as he could at the rotting limb, breaking it clean off at the wrist, sending it flying towards the masses of foulness pursuing them. 'We need some help Molly! You need you to use the bracelet. Look!'

Peter pointed in the direction they were going. Dozens more creatures were pouring out of the earth, blocking off their escape route.

Molly frantically searched the trinket, hoping the answer was there. Hoping something would jump out at her. 'I can't see anything Peter! There are no symbols on my bracelet.'

The trinket was blank. Not one symbol remained. 'How can that be?' asked Peter as he desperately grabbed Molly's wrist, not quite believing what he heard.

'Maybe we've used them all.' She said, all hope beginning to drain from her.

Peter suddenly looked up, distracted by a tall figure in the distance wielding a long thin object. 'Is that Bones?' asked the young man.

The gravedigger seemed to be shouting something as he swung the object around his head. 'Run!' Came the cry.

Suddenly, the storm began to calm, making it easier for the two friends to quicken their pace.

The battle between Mikaeus and Bones raged around them. Both beings trying to control the elements as the undead seemed to move quicker, aware that their prey were nearing their escape.

'We're still too far away, Molly,' said Peter, noticing they were soon going to be cut off, outflanked by their pursuers.

'I can see the door,' replied the girl, unaware of the creature inches behind her.

Without warning, the zombie grabbed hold her shoulder, separating the two humans. Molly screamed as the creature managed to overpower the exhausted young girl, bringing her crashing to the ground.

Peter stopped dead in his tracks, knowing his friend was done for if he didn't react quickly. Grabbing the nearest stone, he could find, the young man ran towards the creature that was straddled on top of Molly, smashing the stone hard against its head, sending it clean from its shoulders. 'Quick, grab my hand!' He screamed, before hauling her off the ground.

Mikaeus's power was beginning to overpower the gravedigger as the storm began to build once more, the undead hindering his efforts to fight back the winds, attacking Bones from all sides.

'You must hurry!' Urged Bones as he tried beating off the creatures, one by one whilst losing the fight to control the storm.

More and more of them seemed to come from all directions, overpowering the gravedigger. 'I can't hold them off much longer!' He cried, the undead now only metres away from the humans.

'It's too late!' Cried Peter, resigned to their fate.

'The golden band! Look at the golden band!' Commanded Bones, the creatures now overwhelming the gravedigger. 'You must use the timepiece. It's your only chance,' he continued.

'Timepiece?' Questioned Molly as she frantically scanned the bracelet.

Suddenly out of nowhere, appeared the symbol of what looked like a stopwatch.

'Hit it!' Ordered Peter as the storm began to rage once more.

Molly quickly tapped the symbol, causing the trinket to use its magic once more.

Mikaeus launched his staff towards the humans, instantly realising the young girl's intention.

Molly quickly grabbed the watch from out of thin air, before a stifled cry from the mass of bodies echoed through the wind.

'Press the—!' Before he could finish, the gravedigger was engulfed by dozens of the creatures, tearing his dilapidated body limb from limb.

Molly immediately knew what their fallen saviour was about to say before being consumed and hit the button on top of the timepiece.

Silence, as deafening as the carnage before it, filled the air. The corpses of the undead frozen in time stood motionless, only inches away from the girl.

Mikaeus's staff, air bound, not much further away. Still, like the hands on her stopwatch, as if it had been stopped dead in its tracks. Everywhere around her motionless, like someone had taken a picture of a battlefield.

Molly immediately looked at her friend, sensing something was horribly wrong. 'No! This cannot be!' She exclaimed, shaking her head as the still figure of Peter stayed as motionless as the picture around her, his face stuck fast, about to say something before it was halted by the sudden click of a button.

'Peter?' Nothing. Not a sound. 'Peter!' She cried.

The girl approached her friend, slowly reaching out for his hand. A tear trickled down her cheek as she placed her hand in his.

Without warning, Peter sprang into action, released from the time lock. A single word bellowing out from his mouth. 'Run!'

Molly flew back, surprised by the, suddenly animated Peter. 'Oh my god,' she said with delight. 'You're alive.'

Peter reacted with a confused, but curious look. 'What do you mean, I'm alive? Why would I be anything else?'

The young man stood back, startled by the strange frozen like status surrounding them. 'Molly, what on god's green earth is going on here? And what's the matter with you? Have you been c__?'

Molly grabbed tight hold of her friend before he could finish, stunning him into silence.

Peter, slowly wrapped his arms around her, feeling her trembling in his embrace. 'Hey,' he said softly. 'What's all this?'

The young man gently lifted her chin, softly wiping away a solitary tear. 'It's ok. I'm here,' he continued, a little confused by her sudden affection.

'You were frozen in time,' she replied, her voice still a little shaky. 'The stopwatch that came from the bracelet stopped time.'

'I can see that,' interrupted Peter, surveying their surroundings, still holding onto her.

'Yes, but you were stuck too,' she continued. 'But as soon as I touched you, it was like it hadn't happened. You just continued where you left off, like it never really stopped.'

Peter frowned at his friend, smiling at the same time. 'But that's how it felt. Nothing really stopped as far as I'm aware. Weird,' he said, shaking his head. 'Are you okay?'

The young man rested his hands on her shoulders, a warm feeling coming over him as he looked longingly into her teary eyes.

Molly nodded, returning his adoring smile with one of her own. 'I am now.' She said blinking, forcing another teardrop to escape from the corner of her eye.

The couple stood staring at each other. Both fully aware there was no use denying the plain and obvious feelings that stirred inside them. Peter searched her face, as every worried line slowly disappeared.

'I have to tell you something' He said softly, inching ever so slowly towards her parted lips.

'What's that?' She replied coyly, a dozen butterflies dancing around inside her, making her breathing shallower, anticipating their connection as he opened his mouth.

'I... I...'

A loud clunking sound jolted them from their trance like state. Molly and Peter wheeled around to see the timepiece lying on the ground, the second-hand trembling, fighting to spring back into action.

Slight movements around them confirmed what they suspected. 'We need to move!' Warned Peter, breaking away from his, friend? 'We must only have a certain amount of time, before the watch continues, releasing them from the time lock.'

'Quick, the door!' Screamed Molly, grabbing his hand as they quickly ran towards the door.

A loud ticking noise alerted them that time was up as the creature slowly began to move.

Like a javelin, Mikaeus's long staff flew right in between the two humans, impaling itself into the door, closely followed by a cascade of creatures.

Molly and Peter lunged towards the entrance with the creatures only a few steps behind, bursting through the door with the frustrating screams of the dead cut off as the door slammed shut behind them.

'Not here again!' yelled Peter in anguish.

The two friends slowly picked themselves off the floor, exhausted from their ordeal.

The young girl looked at the Galpherin as her friend sighed deeply, shaking his head disappointedly.

'I'm sorry my young friends, you have one final choice left,' said Shifter regretfully.

Peter flung his head skywards, a loud and frustrated cry bursting from inside him.

'Peter!' shouted Molly surprised by his lack of control. 'you've got to stay calm, for both our sakes.'

The young man raised a hand, acknowledging his behaviour. 'I'm sorry. I'm just worried we're never going to get out of here.'

Molly nodded sympathetically, feeling his frustration.

'I appreciate that this is difficult,' interrupted Shifter, but your friend is right. Your ability to control your feelings will be the difference between success and failure.'

Molly walked towards the old man, the cogs in her head grinding. 'One thing puzzles me.' She asked calmly. 'I feel more at one with the bracelet than I've ever been. But twice, I've wrongly read the signals from it now, so how am I to trust it.'

The old man looked thoughtfully for a moment. A knowing smile upon his face. 'The trinket is not able to control your actions, Miss Miggins. If you try to second guess it, you will make the wrong decision. You are not, two separate entities. You are one. Let your mind flow, inhibited by thought or decision. And acceptance from both, you and the golden band will be complete.'

Molly looked at the bracelet, breathing deeply as she caressed its perfectly smooth surface. 'Okay,' said Molly, buoyed by the Galpherin's speech. 'I'll try.'

The old man drifted to the centre of the room, before presenting the remaining doors.

'One more question,' said Molly, before he could speak.

The old man tilted his head, curiously waiting for her question.

'Why haven't we encountered the Origin in this realm.'

Shifter raised his eyebrows, surprised by the young girl's query. 'The reason you ask that question, leads me to believe that you are more at one with the trinket than you think, young lady.

Molly smiled, encouraged by his reply.

'The realm of hopes and fears is, a virtual reality. The Origin can only influence realms in the real world. You see, as I've said previously, even the Origin must abide by the written laws of this world. Any intervention, no matter how small, has a cost. The cost to him for breaking the laws, is a breach of the contract, signed by both parties, therefor forfeiting his claim over your life force.'

Molly nodded, satisfied with the old man's explanation.

'Are you ready to make your final choice?' asked the Galpherin, readying himself to open the deciding door.

Molly took a long deep breath, calming herself as she closed her eyes. Clear your mind. She said to herself, trying to feel the bracelets energy. No vibration, she thought. Don't panic, just breath.

A warm sensation coursed through her body as she sensed an unmistakeable connection. 'Duo,' came the sound in her head. 'Duo!' Louder now.

Molly's eyes snapped wide open, the number tittering on the end of her tongue. 'The second door.' She said calmly, a sense of euphoria flowing through every part of her being.

The old man's smile had a look of relief as he opened up his arms. 'Please enter, Arenam,' he announced as the door swung wide open.

'The arena?' asked Molly, looking for the Galpherin's approval.

The old man gently nodded, the smile on his face remaining.

Molly walked over towards Peter, taking his hand in hers.

'Do you think it is a coincidence that you always hold your friends hand, before you pass through the door's?' asked Shifter suddenly.

The human's stopped, turning towards the old man, surprised by his question.

'It is because, only the bearer of the golden band can pass through. By taking his hand, you become one. Without it, Peter would be stuck in whatever realm you left him.'

Peter looked at Molly wide-eyed, gripping tight hold of her hand. 'Don't you ever let go?' He said, the thought of being stranded sending him into panic mode.

Molly smiled sweetly as she gently stroked his hand with her thumb. 'Come on, let's do this.'

The two friends, took their traditional deep breath, holding it, before stepping through the last of the liquid like doors.

Chapter Seventeen

A cascades of streamers and confetti of all colours filled the sky as the fanfare parade welcomed the humans. Huge golden gates patterned in the most exquisite detail stood before them. A sign displaying the word, Arenam, hung high above, as two rows of soldier like, Centaurs lined up in perfect symmetry, sounding their trumpets as the two friends watched in awe. Different species, some familiar, some alien to them, roared as the gates slowly opened, revealing something familiar waiting to receive them.

'Is that a human being?' asked Peter surprised, unsure if his eyes were playing tricks on him.

The two friends hesitated, before the man raised a hand, gesturing them towards the entrance.

Molly and Peter walked cautiously between the Centaurs as they creatures continued to sound their instruments.

The familiar looking host smiled as they reached the gates, holding out a hand to greet the new arrivals.

The friendly looking individual was a welcomed sight, considering the amount of strange beings they'd come across. Even more strange though, was the humans attire. Dressed in a three-piece suit that looked like it had been tailored to fit perfectly, it resembled something out of a 1940's gangster movie. Of medium height, the man wore a pair of black rimmed spectacles. His slicked back mousy brown hair that also reflected a look of the same period.

'Welcome to the, Arena,' said the man, enthusiastically shaking the young girls hand. 'My name, is, Michael,' he continued, greeting Peter just as eagerly.

His two fellow humans looked at each other, a little lost for words, still a little shocked to see someone of the same species.

His accent had an American lilt to it. A little faded, but still obvious enough to detect. 'Err, hello to you too,' replied the young girl. 'I'm Molly. And this is My friend Peter.'

Michael smiled as he held up a hand, halting the fanfare into silence. 'Sorry, I can't hear anything above that racket. Would you both like to follow me please.'

Molly and Peter, a little confused, waited before going any further. 'Just a second. Where are you from? How did you get here?' asked a cautious Molly.

The man laughed, before ushering them through a doorway under the arena. 'I'll explain everything soon. We must hurry. Each of your games will be starting very shortly.'

Peter stopped, unsure if they should go any further. 'Hold on! What games? We're not going any further until we know exactly what's going on.'

The smartly dressed man stopped, before checking his watch, a little flustered by their lack of urgency. 'Please. I promise I will answer all of your questions as soon as we get you ready. I expect you both must be hungry.'

Molly, instantly lifted at the thought of food, nudged her friend, ushering him to move.

'It's just through here,' said the man, opening another door.

A large rectangular room that sported a host of combat memorabilia welcomed the pair. A dozen fairy folk, busy preparing refreshments, flitted to and fro, filling up jugs of liquid as well as an array of juicy fruits and sweet meats.

Molly couldn't help but feel a little sorry for the fairies. Is this all they were used for? She thought to herself.

Pictures, boasting the triumphs of previous competitors, hung proudly around the room. Beings of all types of species captured; tearing their opponents limb from limb.

A dull rumble echoed around the room. The crowd from the arena outside, waited impatiently for their entertainment, as it became clearer by the second what fate awaited them.

Michael unbuttoned his suit jacket as he sat down at the table. 'Please, you must be hungry,' he said, offering a seat to his guests.

The fairies quickly left the room as the man clicked his fingers, causing Molly to frown at his dismissive manner. 'I'm sure their purpose was meant for something more than serving food,' said Molly, a little judgementally.

Michael looked over his glasses at the young girl, sensing her disapproval. 'I don't determine what rolls other beings are assigned to ma'am,' he replied defensively.

Molly sat back, studying the man as she picked at the berries on her plate.

Suddenly, a loud roar came from above, startling the duo, causing Peter to spit out the contents of his mouth.

'Another contest decided,' said Michael, unmoved by the interruption.

'How did you get here?' asked Molly, changing the subject. 'How long have you been here?'

The man stood up, lowering his head as he prepared to answer the question, before Peter suddenly realised who he might be.

'Wait a minute! I think I know who you are!' Said the young man, recalling a story he read. 'Aren't you, Michael Rockefeller?'

Molly quickly looked at her friend, confused by the revelation. 'Michael who?'

Peter stood up, focusing intently on the familiar human. 'Michael Rockefeller,' he repeated. 'I remember reading an article a few years ago. It was a piece on people that had gone missing in the twentieth century. Those that had disappeared without a trace and never been found. If I remember correctly, Michael Rockefeller went exploring somewhere off the coast of Australia. Papua New Guinea if I recall, sometime in the early sixties. I don't remember all the details. All I know is, the body was never found. The rumour was, that he'd been captured by cannibals. The rest you can surmise by yourself.'

Molly looked at the man, a knowing smile appearing on his face. 'Is that true?' asked the girl, in disbelief.

Michael raised an eyebrow, surprised by the theory. 'Eaten by cannibals? So that's what people thought happened to me.

The American paused for a second, memories of that fateful day returning. 'Tell me, what year is it now on Earth?'

Molly, quickly slumped back down on her chair, bewildered by how ludicrous it all sounded.

'The year is 2017,' replied Peter, unsure himself really, aware that time itself was moving on considerably faster than it was here.

'Forty-six years!' Said Michael, shaking his head. 'Has it been that long?'

Molly leaned forward, curious to know the details. Wondering if they were similar to their own. 'What happened to you, Mr Rockefeller? Can you remember?

The man pondered the question for a moment, trying to recall memories he'd long since forgotten. 'The cave,' he replied, staring into space, pictures flashing through his mind, reminding him of memories he'd tried hard to supress.

'Somehow I'd gotten separated from my expedition that day. We'd been tracking a tribe in PNG for some days. Research you know. Anyway, I'd veered off track, distracted by a sound coming from an old mine. I'd heard stories that a hundred years or so, ago, people had attempted to mine gold in the area. Over the coming months, some of the minors strangely began to disappear. Eventually, in fear for their lives, they abandoned the place. Returning home without their colleagues.'

Molly and Peter sat motionless as the man continued with his story, the similarities of which, seemed unnervingly alike to their own. The bracelets he'd found in the mine. The sound that got louder when he put on the trinket. His experience when travelling to, Kaplon.

The two friends looked at each other, dumbstruck. 'So that's why no one came to rescue you.'

The American looked confused, wondering what the young girl meant.

'You said there were two bracelets, yes?'

The Man nodded quickly, eager for her to continue.

'I'd be curious to know if any of your family helped in the search.' She continued, trying hard to explain the rules the Galpherin had told her. 'You see, from what I've been told, the second bracelet can only be used by someone of the same blood. One of your family, would have had to have found the second bracelet in order for them to be transported to this world. Only then, could they take on the challenge of the realms, completing all three to recue you.'

Michael sat back in his seat, a resigned look on his face saying all they needed to know. 'It makes little difference now, Miss Miggins. My life force was taken from me long ago. I only exist in this virtual reality now. I was defeated in the realm of hopes and fears. You see, I don't know if you read much about me,' he said, diverting his attention towards Peter. 'But I was an inspiring young wrestler in my college days.'

Peter nodded, recalling something of that kind in the article.

'Well, when in the realm of hopes and fears, the Arena will pit you against someone or something of your chosen sport. Mine was wrestling. I had to go head to head with Palaestra, the Goddess of wrestling. The bracelet gave me a golden leotard that was meant to hand me the advantage I needed to defeat the creature. Unfortunately for me, I wasn't as good as I thought I was and was subsequently defeated. So, there you have it. With forty odd years already passed on earth, the chances of anyone coming to my rescue are pretty slim, don't you think?'

The noise from the arena outside began to grow louder as the impatient hoard waited for their entertainment. 'It's time my young friends,' said the American, reacting instantly to the restless crowd.

The two humans flinched as they stared at each other, each one terrified at the thought of what they might face.

'Your preferred sports have been recorded,' said Michael, as he turned to Peter. 'Yours is boxing I believe, young Peter,' he continued as a virtual screen appeared on the wall.

Peter watched, amazed as the memories of his bouts played out, reminding him of some of his fights.

'And you are a runner,' continued the American as he switched to Molly, revealing the memories of her competing in track events at school.

'I'm not a runner!' Said a shocked Molly as she watched herself crossing the finishing line in first place. 'I mean, I enjoyed the sport, but I never inspired to be a runner.'

Michael waved a hand, deleting the images as he walked towards the door. 'Nether the less, these are the memories that were taken from you on your journey to, Kaplon. These are the events that you must compete in and win if you are to continue going forward. Remember, you are lucky.'

Peter scoffed, surprised by the American's comment. 'Luck? I don't feel lucky. We'll be more than lucky if we come out of this one alive.'

Michael walked over to the two friends, a sympathetic smile on his face. 'You have each other. I had no one to help me. Not many beings do. I'm sure you've been made aware that it's very rare indeed, to have two beings together on Kaplon at the same time. So, make the most of it. Help each other when you can. Although you will be competing individually, you should make the most of the others support. The encouragement and advice you receive from your companion will be crucial against your opponent.'

Michael opened the door as the two friends held each other's hand, reluctant, but ready to face their fears.

The arena erupted, as they entered. Boo's, hisses and jeers echoed around the intimidating extravaganza. Michael opened out his arm's, presenting the two challengers as they walked slowly towards the centre of the arena. Beings of all species filled the galleries to witness the spectacle. Gargoyles, Amarok's, Hybrid's, Golem's and Troll's were just but a few they were able to identify, all baying for their blood. The two humans wilted as the crowd cried out demands for their demise.

Peter's eyes widened as he spotted the ring. Its sides dressed in golden napes that hung from each corner.

Michael approached the young man as the crowd cheered in anticipation, knowing the battle was imminent. 'You will be first, Peter,' he said, pointing towards the fight arena. 'You'll compete in three, two-minute rounds. The victor will be the one left standing at the end. If you lose, you will be condemned the realm of hopes and fears, therefore forfeiting your life force. If you do manage to go the distance, the three judges will determine the winner.'

The host leaned in close towards the young man, whispering in his ear. 'If I were you, I wouldn't leave it up to them. They're not what you would call.... the most trustworthy of beings.'

Peter looked around, searching out his opponent. 'Compete against who?' asked the anxious young man.

Suddenly the crowd roared and applauded as a figure appeared from the entrance on the opposite side of the arena.

'What the hell is that thing?' exclaimed Molly as her blood ran cold, fearing for her friend's life. 'You can't expect him to fight that.' She said, pleading with the American.

The beast walked towards the ring, his huge muscular arms held aloft, accepting the crowd's adulations. The creature, half man half bull roared, beating his chest as he looked menacingly at his opponent. Its legs must have been as thick as Peter's waist, its thighs rippling with every step taken. Its chest barrel like, as if bullets from a gun would simply ricochet off its surface.

The beast blew gusts of air from its nostrils as the solid gold ring that hung from its septum lifted from the power behind it. The two horns protruding from its head, glistened from the water being sprayed on them by his corner men.

Peter struggled to swallow; his throat dry with fear. 'Molly's right. I can't fight that thing, I'll get killed!'

Michael pointed to the bracelet on the girl's wrist. 'Choose your tools young Peter,' instructed the host, a strange confidence in his voice.

Molly lifted her arm, looking for the symbol he needed. 'I don't see any boxing gloves,' said the girl, as she twisted her wrist trying to find the instruments. 'Wait, can they be what we want?'

The symbol of a pair of gauntlets etched onto the trinket shone out at them, one crossed over the other.

'They're not boxing gloves,' said the young human, confused at the choice of implement.

'Do you see any boxing gloves on your opponent?' asked Michael as they looked over at the beasts hands.

The creature's fists were bare. Knuckles, like jagged rocks cracked as he clenched his fists, smacking them together like mountains colliding.

'Make your decision, its time. And good luck,' said the host as he made his way towards the ring.

Molly looked at her friend, trying hard not to show her concern. 'Don't worry Peter, I'll be with you. You can do this. You're a good fighter, I've seen you in action.'

Peter turned to the beast, watching as it jumped up and down beating its chest, whipping the crowd into a frenzy. 'You'll be with me?' asked her friend sarcastically. 'Not in that ring you won't. I'm going to die Molly! There's no hiding place in the four corners of that ring. I'm on my own in there.'

The young girl took hold of her friend's hand, a determined look on her face as she squeezed tight. 'We've come so far Peter. I believe in you, I really do. You've saved my neck on more than one occasion. And I'm not just referring to this place. You're the most driven person I know. And you never give up, no matter how daunting the challenge. There's not a doubt in my mind you will do this!'

Peter took a deep breath, buoyed by his friend's speech. 'Okay, let's do this. Hit that symbol.'

Molly tapped the bracelet, releasing the golden beam. The trinkets power etched out the gloves as the young man raised his hands.

As if sucked by a vacuum, the golden gauntlets quickly jumped onto Peters hands.

The American host climbed through the ropes. The crowd went wild as he took hold of the microphone.

Molly and Peter made their way to the ring, the three strange looking judges observing the humans curiously. A wrinkled old goblin wearing spectacles sat on one side of the ring, muttering to himself as he scribbled something on a piece of paper. On the nearside, sat a fat gargoyle, coughing and spluttering. Spittle dripping from his mouth. Over on the far side, sat an angry looking troll, shaking his hands victoriously at the beast inside the ring.

'Great,' said Peter to himself, climbing into the ring. 'Good to see we're all on a level playing field.'

The beast growled as he paced around the ring, its cold black eyes never leaving his challenger.

'Don't look at him, look at me,' said Molly as she turned him towards her. 'He's just trying to intimidate you.'

Peter laughed nervously as she shoved the gum shield into his mouth. 'Well he's doing a 'loody good jo' of it,' he replied sarcastically, unable to pronounce the B's because of the gum protector.

'Where's the referee?' Shouted Molly suddenly, noticing they were one official short.

Michael looked over, shaking his head as the realisation soon dawned on them that there was not going to be any need of a referee.

Peter looked skywards, wondering if anything else could go against him.

'Maybe it's a good thing,' said Molly, sensing his anxiety escalating. 'Let's face it, I doubt he'd be on our side anyway. I mean, look at the judges.'

Peter looked at each of the three officials as they gestured encouragement towards the beast.

'You can't rely on the judges, Peter. You'll have to finish this inside the three rounds.'

Peter shook his head, unsure if his friend were trying to show (disingenuous) faith in him or had delusions of grandeur.

'Remember your strengths. Your speed and movement. Look at him, he's big and clumsy. Use your speed to your advantage. Just stay out of his reach and catch him on the counter.'

Peter looked at his friend, surprised by her knowledge of boxing.

'Don't look at me like that. I've been to plenty of your training sessions. I do listen to the trainers ya know. What do you think I do? Just sit there twiddling my thumbs.'

Michael raised a hand as the bell sounded indicating it were time for the introductions. 'Welcome everybody, to the co-featured event of the day!' Announced the animated host as he played to the crowd. 'This bout is scheduled for three, two-minute rounds, that will determine your winner. First, in the red corner, introducing the challenger. His record stands as a perfect one. Three bouts, with no defeats. Hailing from the planet earth. Please give a round of applause to. Peter…! Hughes…!'

Boos and jeers echoed around the stadium as the young man raised his hands up high, saluting the hostile crowd.

'Introducing his opponent in the blue corner. A being that needs no introduction. His career, also a perfect one. With two thousand, one hundred and thirty-one fights. All coming by the way of knockout or death! The multi-weight champion of the universe! Show your appreciation for the one, the only! Miniton!'

The crowd burst into rapture as the beast raised his hand, accepting the adulation from his fans.

Peter turned to Molly; a look of desperation etched across his face. His friend, trying hard not to show her concern, shook a clenched fist, urging him to stay focused.

'Remember, use your speed and movement. You can do this.'

'Seconds out, round one!' Came the announcement as the bell sounded, indicating the start of the bout.

The beast, instantly tore out of his corner, hurling a straight right hand towards his opponent.

Peter, caught a little off guard, swiftly stepped to the side as the juggernaut narrowly missed his head.

'What the hell!' Said Peter surprised, feeling the rush of air that followed.

'Stay on your toes. Move around and tire him out,' came the instructions from his corner.

That was the answer. Thought The young man as he circled the ring. Tire him out.

Peter danced around the four corners as the beast grew angry and frustrated.

Another assault as the half man, half bull catapulted itself towards its opponent, swinging wildly.

The human quickly stepped to his right as the beast threw a wild left hook.

Peter saw the opportunity he'd been waiting for, sending a swift right hook of his own crashing into, Miniton's ribcage.

The creature howled in pain, covering the left-hand side of his ribs as he spun around from the force.

The young human stared at the gauntlets, shocked by the power they expelled. 'Oh shit!' He said, looking up at the beast.

Miniton roared furiously as the crowd booed at the human's successful strike.

'That's it Peter!' Screamed Molly, jumping up and down with excitement. 'Keep doing what you're doing!'

Miniton began to pace around the ring, breathing heavily. His huge mass, clearly causing him problems.

'Thirty seconds to go, Peter!' Screamed the young girl as the beast stomped towards his tormentor.

Suddenly, the creature raised his huge leg, sending it crashing into, Peter's chest. The young man hurled through the air, crashing into a neutral corner.

'What the hell was that!' Screamed Molly as her friend lay motionless on the canvas.

The creature raised its hands aloft as the animated crowd burst into life.

'That's not boxing,' complained the girl as the bell rang, signalling the end of round one.

The three judges waved their hands, dismissing the human girl's objections as she helped her friend back to the corner.

'Sit down Peter,' said Molly, carefully helping him to his seat.

'Is it over?' asked a confused Peter, clearly still dazed from the blow.

'No, that was the end of the first round. He's cheating. The bugger kicked you.'

Peter gritted his teeth, furious as he stared towards the opposite corner.

'Here, drink something.' Molly poured some of the liquid into her friend's mouth, instantly rejuvenation the young man.

'Wow! What is that?' asked Peter, surprised by the new lease of life.

'Dunno,' she replied, making sure he consumed as much as possible. 'Maybe it's the same stuff we had when we arrived. It must have some kind of healing powers.'

'Corners, ten seconds,' came the hosts announcement.

'Listen!' Said Molly urgently. 'They're obviously intent of using every dirty tactic in the book. Be ready for anything. You were doing great up until that point. Just keep doing what you're doing. You can do this.'

The girl looked at her friend, touching his face gently, before climbing out of the ring.

The beast, true to form, flew out at the sound of the bell, determined to finish off his opponent as quickly as possible.

Peter ducked, anticipating the beast's intentions as Miniton began to throw a combination of lefts and rights, eventually clipping the top of Peters shoulder.

The human winced, stumbling against the ropes, bobbing and weaving as the beast threw punch after punch, missing his rival with every swing.

'Get out of there!' Ordered Molly, frantically waving her arm, urging him to move.

Peter noticed the creature blowing heavily as he quickly threw a straight right hand, hitting the beast, right in the centre of his abdomen.

Miniton flew backwards with the force of the blow, doubling over in two, eventually landing prostrate on the canvas.

Peter jumped up and down, anxious for the count to begin.

'Why aren't you counting!' Screamed Molly as she looked over at Michael.

The host, clearly stunned by what he had seen, quickly picked up the mic as he began the count.

Miniton, one arm holding his midriff, slowly began to get to his feel.

'Five, six, seven,' continued the American.

The beast clung to the top rope, eventually getting to his feet on the count of nine. Peter looked to the heavens, a sense of hopelessness filling his soul.

Miniton turned to his rival, still feeling the effects of the blow. Its dark menacing eyes narrowed as it cried out. Its anger, reaching to a crescendo, before another assault began.

Suddenly, to the human's relief, the bell rang signalling the end of round two. Miniton growled, blowing gusts of air from his nostrils as he walked tentatively back to his corner.

'That was brilliant!' Said Molly, as she placed the stool on the canvas. 'That fight was over.' She continued, sending a look of disgust towards their American friend.

Michael shrugged coyly, knowing instantly why he were being chastised.

'Let's forget about that now. You're doing great. Just one more round to go. You're too quick for him, Peter. He's getting frustrated. These gloves are really powerful. A lot more powerful than he'd bargained for, I think. Just stay out of his way and wait for your opportunity. One good punch to the head should do it.'

Peter nodded, breathing heavily as he stared over at his agitated opponent.

'Corners ten seconds,' came the announcement as the young man lent forward, ready for the final round. 'I'll take another drink of that liquid,' said

Peter, tilting his head back as he took in as much of the invigorating juice as he could.

'Please give a round of applause for both competitors, as they begin the third and final round,' said Michael, whipping the crowd into a frenzy.

The bell sounded as the two exhausted beings, cautiously stalked each other, each one waiting for the other to make the first move.

'Come on,' whispered Peter, urging the beast to make the first move.

Miniton, now wary of the power the gauntlets possessed, snarled as the crowd began to heckle towards their hero.

'Coward! Kill him! Boo…!' Came the hostile heckling from the galleries.

Miniton barked at the crowd, furious at their lack of loyalty. Suddenly, frustrated at the human's refusal to take the initiative and aware the fight was drawing to its conclusion, the beast spun around. A flailing backhand catching the surprised human off guard as it caught him heavily on the side of the head. Peter flew back against the ropes as the arena began to spin.

'Look out!' Came the cry from his corner.

Still a little dazed, Peter tried to steady himself as he caught sight of the beast bounding towards him, before leaping high into the air. The dramatic movement seemed like it was in slow motion as Miniton, fist clenched high above his head, descended. Peter moved quickly into position as the beast began to throw the fatal blow, its evil eyes wide open, confident of victory.

Suddenly, with a well-timed move the young boxer, with every last bit of strength he had left, threw a devastating uppercut that connected flush under the beast's jaw, sending it souring six feet into the air.

Molly jumped into the air, before quickly turning her attention towards the host, pointing to the microphone. 'Start now!' She demanded as Michael began the count, dumbfounded at the sight of the beast lying flat out on the canvas.

Peter, quickly went to the nearest neutral corner as he watched anxiously, praying that the beast stayed down. 'Four, five, six,' Announced the host as Miniton began to stir.

'Stay down. Stay down,' pleaded Peter, the thought of its resurrection making him anxious.

'Eight, nine and you're out!' Screamed the American.

Peter leaped high off the ground as Molly jumped through the ropes. To their utter amazement, the crowd began to cheer, Applauding the unlikely victor as they chanted his name. Molly hurled herself into her friend's arms. Squeezing him tight, as she shouted into his ear.

'Steady on Moll's,' said Peter, covering his ear. 'Do you want me to go deaf?'

The young girl smiled as he lowered her to the floor. 'You did it!'

Peter jabbed her softly on the shoulder as he gathered himself. 'No, we did it.'

Michael climbed into the ring as the beast's trainers helped their defeated warrior off the canvas.

The bell sounded around the arena, prompting the host to make the final announcement. 'Please offer your appreciation to these fine warriors.'

The crowd went wild as the humans made their way to the centre of the ring.

'At the time of one minute and forty seconds of round number three, Miniton failed to get to his feet at the count of ten. Therefore, the winner coming by way of knockout. And still undefeated. Peter…. Hughes…!'

Everyone in the stadium stood and applauded as the host lifted the humans hand aloft in victory. 'Well done young man,' said Michael, attempting to shake Peter's hand. 'I think we can dispense of these now can't we.'

Peter held out his arms, as he watched the gauntlets disappear, revealing his unblemished hands. 'Thanks. I thought I was a goner there for sure.'

Molly's expression turned from one of delight to concern as she realised it was now all up to her.

Peter placed a hand on her shoulder, sensing her concern. 'You've got this Moll's. It's my turn to support you now. If I can knockout a four-hundred-pound beast, you can certainly win a running race. Remember, you will have help,' encouraged Peter, motioning towards the bracelet.

The three humans made their way over to the track, as Michael explained the rules of the challenge. 'This is a two-horse race. You will compete against one other being. The distance is over one thousand meter. The first one to make it to the finish line will be the victor. Just beyond the finish line is the gate that will take you to the realm of spells.'

Peter and Molly looked at each other, shocked by the revelation. 'So, that was the right choice,' said the girl, relieved.

The American smiled, confirming her suspicions.

'Wait. Where is the gate?' Interrupted Peter as he looked carefully around the stadium, unable to see the portal.

Michael ushered the two friends towards one end of the arena, before spreading his arms wide open.

Suddenly, the arena began to split in two. Both sides slowly parting, before stopping to reveal the most spectacular sight.

The perfectly straight track stretched far into the distance. A single white line separated the two lanes. Indicating lanes, one and two. Galleries on either side, stretched the full length of the track, filled with beings that roared and cheered as they caught a glimpse of the first competitor.

Peter's eyes opened wider as he spotted something bright in the distance. 'Is that__?'

'Yes. That is the gate that will take you to the realm of spells,' interrupted the American. 'But, be warned,' he continued. 'Fail to reach the finish line before your opponent and you will be condemned to this realm. Forfeiting your life force.'

Molly turned towards the host, giving him one of her icy stares. 'How can you say, by having two of us here we have some kind of advantage? Peter won his battle. What happens if I fail? Does Peter get to continue?'

'Michael hesitated, realising he needed to be as diplomatic as he could. 'I'm really sorry Molly. I don't make the rules, I'm afraid. Unfortunately, both of you have to be successful in order for you to continue. It's unfair I know.' The host hesitated again, unsure if he should continue.

'Come on, spit it out!' Demanded Molly, getting irritated by the lack of clarity.

'Well, unfortunately Peter must wait at the finishing line. If you are defeated, both of your life forces will be extracted together.'

Peter took hold of his friend, sensing her anxiety. 'Come on Moll's calm down. Remember what you said to me. You can do this.'

The volume around the stadium, began to increase as the young human's opponent appeared, waving at its supporters from the entrance.

Both, Molly and Peter stood rooted to the spot mouths open, as the being fixed a sinister stare towards its adversary. 'I'm racing against that?' Exclaimed the girl as the strength in her legs wilted from the sheer presence of her foe.

If she were feeling insecure before, the mere sight of the gargoyle left Molly paralysed. The size of its muscular legs, moving quickly across the ground, confirming its ability to leave the human in its wake once they began the race.

Molly concentrated hard as she studied the monster, realising she had seen this beast before. How could that be? She thought to herself. Why did it look familiar?

'My dream!' Said Molly loudly.

Peter turned around towards his friend, distracting his attention from the beast. 'What was that?' He replied, curious by her bizarre comment.

'Remember that dream I had? You know; At aunt Olivia's.'

The young man nodded, recalling her strange ranting and behaviour at the time.

'That was the thing I was running away from. It's all coming back to me now. The crowds on either side of the track. Everything about this place, is similar to the dream I had that night. I thought I was experiencing déjà vu. But seeing that thing now, confirms it.'

Peter turned back at the beast, then returned to his friend, shaking his head in disbelief. 'That's impossible,' he said, confident she must be hallucinating. 'How could you dream about something that hasn't even happened yet?'

Molly shrugged her shoulders, unable to answer. 'I don't know. But what is impossible? Nothing about this whole experience makes any sense.'

An eerie, but familiar noise distracted the humans attention as they noticed two winged creatures, descending from high above the arena.

'Peter has to leave us now,' said the host as the creature drew nearer.

'What's going on!' Asked the young girl, anxiously.

'Don't worry. The Harpies will take Peter to the finish-line. He will not be harmed; I give you my word,' promised the American as the winged demons hovered above, waiting for the signal to proceed.

Peter urged the Harpies to wait for a moment before he was taken. 'Look at me Molly!' exclaimed Peter as he stared intensely into his friend's eyes. 'I'll be waiting for you at the end. No matter what, we are in this together. All you need to do, is relax and concentrate. Focus on the finishing line, I'll be there cheering you on.'

Molly nodded, a worried expression on her face, wondering if she'd ever see her friend again.

Michael gave the instruction as the Harpies lifted the human high off the ground. A high pitched squawk echoed around the arena, causing the girl to cover her ears as she watched her friend slowly fade away into the distance.

The two competitors made their way towards the starting line as the crowd cheered with expectation.

'Choose your tools,' said the host, gesturing at the trinket.

Molly quickly checked the bracelet, almost forgetting she'd need help from the golden band if she were to have any chance of success.

After dismissing a number of symbols, a pair of sandals caught her attention, leaving her in no doubt they were what she needed.

The illuminating beam rapidly etched out the running aids, before instantly wrapping themselves around her feet. Molly stared at the golden sandals, feeling light on her feet, as if she were floating on air.

The host picked up his mic once more, gathering himself, before the final announcement of the games. 'Good luck,' whispered the American.

A regretful expression appeared on his face as he said his goodbyes, as if he longed to be free from his prison.

Molly smiled sympathetically, secretly wishing there were something she could do to help him escape from this hell he was trapped in.

Michael stepped back, before raising the mic to his mouth 'Please, give your appreciation for these two competitors as they go head to head to determine the winner of the thousand metre dash.'

The crowd from the arena, as well as those that lined the galleries in front of them went wild as the host continued.

'First, in lane number one, representing the planet Sargonia. The fastest being in the multi-verse. Demona!'

The horde of beings cheered as the beast raised its arms, in appreciation.

'Her opponent, in lane number two, representing the planet Earth. Molly…. Miggins!'

The expected cascade of boos and jeers whistled around the stadium as Molly tentatively raised her hand half mast, whilst trying hard not to show her vulnerability.

The host took a few pace back, as he picked up the starting pistol. 'Runners, take your marks!'

Molly took a deep breath as the two competitors took their positions on the starting line.

Demona growled at the human as they crouched. 'You're mine!' Barked the beast, in a high-pitched, spluttery voice, as if it were gargling on a pint of spittle.

163

The young girls blood turned ice-cold, from the sudden threat, making her legs feel like jelly.

'Set...!'

Both athletes bolted from the starting line as the crack from the gun sounded out around the stadium. A roar of excitement burst from the galleries as they watched the rivals flying down the track, neck and neck.

The beast slowly edged ahead, a sinister giggle comming from it spurring Molly into action as she dug in deep, trying to claw back Demona's advantage.

'This is amazing,' whispered the human, as she began to overtake her rival.

The beings sitting in the stands were a blur as she moved at an unnatural speed. Demona swung out her arm, attempting to grab hold of her opponent as she effortlessly breezed past.

'What the hell!' Yelped the startled girl.

Molly pressed on the accelerator, remembering the dirty tricks tactics tried in Peter's fight.

Suddenly, Molly spotted an animated figure in the distance. 'Peter,' she muttered hopefully, injecting a renewal of strength that urged her on.

The heckles on the back of Molly's neck stood on end as she noticed, two familiar looking shadows on the ground, becoming darker with every stride. The malicious squawks that pierced through the air, confirmed her fears as the Harpies began to chastise the human, clawing at her golden hair. The young girl cried out in frustration, waving her arms as she tried to defend herself from constant tirade.

Demona, quickly began to gain ground on her opponent as the human, under constant assault from the Harpies began to slow down.

'Run....!' Came the cry from up ahead as Molly recognised her friend, urging her on at the finish-line.

Peter seemed to move in slow motion the closer she got, blurred by the bright light that shone behind him.

'That must be the gate.' She said hopefully as another claw, grabbed at her shoulder.

The young girl beat away her tormentor with a flailing arm, causing the Harpy to retreat as it readied itself for another assault.

'You're almost there!' cried Peter, a concerned expression on his face indicating her pursuer was close behind.

The young girl looked over her shoulder, sensing her rival was only a few meters away.

Molly suddenly cried out, shocked as the beast suddenly revealed its secret weapon, strategically hidden from sight.

Appearing out of nowhere were a pair of wings that flew out, lifting the beast high off the ground.

'No…!' Screamed the human as the beast made a last-ditch attempt to thwart her opponent.

Memories of the dream came flooding back to her as she witnessed the same events unfolding before her eyes.

Filled with feelings of anger and determination, the human gathered every last bit of energy she had and threw herself over the finishing line, beating her rival by the narrowest of margins.

'Are you okay?' asked Peter, helping his friend to her feet.

Exhausted and out of breath, Molly stared over at the beast, lying in a heap on the ground. 'We've done it.'

'You've done it,' said the young man.

Molly still physically drained from her ordeal tried to reply, before spotting a small but familiar figure lurking in the background. 'Shifter?' Queried the girl as the old man walked slowly towards her.

'Congratulations miss, Miggins,' replied the Galpherin, looking up at the exhausted girl, a look of pride etched across his face. 'You are victorious and have earned the right to enter the final realm. Please, will the two of you make your way into the realm of spells.'

The old man opened his arms as the gate opened wide, revealing the doorway to their final challenge.

The three beings walked towards the entrance as the Galpherin's expression turned to horror, before disappearing through the door.

Molly and Peter screamed as the Gargoyle descended. Its jaws opened wide, revealing its razor like teeth, as it bit down into Molly's shoulder.

The injured girl fell to the floor, screaming out in pain as her blood dripped from Demona's fangs, roaring with ecstasy, pleased with its conquest.

Pre-occupied with the girl, the beast failed to notice her friend, who quickly jumped onto the creatures back.

Peter grabbed hold of the creatures wing and with all his strength, ripped the fragile tissue from its shoulder. Demona whaled in agony as her wing dangled precariously, attached only by a single tendon. The demon writhed around in agony as it struggled to reach for its wing.

There was little time to lose as the beast, frustrated by its failed attempts to save its wing, fixed an evil glare towards its assailant.

'Molly….! Get up….!' Ordered Peter, grabbing his friends hand.

The badly injured girl, numbed by the adrenaline coursing through her veins, scrambled to her feet, as the two humans, closely pursued by the demon, launched themselves through the doorway, leaving Demona and the realm of hopes and fears far behind them.

Chapter Eighteen

The realm had an eerie feel about it as the young girl lay on the ground. Peter, careful not to hurt his friend, peeled back the suit from her shoulder.

'What are we going to do?' asked Peter, a concerned look on his face.

The old man smiled sympathetically as he approached the humans.

Shifter examined the wound, pausing for a moment before giving his opinion. 'The young lady will be fine master Peter,' replied the Galpherin. 'The wound will heal in time. She is extremely lucky. Not many survive a bite from a gargoyle. Any deeper and the damaged flesh would spread and deteriorate dramatically. The suit will help with the healing process. I would suggest you rest for a while. Keep her wounds covered with the suit and after some well needed sleep, she should be back to normal.'

Peter gently covered the wounds back up, closing the suit. Molly winced as she attempted to sit upright, her eyes trying to adjust to the darkness.

'Where are we?' asked Molly, a little groggy from her ordeal.

'This is the realm of spells,' replied the old man. 'This is your final challenge. Beyond the forest of the dead, lies the castle of the witch, Hecate. In order for you to succeed, you must defeat the witch. A most formidable opponent, her powers are legendary, second only to the Origins. She is the Origins right hand, so to speak.'

The Galpherin raised an arm, pointing into the distance. 'That is the witches castle,' he revealed as the humans followed his direction, just making out the dark fortress looming out of the night.

The two friends fell silent for a moment as they contemplated their fate. 'Is that where my father is held captive?' asked Molly, eyes firmly fixed on the castle.

'Your father is trapped in the tree of souls, which guards the door that will free you from the realm of spells. Unfortunately, Norman Miggins failed to defeat, Hecate and was taken by the tree of souls. Defeat the witch and your father will be released. Fail and all three of you will be condemned, your life force lost forever.'

Overwhelmed with all the information, along with the throbbing pain from her wounds, Molly slumped to the ground, her body and mind unable to bare another battle.

The Galpherin's expression softened as he approached the girl, placing his hand gently into hers.

His ancient hand felt surprisingly soft to the touch as he looked into her eyes. 'Miss, Miggins,' said Shifter sympathetically.

The young girl raised her head, her eyes moist as she tried to suppress the tears.

'Never have I witnessed a braver or heroic being than you. I have served in this world for many a millennia and most, if not all have failed long before now. This is your final challenge. I would be remiss in my duties if I didn't prepare you for the perils you must face. This realm, although the smallest, is the most harrowing. You will both no doubt face your worst fears. But you will face them together.'

Peter nodded his head in agreement, he too beginning to feel the effects of their ordeal as the adrenaline started to wear off.

Molly groaned as the pain in her shoulder intensified. 'I knew that was going to happen,' said the girl, annoyed with herself.

The Galpherin raised an eyebrow, unsure of what she meant.

'The race—The attack from that creature. I knew; I dreamt about it.' She continued, recalling the dream. 'I should have reacted quicker.'

The Galpherin looked puzzled at the human, unsure of what she meant.

'I dreamt of the race, before we even arrived in this world. The beast; You, all of it. How could I dream of something that hadn't happened?'

The old man smiled as he drew her attention towards the bracelet. 'The golden band has powers not even I understand my young friend. You see, it belongs somewhere out there. Somewhere beyond these worlds and universes.'

Molly stared at the trinket, feeling its presence as she marvelled at its wonder.

'Its power even supersedes that of the Origin. That is the reason no being can question the written laws. Not even him. The golden band is all powerful. Those that have failed to conquer the realms, have not failed because it was beyond their capabilities. But because they were not able to be as one with the golden band. You, my dear friend, are one of the few that have made it this far because you and the trinket, are as one.'

Shifter, complaining from the stiffness setting into his old bones, stood up, before he finished. 'I must leave you both now,' said the old man as he made his way to the doorway. 'But remember, nothing is always what it seems.'

The Galpherin turned, before disappearing, recalling one more bit of advice. 'Oh, and one last thing. listen out for the spells that fill the air.'

With that, the old man vanished through the door, leaving the humans confused, ceiling the entrance for good.

Molly and Peter stared into the dark forest ahead, either one reluctant to take the first step.

'Listen, there's no point continuing until you are fully healed,' said Peter, hoping his friend were of the same mind.

'To be perfectly honest with you, if I walked much further, I think I'll collapse.' She replied, carefully moving her shoulder in a more comfortable position.

Strange noises echoed around the night sky. The forests inhabitants concealed from sight as the sound of, the breaking of fallen branches, confirmed their presence. A thick low mist moved gently across the floor; the terrain underneath hidden by its density. Trees, their crooked branches bare, entwined with one another as if one unit, looked alive, enhanced by the silhouette from the moonlight.

'Look, there's a hollow in the ground over there,' said Peter, pointing towards a mound just above the mist.

The dip in its centre looked perfect as he helped his friend off the floor. A large thick tree that looked like a, Baobab, rooted deep into the ground sheltered them as they sank into the thick layer of dead leaves, a little damp, but bearable.

The two friends, although beaten and exhausted, fought hard to stay awake, the forest of the dead reminding them of the dangers that lay in wait.

'I've a bad feeling about this place,' said Molly, trembling as her head swivelled, sending her senses into overdrive.

'We've got to try and stay calm, Moll's,' said Peter, trying desperately hard to stay positive. 'You need to rest or you won't heal. We'll sleep in shifts. You go first and I'll keep watch,' he suggested, wondering if being awake on his own was a good idea.

Molly nodded, hesitantly as she moved close to him, wrapping her arm slowly around his waist. Hundreds of tiny butterflies danced feverishly inside his stomach as he lifted his arm. The weary young girl nestled her head on his chest, letting out sound of contentment, soothed by the sound of his heartbeat as she soon, drifted off into a deep sleep.

The scent of her golden hair intoxicated him. The turmoil of the day, as he too, fell fast asleep, leaving them vulnerable to the creatures of the night.

Peter woke with a start, shocked by the sight of dozens of winged devils clawing at his hair. Still dazed from his sleep, frantically waving his hands in the air, the young man cried out desperately trying to alert his friend who was lying motionless on the ground. The creatures swarmed around them, a black mass of torn flesh and bones feverishly attacking them at will.

'Not more of these things!' Cried Peter, recalling the Vespertilio. But these were different, he thought to himself. Their decaying bodies, mostly rotted away exposing their skeletal frames, looked like they'd been dead for many years. Their hollow eye-sockets, revealing the darkness behind their soulless corpses. 'Molly! Wake up!'

The girl screamed, instantly jumping to her feet as one of the decrepit bloodsucking creatures ripped a clump of her golden hair from her head. 'Get them off me!' Cried the girl, her flailing arms thrashing in vein at her assailants.

Overwhelmed by the torrent of attacks, the two humans, not quite with it after their deep sleep began to fade under the constant assault.

'You need to use the bracelet Molly! Cried Peter desperately failing to fend the creatures off.

The young girl screamed in frustration as the creatures, somehow aware of her intentions, grabbed tight hold of her arms preventing her from reaching the trinket.

A loud crack, bellowed through the air, startling the winged devils, staying their attack.

The large tree that sheltered them while they slept, suddenly began to move. The bark seemed to splinter; a distinctive shape beginning to form. First an arm, then another. The Vespertilio shrieked in complaint, gathering in one black mass as the transformation continued.

Molly and Peter, both fell back watching in awe, mouths wide open as the figure emerged, breaking free from its prison.

The tall oak like figure stood poised, ready for battle, before swinging its long impressive limb, crashing into the swarm of bloodsuckers, scattering their fragile bones in all directions. The Vespertilio that remained, sprang instantly into action, laying siege towards the being one by one. The beast, deceptively quick for its size, ripped the zombie like creatures from its bark, crushing them effortlessly with its branch like fingers. The two humans could only watch, dumbfounded by the massacre that continued before them. The tree like figure let out a cry, that didn't quite fit its stature, as one of the creatures tore off a small branch attached to its shoulder.

Was it female? Molly asked herself, shocked by the sound. 'We need to help it!' She insisted, checking her bracelet. 'There's nothing here.'

The human scanned the trinket, desperately looking for a weapon.

'I think it's doing just fine on its own,' answered Peter, motioning towards their saviour.

Suddenly, the creature leapt high off the ground, landing heavily, sending the last of the winged devils attached to its body crashed to the floor. One by one, the bloodsuckers splintered into pieces as the creature slammed its stump like feet onto their fragile bodies.

Both humans sat still, unable to speak as the creature kicked the; lifeless corpses, checking they were dead (Again). Molly and Peter looked at each other, a little concerned as it approached, still unsure if it was friend or foe. Slowly rising to her feet, Molly gasped quietly, shocked as it came clearly into view, its feature lit up by the moonlight.

Its face was almost human like. Its delicately pointed chin softened by its high cheekbones, looked almost elfish like. Lips, as dark as mahogany glistened from the sap that seeped from its mouth. It's clear, deep blue eyes gave off a feeling of warmth as it slowly leaned down towards the two nervous looking beings.

'Don't be afraid,' said the creature, smiling as it tilted its face curiously to one side.

From the top of its head, grew thin twig like branches that intertwined, spiralling up into a point. Tiny unflowered buds decorated the stems, hibernating as they slept soundly waiting for the sunlight.

'My name is, Etherine. I am the guardian of the forest.'

Molly returned the smile, relaxing as she extended an arm. 'Very pleased to meet you, Etherine. I'm Molly Miggins. And this is my friend, Peter.'

Etherine, gently shook the girls hand. Her thick branch like fingers, felt rough as they curled around her skin.

'Are you both okay?' The creature began to stroke Molly's hair, noticing it had been through some turmoil.

'I'm fine, thank you,' replied Molly, discreetly pulling away. 'I've been through far worse.' She continued, feeling for the wound on her shoulder. 'Oh! It's healed.' She said, pleasantly surprised.

'Thanks for your help,' interrupted Peter, still feeling a little intimidated by the creature. 'I don't know what we'd have done if you hadn't appeared. Molly's bracelet wouldn't work.'

'The golden band will assist you when you need it,' said the creature.

Peter laughed, surprised by her response. 'I don't mean to be rude, but I think a colony of bloodsucking beasts would signify the need for its help, wouldn't you?'

The forest guardian smiled sympathetically at the humans lack of understanding. 'The golden band knows when you need help. That is why I am here. When the trinket and its wearer become one, it subconsciously knows when you are in danger. It sensed the young lady was confused, unable to react to the threat, therefor sending out a signal for help. I am that help.'

'You mean I don't always need to physically touch the bracelet for it to give me what I need?' asked Molly, beginning to understand.

'Precisely,' confirmed Etherine. 'As I am sure the Galpherin has explained to you already. The golden band has many powers. Some of which are still unknown. But the more the wearer accepts the trinket, then the less need there is for symbols. Your mind will subconsciously select what you need.'

'But why are you still here?' asked the young girl. 'Everything the bracelet has provided, disappeared almost immediately after.'

'My work here, is unfinished miss, Miggins. When you evolve, the band evolves with you. Giving you stronger powers, able to summon beings, as well as objects to help you.'

'But I didn't summon you.'

'Didn't you?' asked the forest dweller, implying the opposite were true. 'You are the golden band. The golden band is you. Don't you understand that by now? The psychic link between you and your charm, is extremely powerful. Without that understanding. Without that bond, the golden band is useless to you, no more than a decoration.'

Molly listened carefully. Trying to take it all in. Some of it made sense, some of it incomprehensible. Sure, there were things in the universe, (or multi verse) that we didn't understand, things too complex for the human mind to comprehend, but why were she finding it so difficult to except? And if that were the case, then why didn't the bracelet sense that? Did she understand more than she thought? Maybe. It was all too much to take in. Her father, the time loss. Oh, the time loss, she suddenly thought to herself. Her mother, what had become of her mother? How old would she be if she ever returned home? Would there be a home for her to return to? And Peter. Molly looked over at her friend. Her loyal devoted, friend? He'd sacrificed so much for her. What of his family?

He was their only son. The feelings. What were these feelings she was having? Was he just a friend? The butterflies, the warm glow that flushed her cheeks every time she got close to him. Did he feel the same? She couldn't be sure. She didn't want to look a fool by making the first move, only to be ridiculed. She'd never live it down.

But that look he gave her. She could feel it, his eyes looking deep into hers, as if penetrating her most secret thoughts. No, it would have to be him, she decided. The price was too high. Maybe it was the bracelet! If it was as powerful as everyone claimed, then maybe it was controlling her feelings. Maybe these unexpected desires were why she were behaving this way. But what if the trinket were bringing out her true affection? It was a part of her now after all.

'You okay Moll's?' asked Peter, disturbing her from her trance like state.

Molly snapped out of her daydream, an awkward look on her face, wondering if he could read her thoughts. 'Yeah, I'm good thanks.' She replied, quickly dispelling all foolish nonsense from her mind.

'We need to go,' interrupted Etherine. 'I'm unsure how much time I have. If you are to reach the castle of Hecate, you will need all the help you can get. There will be many dangers waiting for in the forest of the dead. She will be watching, waiting for the right time to cast her spells. You must be on alert, Molly. Only the wearer of the golden band has the power to hear the witch's spells, so listen carefully. It may only be a whisper, but you will need to react quickly. Translate the spell and the golden band will act accordingly.'

Molly nodded her head pretending to understand, apprehensive about asking the forest dweller to explain further.

'This way,' said Etherine as she pointed towards a clearing in the forest.

Molly stared at her friend. A look of fear and apprehension in her eyes, the consequences of failure weighing heavy on her mind. Peter nodded, a look of determination on his face reassuring her as he took her hand.

The creatures of the night fell deathly silent as the three companions entered the dark forest. Strange shapes seemed to move within the trees, becoming still when aware they were being watched. Molly's eyes danced from side to side, her peripheral vision alerted to the slightest motion. Sudden cries pierced through the dank air high above the sparsely covered branches, sending her nerves on edge as they continued through the forest. The tall tree dweller moved deliberately, poised to react to any sudden danger. Small streams of moonlight, fought in vein to penetrate the darkness through the lofted canopies, making the pathway ahead difficult to navigate.

A clearing up ahead loomed in the distance, giving them some comfort. 'Be ready,' warned Etherine as she moved slowed, expecting the unexpected.

Half a dozen headstones, randomly dotted around the ground, separated them from the forest. It seemed like a graveyard, yet the usual characteristics were mostly absent. No discernible graves were present, only the headstones. No signs depicting its inhabitants.

Molly froze, a coldness running through her veins, chilling her blood as she remembered the valley of bones.

'We must re-enter the forest on the other side,' whispered Etherine quietly. 'Don't make a sound. We need to be as quiet as possible. Molly Miggins, remember, listen carefully. If you hear anything you must act quickly.'

Molly nodded hesitantly, still a little confused as to what she were listening for.

'Don't worry young lady, you will know,' continued the forest dweller, as if it knew what the human was thinking.

Slowly, the three companions quietly crept through the unmarked graveyard, each footstep deliberately cautious as they passed the first headstone.

HIC JACET BAGGOT FERTUR LYCAON EODEM TEMPORE AFFLIGUNTUR DAMNATI OMNES; Read the inscription carved into the headstone.

Instantly translating it in her head, Molly whispered the inscription. 'Here lies Baggot Lycaon, damned for all time.'

Peter and Etherine quickly turned towards the young girl, shocked as her softly spoken words echoed around them.

Molly held her breath, surprised at how loud she was as a gentle breeze blew through her hair, lifting her golden locks from her shoulders.

'It's happening,' said Etherine softly, searching for any movement around them. 'What do you hear Molly?'

The human listened tentatively as the strange chanting, a faint whisper at first, got louder repeating over and over again.

LYCAN ORIRI MEAM ET TESTAMENTUM TUUM. SPIRITUS MOVET. OCCIDITIS: OCCIDITIS, OCCIDITIS.

'Quickly Molly, what does it say!' Repeated the tree dweller, by now unconcerned of how loud she sounded.

Molly began to stutter, aware of the urgency. 'Err! I'm not sure.' She replied, desperately trying to make sense of the foreign chanting. 'Rise? Yes, rise my Lycan and do thy will…Move like the wind. Kill, kill, kill.'

Everything fell silent for a moment, as if all around had held its breath. Even the soft breeze hushed, as if waiting, anticipating the horror that was to follow.

'Run!' Screamed Etherine as the ground began to shake beneath their feet.

They burst out from the soil. One, no two, three four five. Half a dozen of them. Howling at the moon in delight. Famished for the taste of flesh. Trapped in their graves for hundreds of years, waiting. Waiting to be freed, allowed to hunt once more.

Molly gasped in horror at the mere sight of them. Their human like bodies, covered with course hair, some as black as the night, others a lighter shade of brown. But there was one; one that stood out, one that had fixed its devilishly black eyes, solely on her.

Baggot Lycaon, she said to herself, remembering the inscription on the grave.

The white werewolf snarled, baring its razor like teeth. The sound of its jaws snapping pierced through the night air, a single growl bringing its companions to heal.

The beings raced towards the woods as the Lycans gave chase. 'We won't make it!' Cried Etherine. 'You must concentrate. We need the help of the forest.'

'I don't know what I should do!' Replied Molly, desperately looking at her bracelet. 'There's nothing there!'

'Clear your mind!' Ordered the tree being.

Suddenly, Molly drifted into a trance like state as the bracelet sparked into action, creating the instrument before her very eyes.

Still trying to come to terms with the new order of things, the young girl grabbed the ivory horn from thin air.

'Blow the horn!' Instructed Etherine as one of the werewolves lunged its snapping its jaws inches from Peter.

'Do it now Molly!' Screamed Peter, quickly changing course, avoiding the beast as its momentum sent it sprawling to the ground.

The human placed the horn to her lips, blowing hard into the mouthpiece. The deep booming sound, filled the void around them as the Lycan suddenly stopped in their tracks as if fully aware what was to follow.

'Look!' Said Peter, pointing towards the trees.

The forest suddenly came to life, roots ripping out from their beds as the lumber sum figures bounded towards them, a deep hum penetrated through the air, like a signal to charge.

The werewolves, unsure which way to run scattered like frightened dogs, desperately trying to escape. A sickening yelp pierced the night air as one of the tree creatures picked up its prey, tearing it limb from limb, strewing the bloody mess across the graveyard.

'Protect the girl!' Ordered Etherine as she spotted the white wolf, undeterred by the slaughtering of its kind, in full flight determined to fulfil its task.

Molly wheeled around, willing her legs into action as she made for the forest. The creature picked up its pace, an evil self-satisfying look on its face, knowing it would, at least have its kill before its demise.

Molly screamed, wheeling around to face her attacker as the beast pounced. Everything went into slow motion as the once, Baggot Lycaon opened its jaws, its sharp fangs dripping with spittle, claws extended, pinned her to the ground.

Molly closed her eyes, feeling the creature's hot rancid breath on her face. The terrified girl whispered in prayer as her assailant paused, savouring the moment before the end.

A loud stomach curdling cry pierced her eardrums, forcing her to open her eyes. Molly's face grimaced as she watched her attacker being brutally torn apart, the two tree beasts scattering the body parts far and wide.

The scene was like something out of a war film. The ground, wet with blood glistened, appearing black against the night. Body parts, changing back into their human form, lay lifeless on the ground. The defining silence reverberated around them as they surveyed the scene of horror.

'Is it over?' asked an exhausted Molly, looking warily at the colossal tree creatures as they gathered, their blood-soaked limbs dripping with the dark liquid of their victims.

'These are our friends Molly,' replied Etherine, sensing the girls agitated state. 'They are the keepers of the forest. You have nothing to fear from them.'

'I thought you were the keeper of the forest,' interrupted Peter looking up at one of the trees, causing a gentle breeze to disturb his hair as it passed by him.

'That I am young Peter. We are all guardians of the woodland. There is no hierarchy here, but unlike me, our friends can only be summoned if, Baggot Lycaon rises from his resting place. Hecate has been saving him for the one who possesses the last golden band. Up until now she has used, let's say, other more conventional methods to defeat the Origins enemies. Unfortunately for her, she'd underestimated you.'

Etherine Turned towards the young girl, lowering her head in respect as the guardians of the forest, one by one, knelt down before her.

Molly watched in awe as the hoard of guardians, lowered their trunk like heads to honour her.

'All hail Queen Molly,' joked Peter, slightly amused at the absurd spectacle.

The young girl scowled at her friend, feeling a little embarrassed by the whole thing. 'Please, stand up,' urged Molly. 'I'm no hero, I'm just a girl trapped in this world trying to find her father.'

Etherine, slowly raised her head, followed by her companions. 'You don't understand, Molly Miggins. We have been waiting a long, long time for you. The white werewolf and his army of Lycan have lay, desecrating this land for many moons. Your arrival has prompted, Hecate to use her most lethal weapon. Now that weapon is no more, leaving the guardians of the forest to live and their roots to flourish from the ground once more.'

The young girl placed her hands over her face, her mind struggling to process what she was being told. How could this be, she thought to herself. Could the bracelet and her really be as one? She often felt confused, unsure of what to do. But at every stage up to now, every choice she made, was the correct one.

Molly studied the trinket, hypnotised by its perfect symmetry. Feeling its power coursing through her whole being, whispering an ancient language unknown to her, yet understanding its meaning perfectly. She felt like her mind was developing, expanding her knowledge. Strange images began to flash through her mind. Her father. Crying out in agony. Lost in limbo, damned for eternity. What was he saying? Molly concentrated, tightly closing her eyes, the images becoming clearer.

'Help me Molly! Please hurry!'

Peter grabbed hold of his friend, startling her as she snapped out from her trance like state. 'My dad Peter. My dad was calling me. We have to hurry; I don't think there's much time left.'

The young man held on to the girl, trying to calm her down as she began to hyperventilate. 'Okay Moll's relax. What did you see?'

'I don't know. Just these images flashing through my head. He's here Peter, he's trapped, in pain. He was calling out my name, he knows I'm here.'

'You're father senses you are close, Molly Miggins,' said Etherine calmly, unsurprised at the revelation. 'The closer your golden bands get to each other, the stronger the connection will be. That is why you are beginning to see these images, he's become alerted to your presence, desperate to escape his captor.'

'We have to go now!' Exclaimed Molly. 'Please help me!'

'We'll find him Moll's, take a breath,' said Peter calmly, embracing his friend. 'There can't be much further to go now.'

'There are still many dangers to avoid,' said the tree dweller. 'We must be vigilant if we are to reach the witch's lair. She will be even more determined to destroy you now. You have defeated her most valuable asset.'

Molly and Peter watched as the guardians of the forest, slowly made their way back to their habitat, their long roots digging deep into the ground as they extended their impressive limbs, as if they were stretching, before finally sleeping, becoming still once more.

Chapter Nineteen

The three companions moved quietly through the forest. Listening intently as each sound perked their senses. Small branches cracked around them, each one warning them they may not be alone.

Molly felt the hackles on the back of her neck stand on end as the bracelet began to warm her wrist. Was it a warning? Molly thought to herself, still a little unsure she understood the signals.

Etherine stopped, alerted by something moving in the distance. The ground up ahead seemed to ripple, forcing them to step back as it got closer and closer.

'Go back!' Ordered the tree dweller, retreating swiftly from the threat. 'What do you hear, Molly!' She continued, desperately urging the human to concentrate.

Molly listened, hoping some sign would come to her. 'I hear nothing!' Replied the girl, worried she'd lost the power to hear the witches spell.

Suddenly, the trio began to fall as the ground opened up around them, sending them tumbling through to the depths of the realm.

The vast space around them seemed dank and musty. The only form of light, the reflection of the moon, bouncing off gem like crystals buried into the walls of the cavern, twinkling as the Lunas light that seeped down through the space above.

The eerie cavern stretched far into the distance, the light fading, turning blacker the deeper it went. The ceiling high above formed a type of patterned structure. Long rectangular shaped objects seemed to protrude out of the surface, their dimensions, off at each side, leaning out then back in, three quarters of the way up. Dozens of them lined the high vaulted rooftop, continuing through the passageway ahead.

'Are you both okay?' asked the tree dweller, shaking the earth from her soiled limbs.

Molly and Peter helped each other to their feet, spitting the decrepit soil from their mouths as they looked up at large gaping hole left from the earthquake.

'Where in the hell are, we!' Asked Peter angrily as he held his shoulder, feeling the effects of the fall.

'I'm not sure,' replied Etherine, confused by her surroundings. 'I'm not familiar with this part of the realm. It must be the work of, Hecate. Her spells are powerful; she has the ability to change parts of the realm. I haven't witnessed this change in design. The witch is usually methodical; this sudden change can only be considered a victory.'

Peter laughed at the concept. 'A victory? I fail to see any kind of victory here. She has us trapped in some sort of, underground fortress of some sort.'

'You don't understand, young Peter. The realm of spells has a tried and trusted design that has served, the Origin for more than a thousand challengers. For the witch to change the design now, can only mean one thing.' Etherine turned to Molly, before revealing her opinion. 'You, Molly Miggins.'

The confused young girl looked unbelievingly, between the tree dweller and her friend, waiting for the punchline.

'What, me?' asked Molly, by now overwhelmed by the constant expectation being bestowed upon her. 'How on earth am I important enough to force these changes. I'm tired of everyone, every being, telling me I'm someone special. Like I'm someone who can save the whole world.'

The forest guardian smiled sympathetically as she approached the human, feeling the weight of the heavy burden she bore. 'I am sensing how difficult this is for you, Molly. And I am sorry that you are the one that has to carry this charge. But you are the one that wears the last golden band. It is more powerful than any of those that came before it.

'Why didn't Shifter tell me?' asked Molly, beginning to understand the magnitude of the task that was forced upon her. 'I didn't ask for any of this.'

'The Galpherin, knew if he told you before you were ready, the chances of failure would be far greater than success. He knew that, if the wearer of the last golden band were unsuccessful, the Origin would have complete control to summon more beings from other worlds, including your own. You see, the beings of this world, want the challenges to stop. The more beings who fail to succeed, the more powerful the Origin becomes.'

'But why tell me now? I need to speak to Shifter! I don't want this, all I ever wanted was to free my father and return home to my family.'

'You may summon the Galpherin if you wish. But he will only repeat what I have already told you. It wasn't my plan to reveal your true quest at this point, but you looked so defeated, despondent, that I felt I had little choice. We are so close to ending the suffering inflicted by the Origin and his minions, that you needed to understand how important you are to this world and others. You are stronger than you realise, Molly Miggins. I cannot recollect the last time Hecate has been forced to change the design of this realm. You have done that, Molly. You!'

Peter moved closer towards his weary friend, placing a comforting arm around her shoulders. 'Etherine is right Moll's. If we'd have known what was expected of you, the chances are, knowing you like I do, you may have been more cautious, therefor making more careful decisions. Would we have got this far? Who knows? What I do know, is, you made the right decisions, at the right time. Everything, up to now was meant to happen. Maybe knowing what you know now is, meant to happen. All I can say is, whatever happens to us, I will be right there with you.'

Molly looked longingly at her friend. These feelings were real. She knew that now. Any thoughts of the bracelet manipulating her senses, quickly expelled. Nothing that felt this strong, could be controlled.

Molly's heart began to race, causing her to breathe deeply as she felt its physical presence. Hypnotised by his penetrating gaze, the space between them began to close, inching ever nearer.

Can this be happening to me? She thought to herself, helpless to resist the inevitable.

The young girl took in a sharp breath as their lips touched. His warm moist mouth, pressed gently against hers, causing her legs to buckle underneath her as he pulled her in tight, sensing her surrender. The electricity between them charged the atmosphere, creating a heat that she'd never experienced before, afraid that if she let go, it would never return.

Suddenly, the spell was broken. Pieces of the earth began to fall down from above, separating the two lovebirds.

'What's going on!' Screamed Molly, annoyed by the sudden interruption.

'It's happening!' Cried the tree dweller, noticing the sarcophagus's protruding out from the ground above were splintering. 'Quick, Molly, we have to move. What do you hear!'

The young human concentrated hard as the trio ran towards the dark void. Suddenly, the golden band began to glow, a bright amber light dispelled the darkness, lighting the way ahead.

'I can't make it out!' Complained Molly, an intelligible whisper floating in the air.

The foreign spell, repeating over and over again began to get louder, disturbing the inhabitants that lurked above them.

'Molly, they're breaking through, you must translate the spell, before it is too late!' Pleaded Etherine as the coffins began to break apart.

The young girl began to mumble the ancient language, its meaning becoming clearer the louder it got. 'ARAPHA DE GENERE TUO DEEXPERGISCIMINI SOMNO POLLENTIUS HYDRA. UT OPORTET ME ADDUCERE, ET INIMICOS I.'

'What does it mean, Molly? You must translate the spell!' Repeated the tree dweller.

'Descendants of the Hydra awaken from thy sleep. And bring me our enemies I must keep!'

The announcement of the spell seemed to spark the beasts into action. The sarcophaguses exploded into pieces; fragments of rotten wood rained down from above as the horrors, once concealed inside revealed themselves. One by one, their skeletal figures dropped down from their resting place.

Peter yelled in terror as one of the creature dropped heavily on top of him, sending him crashing to the ground. The sudden rush of adrenaline spurred the young man into action, kicking the surprisingly light, frame of bones into another.

'Molly! We need some help! There's too many of them!' Cried Peter, struggling to his feet.

It was like death itself had been drooped from above. Hundreds of skeletons that had broken free from their resting place, poured down around them, cutting off their escape route.

Etherine began to use her size and strength, smashing the creatures into pieces with her impressive limbs. 'I can't hold them off much longer!' She exclaimed as the creatures began to overwhelm her, their thin bony fingers clawing at her from all sides.

The way ahead was a sea of white bones, each one desperately clambering over the other, intent on fulfilling their goal.

Molly wheeled around, a stomach curdling cry distracting her from the nightmare around them. 'Peter!' Cried the young girl as she watched in horror.

Dozens of the soulless creature began to swam over her friend, like spiders, rushing to consume their prey, eventually covering every inch of his being, until he was gone, buried under a mound of bones.

The space around began to move as the temperature started to rise. The young girl, ignoring the creatures that were ascending her legs, began to glow. A blinding white light surrounded the human, her golden hair turning to fire as she extended her arm. Everything seemed to slow down as a deep booming drone, echoed around the cavern. The creatures, caught by surprise by the unexpected event, slowly began to rise from the ground, drifting in limbo, paralysed by the strange phenomenon. Instantly, a dark void appeared, looming out from the distance, swirling around in a spiral as the cavern began to tremble.

The animated human let out a defiant cry, forcing her arm out once more as one by one, the descendants of the Hydra clawing out in vein, their fleshless hands breaking away from their limbs as they desperately clung on to their victims, disappeared, sucked into the void.

A deafening hush filled the atmosphere as the human slumped to the ground, exhausted from her efforts.

'Peter!' She remembered, rushing to his side.

Gently, she rolled him over, hoping for signs of life. 'Peter wake up!' She cried, desperately shaking her friend.

The thought of losing him now, filled her with dread. What would she do without him? How could she go on? 'Peter please wake up! You can't leave me here alone.'

A single tear, fell gently onto his face as she rested her head on his chest, devastated by what she had caused.

A sharp intake of breath, forced her to move. 'You're alive!' She cried loudly, causing him to wince.

'Yeah, but I'll be deaf if you scream down my ear once more,' joked Peter, scratching the side of his head.

'I thought I'd lost you. Don't ever do that to me again.' She grumbled, affectionately slapping his shoulder.

'Well done, Molly Miggins,' interrupted the tree dweller. 'Now do you believe me?'

Molly helped her friend to his feet, grateful he was alive, before turning to the guardian of the forest. 'I do believe you, Etherine. I knew exactly what to do. It was like the bracelet was talking to me, guiding my every move. But I was the one in control. I was the one making the decisions. It was weird yet made complete sense. All the fear, all the doubt, evaporated.'

Etherine smiled, satisfied the human had finally come to understand her importance. A newfound confidence seemed glow from Molly's face. Her whole demeanour had changed, like she was invincible, ready to take on anything that stood in her path.

'Look!' Said peter, pointing towards an opening up ahead. 'I think that's a way out.'

Moonlight trickled in through the cavern, highlighting their escape route as the tree dweller hesitated, recognising where they were.

'Wait! Said the surprised guardian. 'We are here.'

Molly and Peter stopped, waiting for Etherine to explain. 'We are closer than I thought. By changing the design of the realm, Hecate has forfeited a number of challenges. She has played almost all of her cards. The Origin, in his haste trying to defeat you, must have instructed the witch to use her most powerful spells. Beyond this cavern lies, Hecate's castle.'

Molly's eyes lit up, surprised at the revelation. 'You mean we've done it; we've won?'

'Not quite,' said Etherine, trying to suppress the girls excitement. 'She may have used up the last of her spells, but your greatest challenge is still ahead.'

Peter moaned; His short-lived enthusiasm dashed in a millisecond. 'When are we ever going to catch a break? How many more beasts can these dictators leash upon us?'

'To enter the castle, you must defeat, Hecate's pet.'

'Pet?' asked Molly, guessing it wasn't going to be the fluffy bunny kind.

Etherine paused for a moment. contemplating if telling them what they were about to face were a good idea. 'You need to know what we are up against,' warned the guardian. 'It is known as, The Hydra.'

'Wait, I've heard of this,' interrupted Peter, remembering reading something about the creature. 'It was in a book about Greek mythology. If I remember correctly it has many heads, almost dragon like. I've read that, even if you cut off the heads, multiple others grow back.'

Etherine looked at the young man, surprised by his statement. 'There can only be one explanation for that, Peter. Only someone who has conquered the realms and faced the, Hydra could tell of its existence. As I'm sure, the Galpherin has explained to you, most of the beasts you call, methodical originate from this world, so, those few humans who have successfully conquered the three realms and returned home, have subconsciously remembered parts of our world, therefore written about them believing them to be no more than fantasy.'

Molly looked quizzically at Etherine, something she said perking her curiosity. 'You say remembered? Do you mean, if we leave this world and return home, we'll forget this place?'

'We have found, the human brain once exposed to our world, finds it hard to differentiate itself from its own when back in its habitat, therefore the golden band tries to erase all memories of its time here. However, the brain, as I'm sure you are aware, is a complexed organ. Some of its deepest secrets are still unknown. Often, some of the more traumatising memories are difficult to eradicate or supress, coming back to the human mind, in forms of what you call flashbacks.'

'Good!' Said Peter relieved. 'I don't know about, Molly. But I'm more than happy to forget everything about this place.'

Molly, Peter and Etherine approached the exit of the cavern, the much-welcomed fresh air of the night filling their lungs.

'Oh my god!' Exclaimed Peter as he stood there gawping at the intimidating fortress, a short distance away.

The vast, resplendent and ancient looking castle dominated the landscape. Its traditional looking parapet's rose high into the night sky, circled by large numbers of Vespertilio surveying the ground below waiting for their unexpecting prey. Its bold silhouettes enhanced by light from the many moons that surrounded it seemed to give the fortress a more menacing impression.

At one side of the castle was a large lake that fed all around the fortress, creating a type of island, separating it from the mainland. Its lucid surface turned black against the darkness as pockets of moonlight reflected from its exterior, the stillness portraying an eeriness, giving an uneasy feeling as to what lay beneath.

The three companions approached the fortress, an unnatural silence highlighting their need to be vigilant. Even the winged beasts that circled above ceased complaining.

'Be ready for anything,' warned the forest guardian. 'The Hydra has many weapons. Its breath is said to be poisonous. And its blood, a corrosive element that dissolves its victims.'

'How on earth am I supposed to defeat it if I can't spill its blood?' asked the frustrated girl, feeling unprepared.

'That, Molly Miggins will be decided by you and the golden band.'

Peter stopped dead in his tracks, unable to move as he noticed something moving in his peripheral vision. The young man slowly turned his head towards the lake, its surface disturbed by something deep beneath its depths.

'Stand back!' Ordered Etherine as the water began to bubble and foam, creating a multitude of white horses, erupting like a volcano.

The colossal beast burst out from beneath its hiding place, a series of ear-piercing screeches, causing the few curious Vespertilio that remained, to flee for cover.

The Hydra stood posturing for a moment as it surveyed its surroundings. Gallons of dark lake water flowed down off its body like a waterfall, back to where it whence came. Each of the creature's numerous heads tussled, weaving to and fro, snapping angrily at each other as they battled for supremacy.

Suddenly, the beast, loomed out from the lake, causing the ground to tremble.

'We need to separaie!' Cried Etherine anxiously. 'The Hydras weakness is, its many heads have minds of their own, each one disagreeing with the next. If we separate, we will confuse it, causing it to fight with itself.

All three, quickly fled in different directions, as sure enough, the beast struggled to agree with itself, stumbling awkwardly as it failed to decide which being to pursue.

'Etherine! Look out!' Screamed Molly.

The tree dweller turned, unable to avoid the oncoming collision. The Hydras enormously imposing tail struck the guardian full on, sending her hurling through the air.

Molly looked desperately towards her friend her lifeless frame motionless on the ground.

'You have to do something, Molly,' pleaded Peter, wondering why the bracelet hadn't kicked into action.

One of the beast's heads, alerted by the humans cry for help, arched down towards the young man, taking in a huge gulp of air.

'Cover your face!' Warned molly as the Hydra exhaled a cloud of putrid green poison.

Remembering the tree dwellers warning, the human reacted instantly, diving away from the visible cloud of toxic air whilst covering his face, consciously trying not to breathe.

Molly, angered by her own lack of assistance, stood fast as the temperature in the atmosphere began to rise. The young human thrust her arm up into the air as multiple bolts of lightning, descended from the sky, electrifying the golden band.

An aura of terrific energy surrounded the girl, lighting up the space around her. Her eyes, like two beams of white light, appeared ghostly like as she confidently approached the beast. 'Molly, be careful!' Warned Peter, ducking for cover.

Undeterred, the young human dispelled a single charge from the golden band, severing the first of the beast's heads clean from its neck.

The Hydras remaining heads, simultaneously whaled in agony as the girl, unrelenting in her attack, sent another, then another as one by one, each of the creatures heads toppled from their stay until all that was left, were a mass of headless necks, twisting silently in vein amongst themselves.

With one final assault, Molly sent the beast careering back into the lake, its headless body vibrating as the electric charge made contact with the water, disappearing back into the deep.

Peter quickly rushed over to where the tree dweller was lying. 'Etherine, are you okay?' asked the human as the guardian stirred from her semi-conscious state.

'Is it over? She replied, struggling to make the effort to move.

Peter nodded, smiling as he helped the tree dweller up off the ground. 'She did it. She defeated the Hydra.'

Etherine looked over towards the lake, relieved at the sight of water returning to its stagnant state, a few dying ripples the last bit of evidence there were any signs of a struggle.

Molly stood motionless by the side of the lake, a strange sombreness about her demeanour. Her eyes seemed to be fixed, in a trance like state as she remained focused on the, now still black waters.

'Molly, what's the matter? Are you okay?' asked Peter, a little worried.

The girls face began to change colour, fighting to breath, as if something were restricting the flow of air to her lungs.

Molly starred at her friend, a desperate vacant look on her face, as if she were silently crying out for help. Peter gripped tight hold of her shoulders, violently shaking her, worried he was about to lose his friend if she failed to take some air in the next few moments.

Suddenly, Molly took in a sharp deep breath, her chest heaving as she swallowed masses of air. 'Where…. am I?' asked the girl, struggling to find the energy to speak.

'You're here, Molly, you're with us. You defeated the Hydra,' replied her friend anxiously. 'What happened to you?'

Molly paused for a moment, still recovering from her ordeal. 'I thought I was sinking down with the beast. In my mind, I was fighting the Hydra as we were sinking deeper into the water. I couldn't breathe, the beast was pulling me down, deeper and deeper, I thought I was going to drown.'

'Hecate,' interrupted Etherine, suspecting the witch was responsible. 'It was her last attempt to destroy you. Waiting until you were at your most vulnerable, the witch took over your mind, convincing you, you were still fighting the beast. If Peter hadn't reacted as quickly as he did, you would have drowned.'

Molly, overwhelmed by the revelation flung her arms around him, no longer able to control her emotions as they poured out in waves.

'It's okay, Moll's. You're fine now, I've got you.'

Peter gently lifted her head as he wiped away her tears. His heart began to melt, for the first time in a long while, sensing her vulnerability. He knew her better than anyone. She wasn't the tough, cold hearted ice queen she often made herself out to be. Deep down inside, she was gentle and caring, sensitive to animals and those less fortunate than herself, even more so since her father went missing. Dasher, her rescue dog, a prime example of her caring side. Her understanding of Mr, Wittleworth, feeling his guilt and pain, not judging or blaming him, even though he clearly blamed himself.

Yes, this was the real, Molly. The one he loved, loved ever since they were small children, ever since she pulled tongues at him, hiding behind her mother the first time they met. Nothing would ever separate them. Not in this world or any other.

The three companions wheeled around, alerted by the sound of some kind of movement coming from the castle.

The friends stood and watched as the castles drawbridge started to lower itself, bridging the gap between them and the fortress.

'This is where I must leave you both,' said Etherine regretfully.

Molly and Peter both stared anxiously at the tree dweller, not really knowing what to say. 'What? What do you mean, leave us?' Replied the girl, trying to understand.

'I'm afraid this is as far as I can go. Only the challengers can enter, Hecate's castle. I am the guardian of the forest, therefor must remain in the forest. Besides, there is nothing more you need from me, Molly Miggins. You have both achieved, what very few have. You have conquered the realm of spells. But beware! Hecate will have one last challenge for you, before you can leave the realm.'

'What challenge?' asked Peter despondently, wondering what else they had to do to be free from this nightmare.

'I'm not quite sure, Peter,' replied Etherine. 'As I have explained, we are forbidden to enter her fortress, but it will have something to do with the tree of souls.'

The tree dwellers revelation instantly caught Molly's attention as she remembered her father's prison.

'The tree of souls. That's where my father is being held against his will. But we have done what was asked of us. We have conquered all three realms. What more do they want?'

'They will do whatever they can, within the law, to prevent you from returning back to your world. The Origin, at this point, will be desperate to keep the last golden band here in, Kaplon. Yes, you have defeated all three realms. But now, Hecate will set you one last challenge before she will free your father.'

Molly and Peter stared desperately towards the fortress, knowing they had little choice. Either enter the castle and except the challenge or, stay in this realm and concede defeat.

'It has been a pleasure to serve you, Molly Miggins. And you, Peter. I have every faith in you. Believe in yourself and you will succeed. Good luck to you both.'

Etherine, wrapped her arms gently around her new friends as they said their goodbyes, before slowly walking back into the forest, disappearing amongst her own kind.

Chapter Twenty

Molly and her friend, stood at the mouth of the fortress, staring into the abyss. The darkness inside, refusing to surrender its secrets to the moonlight, an eerie entity all of its own.

Both humans, hesitantly at first, slowly made their way forward. Molly, true to form searched for Peters hand, holding it tightly as they reluctantly entered the castle.

A dull thud echoed around them, signalling their arrival as they passed over the threshold.

No sooner had they entered, two candles, perched upon a pair of golden candelabras on either side of them, magically sparked into life, causing Molly to flinch as they lit up part of the great hall, quickly followed by two more, until eventually expelling the darkness completely, revealed the most spectacular architecture they'd ever seen.

Exquisite intricate carvings littered the granite like walled interior, from the high lofted arched ceilings, all the way down to the stone floor. The impressively detailed battle scenes seemed to move as the two humans made their way, further into the fortress. Tall monuments, made of the same material dedicated to the Victors, as well as the fallen, lined proudly along the wall on either side. Their shadows, enhanced by the subdued candlelight, danced as the flames flickered, disturbed by the gentle rush of air that swept through the great hall.

Molly stopped in her tracks, a strange black and white figure looming at the top of a large flight of steps, stood still, its features undetectable against the false light.

'Come forward!' Commanded the witch, her voice as chilling as her presence.

The two humans looked at each other, each one's expression as unnerving as the others.

'There's no turning back now, Moll's,' whispered Peter, trying unconvincingly to perceive some kind of confidence.

The two friends, still holding tight hold of one another, slowly climbed the stone staircase. Molly's heart began to race, each beat more physical than the last, pounding her chest, as if it would jump out at any second, all the time wondering if the next step taken were their last.

Hecate carefully studied the humans as she paced from side to side like an undertaker, making mental measurements for his unsuspecting clientele.

Molly and Peter stared, surprised by the witch's appearance. Other than the long black gown she wore, Hecate didn't look like your traditional witch. Her face was rather young looking. Not what you would call beautiful, but certainly not unpleasant to the eye. Her well-kept, long white hair shone brightly as it flowed down the full length of her back. Only the sinister look from her darkened eyes gave evidence that something evil lurked inside. Their blackness enhanced by her pale complexion.

Hypnotised by the witch's presence, Molly failed to notice the most important thing.

'Oh my god, Molly look!' Said Peter, his eyes lighting up, surprised by its location.

Stretching out from the stone floor high into the castle, stood what must have been, the tree of souls. Its imposing stature dominated its surroundings. Its thick dark trunk seemed to twist and creek in complaint, against the strange shapes that protruded its surface, desperately trying to escape their prison. Hundreds of lost souls cried out in vein, hoping someone would release them from their living hell.

'Dad!' Screamed Molly, knowing her father were one of the many lost souls trapped in his own nightmare.

'Not so fast young human,' said the witch, delighted by the girls misery. 'You must prove worthy before the tree will release your kin.'

'What do you want me to do? I will do anything,' pleaded Molly, all concerns for her safety a distant second.

A churlish smile crossed Hecate's face as she made her way towards an ancient looking stone table. On the centre of the alter, sat a translucent crystal ball, rotating slowly, a magical aura surrounding its sphere.

The witch gently cupped the object with both hands, lifting it from its station.

Molly and Peter took a step back, looking confused at one another other as the witch began to chant. 'Look deep inside my crystal ball. Which one will read the writing, on the wall?'

The two friends stared, transfixed at the crystal ball as it began to spin. Faster and faster it went, until suddenly, it stopped.

Peter was left dumbstruck as a picture of his face appeared, staring out at himself. 'What…. What does that mean?' asked Peter, a sense of dread filling his soul.

'The young male will be the first to utter the spell,' replied the witch, a satisfied smile etched on her face. 'Translate the encryption on the wall correctly and you will open the gate, releasing the girl's kin from the tree of souls.'

'What encryption?' asked the young man, aware he wasn't going to like the answer.

Hecate raised her arm, waving it from side to side as the foreign encryption magically appeared on the wall.

Molly gasped, recognising the words. 'I know what it says!' Said the girl enthusiastically, remembering her dream once more.

'Enough!' Ordered the witch, before she could reveal its meaning. 'You will get your chance. First, the male must speak.'

Molly looked worried at her friend. She knew he couldn't read Latin. This was Hecate's evil plan all along. They were finally going to get what they wanted.

'You can't do this! I wear the golden band! I'm the one who should read the encryption! Shifter!'

'The Galpherin cannot help you, Molly Miggins. You were the one who brought this being to our world. In doing so, you have made him a part of your challenge. Did you really think it was going to be that easy? The boy will go first! If you intervene or utter a word, you will forfeit the challenge.'

Peter looked helplessly at Molly, a desperate look in his eyes, knowing it was all about to go horribly wrong. 'We've got know choice, Moll's. Unless the bracelet can magic the translation into my head, I'm afraid we're screwed.'

Molly felt nothing. The bracelet remained still. It was like she'd been separated from the trinket, like it was just another piece of jewellery.

'The golden band will not assist you here, Molly Miggins. It has no power in my castle. It has already given you the power of translation. Even before you entered our world, the trinket gave you the foresight to succeed in this challenge. Do you think we would not take steps to ensure you could not prevail?'

Molly recalled her dream once more. Realising it was the bracelet, communicating with her, giving her the weapons that would save her. But it failed to include Peter in her plans. After all, the golden band was for her alone, it was there solely to assist her.'

'Speak the words!' Commanded the witch, growing impatient with the human.

Peter took a deep breath as he studied the inscription on the wall. 'IN NOMINE PATRIS MEI, HAEC PORTA APERIRE.'

Some of the words looked familiar, like her had heard them many times, in films or in text from some book or other. What do they mean? He thought to himself. He knew, PATRIS meant father. It must have something to do with, Molly's father and how to release him.

The witch began to get agitated, certain he was stalling, hoping for some kind of miracle. 'I'm losing patience. Speak the words or surrender your life force.'

The young man gathered himself, uncertain of the words he was about to translate as he turned to his friend one last time. A look of resignation on his face as he uttered the words.

'IN THE NAME OF THE FATHER, RELEASE HIM!'

Molly, slowly closed her eyes in despair, knowing the translation was incorrect.

Peter wheeled around, alerted by the sound of something moving behind him. The tree of souls began to twist and bend. Thin branches whipped out towards him, curling themselves around his arms and legs.

'Molly! Help me!' Cried the young man as he struggled to free himself, restrained by the trees many vines.

Molly ran towards her friend, trying desperately in vein to free him as the constant tirade of vines and branches continued to wrap themselves tightly around his whole body, before dragging him closer to his doom.

'Peter! Don't leave me!'

Molly watched helplessly as the tree of souls dragged, Peter screaming into his prison. His physical existence becoming one with the tree, his cries for help fading, until suddenly, it was silent.

Molly stood in complete shock as the tree of souls began to rest, its huge trunk pulsing slowly, as if satisfied after consuming its prey, before suddenly, it stopped, another soul, lost to its realm.

The young girl turned angrily towards the witch, a look of hate in her eyes as she approached her tormenter.

'There is nothing you can do for you friend young human,' said Hecate, anticipating the girls intention. 'You still have the chance to free your kin. But the boy is lost forever.'

'That's impossible!' Exclaimed Molly furiously. 'There must be something I can do.'

'You will, have choices,' replied the witch, a smug smile on her face revealing, Molly's choices would probably favour her enemies. 'But I'm sure, the Origin will explain what they are in due course.

Hecate moved to the side as she gestured towards the inscription on the wall once more. 'Now, speak the words, Molly Miggins.'

The girl closed her eyes as she recalled the dream, the words emblazoned in her mind.

'IN THE NAME OF MY FATHER, OPEN THIS GATE!'

No sooner had the words left her mouth, the wall began to change, melting its granite like surface, revealing a translucent door that would lead her out of the realm of spells.

Suddenly, disturbed by a familiar noise, Molly turned around to see the tree of souls pulsing once more. This time there were no vines, no branches protruding from its limbs. Its trunk began to twist and turn, its surface disturbed by something within.

Molly's eyes began to light up as the figure started to emerge from captivity. Fist a hand, them another as the human figure began to take shape, slowly revealing itself, separating from its capture.

The man stood there for a moment, in a trance like state. His vacant expression, the result of his time spent in captivity.

'Dad!' Screamed Molly as she ran towards her father.

Norman Miggins began to blink, alerted by the familiar voice. 'Molly?' asked the man surprised. 'Is that you?'

The young girl flung her arms tightly around her father's neck, sobbing uncontrollably. 'It's me, dad. I'm here.

The two humans embraced each other, all thoughts of their ordeal vanquished for that moment, happily reunited once more.

'I sensed you, Molly. I sensed you were near,' whispered Norman, still holding his daughter close.

Sensing something had changed, Norman gently released his daughter's hold on him. 'Oh my god! How long has it been?' He asked suddenly, realising how much she'd grown.

'It's been two years since you went missing, dad. Two years on earth that is. I'm guessing a few more have passed, since I've been here, so who knows how much time has passed.'

Norman slumped to the ground at the news, devastated at the amount of time lost with his family. 'I wish I'd never found that bracelet. What have I done? Wait! How did you get hold of the other bracelet?'

Molly knelt down as she held his hand. 'Mr, Wittleworth gave it to me, dad. Don't be angry with him. He knew there was something strange about the bracelets. He told me the whole story.'

Norman stopped his daughter as she attempted to explain the details of her ordeal. 'You can tell me everything once we've gotten out of this place, Molly.'

Molly lowered her head, a look of despair on her face. 'There's something else dad,' continued the girl. 'Peter.'

Norman stared at his daughter, a look of confusion on his face. 'Peter? Peter Hughes? What about him?'

'Peter refused to let me go alone. He's been with me the whole time, helping me try to rescue you.'

Norman was speechless for a moment, unable to process what he was hearing.

'He's been taken, dad,' continued Molly. 'Taken by the tree of souls.'

'Oh my god,' whispered her father. 'What have I done? This is all my fault. If I hadn't been so obsessed, so bloody minded, none of this would have happened. All I have done, is, sacrifice one soul for another.'

The human angrily rose to his feet to face his tormenter. 'Haven't you taken enough from us, witch? What more do you want?'

Hecate gave a devilish look towards her accuser, revelling in his misery. 'We want all of you!' Spat the witch, furious at the human's question. 'And thanks to the young males participation, we shall have you. Now, both of you must leave the realm of spells and return to the fortress of the Origin. He is waiting for you.'

'We can't leave here without Peter!' said Molly, desperately hoping her dad would have the answer. 'There must be a way to free him.'

'There is no way, Molly Miggins,' insisted the witch. 'His fate is sealed. You must leave this realm or join your friend. The gate will only remain open for a short while longer. Once it has closed, the power to open it once more will be lost forever.'

Norman turned to his crest fallen daughter, pained by the look of desperation on her face. 'I'm sorry, sweetheart, we must leave. There's nothing we can do here. If we stay, then there's no chance of helping Peter. Maybe there is something we can do on the other side. But if we are trapped here, everything you have been through will be for nothing.'

Molly knew her father was right. Leaving Peter in this realm was unthinkable. But any chance of helping him would be lost if they succumbed to the same fate.

Norman took hold of his daughter's hand, knowing he couldn't take the chance of her changing her mind if they didn't leave together; the guilt of losing her friend trapping her here in this realm if she hesitated.

The duo slowly made their way towards the gate as Molly directed one last comment at the witch who was smiling smugly celebrating her victory. 'You have won nothing.'

Norman gently squeezed his daughters hand, proud of the young woman she'd become as the they passed through the translucent gateway, a dire feeling of regret of leaving their friend behind.

Chapter Twenty-One

The evil ruler began to clap his hands together, laughing triumphantly, mocking the humans as they stood defeated before him.

'At last, victory is mine,' he said magnanimously. 'Did you really think you could outwit me? Do you honestly believe I could be denied what is mine?'

Molly glared at her tormenter, angered by his premature revelry. 'But you haven't won anything yet. I have freed my father. We have earned the right to return home.'

The Origin deliberated silently for a short time, savouring the moment before stating, what she knew was obvious. 'This is true. And yes, you are free to return to your own world. But you will leave without your companion, Miss, Miggins. He belongs to me now, so please, be my guest, leave.'

The smug ruler began to laugh once more, enjoying his cruel mind games with the girl as she struggled to control her emotions.

He knew she couldn't leave without him. Past experience had taught the dictator that the human mind was emotionally weak. Only one who was self-centred, self-obsessed, would take the opportunity to run. His observations of Molly over her time in this world had told him she had neither of those traits.

'You have three options,' he continued. 'The first, is, you and your kin can return to your world. You will face no resistance; you have my word. The second. Both of you will surrender to me and relinquish your golden bands. Then you, your kin and your young friend will be drained of your life force and exiled to the realm of hopes and fears to do my bidding.'

Molly and her father looked at each other, the suggestion of surrendering themselves without a fight, unthinkable. 'And the third?' asked the girl hesitantly.

The Origins evil grin left the humans feeling, the final option was probably less appealing than the last. 'The third, is. You will both return to the beginning. You will be given the opportunity to release your friend by doing it all over again.'

Any remaining energy she had left, drained from her body. The thought of having to do battle through all three realms over again, was unimaginable. The amount of time lost already must have been significant by now. If they were to make it through a second time, how much more time would be lost?

Norman turned towards his daughter, a resigned expression clearly telling her what she already knew. 'We have little choice, sweetheart. We can't return home without, Peter. How could we live with ourselves?'

Knowing her father was right and with no other choice, Molly nodded in agreement. 'Okay, you win,' replied the girl. 'You've given us no other choice.'

'Not necessarily!' Said a familiar voice.

Everyone looked around, surprised to see the old man standing unnoticed on one side of the room.

'Shiftervorgoethryn! What is the meaning of this intrusion?' Snapped the Origin, demanding an explanation. 'You have no business here!'

Molly and Norman remained silent, somewhat confused by the Galpherin's statement, although relieved to see him.

'I am here because you have broken our laws, Your majesty,' revealed the old man. 'I am here to grant Miss, Miggins one wish.'

The evil ruler roared angrily at the Galpherin. 'That is impossible! You have no grounds to grant her a wish! The rules state, a challenger must earn the right to be granted a wish. The human has done what is expected of any challenger and no more!'

'On the contrary, your highness,' replied Shifter calmly. 'You tried to have me destroyed. You ordered the dragon, Glycon to have me killed in the realm of legends. The human, in her bravery, risked her own life to save mine, by standing between me and the dragon. You know full well that a guarding of, Kaplon cannot be terminated without just cause. You realised the young human was a threat, therefor you sought to have me destroyed, so that she would have no one to guide her through the remaining realms. You did this your majesty. You broke our laws, culminating in your own downfall.'

The Origin wheeled around furiously as the room began to tremble. 'This is impossible! You cannot do this to me. I am the ruler of everything!'

Molly and her father ducked for cover, anticipating a barrage of assaults as the Origin Failed time and time again, desperately trying in vain to unleash his powers. 'What is happening? Where are my powers? Give them back to me!'

The Galpherin, confidently approached the evil ruler as it stood there, exhausted, drained by the incessant failed attempts to destroy its enemies. 'It is over your majesty. Your powers have been removed, pending your trial. Take him away.'

Molly watched in disbelief as two centaurs marched into the room. Restraining the Origin on either side, they escorted the crestfallen leader from the room, destined for his own prison.

'You have won nothing human! I will find you! I will find you!' He warned, cursing as he disappeared out of sight.

The old man turned to the humans as they watched the doors close. 'Now Miss, Miggins. What is your wish?'

Molly looked at her father who was smiling, both knowing exactly what she would wish.

'I wish.... I wish, Peter was here with us, released from the tree of souls.'

The old man smiled as he opened his arms out wide. Instantaneously, the gate leading to the realm of spells became translucent once again. Molly's heart began to thump, nervously anticipating her love. Suddenly, her eyes lit up as her loyal friend appeared out from the mirror like entrance, his eyes searching, hoping to see his girl once more.

Their eyes locked as the two humans ran towards each other, embracing, smothering one another passionately with their lips.

'I... thought... I'd lost you,' said Molly, in between the constant lavishing of affection.

'You're not going to get rid of me that easily,' joked Peter, enthusiastically pressing his mouth onto hers.

'Err.... Is there something I should be aware of?' Interrupted Norman as the two lovebirds, forgetting he was there, coyly separated.

'Erm, hello Mr Miggins. I didn't see you there,' replied a slightly embarrassed Peter as he approached the girls confused father, hand extended. 'I'm so happy, Molly was able to free you.'

'Thank you, Peter. It's good to have you back,' said Norman, awkwardly shaking the young man's hand. 'I think you and I need to have a chat at some point in the future, don't you?'

Molly giggled, enjoying the banter between them. 'Come on dad, stop teasing him.'

The old man coughed discreetly, before asking the question they'd been longing to hear. 'Are you ready to go home.'

The three humans looked at one another, each one thinking the same thing. 'We're ready,' replied Molly as she leant down to make eye contact with her friend.

'I want to…. We want to, thank you for everything you've done for us. We couldn't have made it without you.'

The old man smiled affectionately as he took hold of his friend's hand. 'No, Molly Miggins. We are the ones who should be thanking you. Because of you, there will be no more challenges. If justice is served correctly, the Origins rule in the multiverse is over. Beings from all worlds will be safe.'

The old man, suddenly placed his hand on the golden band, causing the trinket to make a strange sound.

'What did you just do?' asked Molly, instantly pulling her arm away.

'Something, one day, you may thank me for, Miss Miggins,' replied Shifter, a mischievous look on his face.

Brushing the incident off, Molly rose to her feet. 'If you see them again, please say goodbye to my friends for me. Chiron, Michael and Etherine. Without them, I certainly wouldn't be here.'

'You can say farewell to them yourself, Molly Miggins,' replied the old man as he waved his hand towards the wall behind them, instantly revealing the images of her most trusted companions.

Molly cupped her hands to her mouth as the three beings began to wave, causing the girl to shed a solitary tear.

The young human wiped her cheek, before raising an arm, bidding farewell to her friends as they slowly began to fade away.

'The time has come,' announced the Galpherin, guiding them into position. 'Peter, you must stand in between your companions. The golden bands on either side will form your armour.'

The young man did what he was told, holding both, Norman and Molly's hand as they readied themselves.

'Goodbye my friends,' said Shifter as the wall began to twist.

Molly looked towards her dad as the trinkets began to take form, spreading themselves, quickly up the arm, before covering their entire bodies until they were completely locked in.

Noticing that gravity had surrendered its hold on them, all three started to rise as one as the vortex took shape, twisting and spiralling into the vast unknown ahead, before suddenly, they were gone, their nightmare over, light years behind them.

Chapter Twenty-Two

The mid-afternoon summer sun shone brightly against the sea. Glistening flecks of silvery light danced off its surface as the waves brushed softly upon the beach. The day was a beautiful one, perfect for the occasion. Each of the family members and friends, gazed out into the horizon as they reflected on past memories. Their heads bowed in silent prayer, each one with their own thoughts of what might have been. The occasional sound of a sniffle, prompting comforting reassurance from their loved ones, interrupting the silence.

Everyone had attended this year. Even, James Wittleworth who had found it too difficult the previous year, blaming himself as he had when his friend disappeared. Peter's parents, Fiona and Robert Hughes, also had found the strength to come along, accepting Gina's invitation, unable to attend the first-year anniversary. And Bailey, now a young man, back from college for the holidays completed the congregation.

Olivia pulled her sister close, the memories too much to bear as the tears began to roll down her face. 'I know sweetheart.... I know,' whispered Olivia, holding her sister tightly. 'I feel it too. We'll get through this together. Would you like me to say a few words?'

Gina dried her eyes as she noticed everyone watching her, their sympathetic expressions causing her to gather herself. 'No, thank you, I need to do this.' She replied, reassuring her sister.

'Firstly, thank you all for being here today,' began Gina, addressing the congregation. 'It's wonderful to see you all, especially those who found it too difficult to come along last year. I know how painful it must have been for you all. Can I start by....'

Suddenly, Gina stopped as a strange sound halting her speech, echoed out from the cave. Everyone turned and stared towards the gaping cavern as the drone got louder and louder, reaching to a crescendo until suddenly, silence.

'What the hell was that?' cried Bailey, eyes still fixed on the cave.

'Wait! There's someone there,' replied Olivia, noticing some movement coming from within.

The whole congregation gasped in disbelief as three familiar figures exited the cave; their appearance clear to see in the bright summer sun.

'Molly?' Uttered Gina, unable to muster anything more as her legs began to give way from underneath her. 'Can it be true? Am I dreaming?'

All three names filled the air as everyone, including the trio emerging the cave, ran towards each other, every emotion pouring out.

As Peter embraced his overwhelmed parents, Molly and her father hastily continued towards their paralysed, Mother/wife, who was kneeling down, arms stretched out, crying tears of unbelievable joy on the sand.

'Please don't let this be a dream!' Cried Gina as she wrapped her arms tightly around her lost loved ones.

'You're not dreaming mum,' replied her daughter, stroking her mother's hair.

'I don't understand... How...? What...? Why...? Norman, my darling, where have you been?'

'Hush now sweetheart, we'll explain everything when the time is right. For now, let's just enjoy the moment.'

'But neither of you have hardly aged. How is that possible?'

'It's a long story mum,' replied Molly, knowing they would need everyone to gather themselves before explaining. 'One best left until we are home.'

'But you are home my love,' said Gina, holding their beautiful faces. 'Both of you.'

Norman stood up as he saw his friend slowly approach. The old man looked shell-shocked, his face showing the years of guilt he'd suffered.

'Hello my friend,' said Norman as he hugged his best friend.

Jim Wittleworth squeezed tight hold of his long-lost companion as years of pent up emotion poured out all at once. 'I knew it, Norman. I knew you'd return,' stuttered James, trying desperately to get his words out without losing control.

'Thank you,' replied Norman. 'Thank you for believing. If it weren't for you, I wouldn't be here. I owe you my life.'

The two friends embraced once more as the congregation gathered in a mass huddle, each one hugging the other as they welcomed back those that were lost.

Molly and Peter followed a short distance behind as the group caught up on stories and memories of the years that were lost.

'Molly, have you noticed something?' asked Peter quietly. 'How are we able to remember?'

The young girl looked at her friend, a single name leaving her lips. 'Shifter. Don't ask me why and he wouldn't say. But he did something to my bracelet before we returned. He said, 'One day I'll thank him for it.'

'That sneaky old bugger,' replied Peter. 'Well, I'm glad I can remember,' continued the young man. 'I mean, what would life be like if we didn't remember what happened between us up there?'

Peter smiled at his new girlfriend as their lips entwined once more. This time there was no doubt. No hesitation. This was real. This was home.

'Err! I think we need to have that conversation now, Peter!' Shouted Norman, catching the couple in the act.

The two lovebirds laughed, a little embarrassed by his teasing as, Molly noticed a warm feeling, coming from her trouser pocket.

The young girl slowly placed her hand inside as a familiar voice spoke to her subconscious. 'REMEMBER MISS MIGGINS. THINGS AREN'T ALWAYS WHAT THEY SEEM.'

Molly looked up at the sky, a heartfelt smile appearing on her face as she took tight hold of her boyfriend's hand. 'Come on. Let's go home.'

THE END...?